PRINCE MATERIAL

NORA PHOENIX

B

Boldwood

First published in Great Britain in 2025 by Boldwood Books Ltd.

Copyright © Nora Phoenix, 2025

Cover Design by Head Design Ltd

Cover Images: Shutterstock

The moral right of Nora Phoenix to be identified as the author of this work has been asserted in accordance with the Copyright, Designs and Patents Act 1988.

Every effort has been made to obtain the necessary permissions with reference to copyright material, both illustrative and quoted. We apologise for any omissions in this respect and will be pleased to make the appropriate acknowledgements in any future edition.

A CIP catalogue record for this book is available from the British Library.

Paperback ISBN 978-1-83656-908-4

Large Print ISBN 978-1-83656-907-7

Hardback ISBN 978-1-83656-906-0

Trade Paperback ISBN 978-1-80635-302-6

Ebook ISBN 978-1-83656-909-1

Kindle ISBN 978-1-83656-910-7

Audio CD ISBN 978-1-83656-901-5

MP3 CD ISBN 978-1-83656-902-2

Digital audio download ISBN 978-1-83656-904-6

This book is printed on certified sustainable paper. Boldwood Books is dedicated to putting sustainability at the heart of our business. For more information please visit https://www.boldwoodbooks.com/about-us/sustainability/

Boldwood Books Ltd, 23 Bowerdean Street, London, SW6 3TN

www.boldwoodbooks.com

PROLOGUE
FLORIS

I sprawled in one of the ancient, wooden loungers that had probably seen more royal butts than the throne itself. The evening sun painted long shadows across the perfectly manicured lawns of Het Oude Loo, the palace that had been my home all my life, and the garden's familiar scents—freshly cut grass, blooming roses, and that earthy dampness from the castle moat that always reminded me of a forest in the rain—wrapped around me like the world's poshest security blanket.

Even better was the company of my three best friends, all princes, like me. We'd met practically at birth and had grown up together in the public eye, though in different countries. Tore was from Norway, Nils from Sweden, Greg represented the United Kingdom, and I was a proud member of the Dutch royal family. Well, mostly proud anyway.

I took a long pull from my Heineken, savoring what might be my last beer for a while. In America, eighteen was old enough to drive, marry, kill, or die in battle, but not old enough to have a beer. Somebody needed to explain that to me as if I were still in elementary school because it made no sense to me. Anyway, I'd have to wait one more year to be allowed to drink.

"You're seriously giving up beer for a year?" Greg's British accent dripped with disbelief as he lounged in the chair next to mine. "That's a human rights violation, if you ask me."

I snorted. "Pretty sure my late grandfather would disown me if he knew. Though I'm confident that despite the legal age, beer will be served at frat parties, right? That's what they always show in the movies anyway. But hey, what's the worst that could happen? I become the first sober Dutch prince in history?"

"The press would have a field day with that one," Tore chimed in from where he was sprawled in the grass. "'Dutch Prince Abandons National Beverage.' They'd probably call it a diplomatic crisis."

The mention of the press made my jaw clench. I forced myself to relax, but not before catching Greg's knowing look. He'd always been the most observant of our little royal quartet, and it had been the British tabloid press that had crucified me without ever bothering to check the veracity of their allegations.

"Speaking of the press," Nils said carefully, "have you figured out how you're going to stay under their radar at Vernon?"

"Yeah." I sat up straighter, warming to the topic I'd spent months planning. "The American press doesn't give a shit about European royalty unless we're getting married or spectacularly screwing up. And most Americans couldn't pick me out of a lineup if their lives depended on it. I'm going to be Floris van Oranje. Drop the Nassau, keep it simple."

"And when someone googles you?" Greg arched an eyebrow. "Your real identity will pop up."

"Then I'll deal with it. But I'm not going to announce it. I want..." I trailed off, searching for the right words. "I want to be normal for a while. Have the opportunity to mess up without it making international headlines."

The others went quiet, and I knew they were all thinking about the video. The edited footage that made me look like... I cut that thought off before it could fully form.

"We know what really happened," Tore said quietly. "That's what matters."

I managed a weak smile. "Yeah. But sometimes, I wonder if being the first openly gay prince is worth all this scrutiny. Every move I make, someone's waiting for me to fuck up again."

"Which is exactly why this year in Massachusetts is perfect timing," Greg pointed out. "You get to be a regular college student. Well, a very tall, very Dutch college student with questionable fashion sense, but still."

"My fashion sense is impeccable," I protested, though I couldn't help grinning. "Even if it's not quite up to your stuffy British standards. But yeah, that's the plan. How's your planning coming along, Tore?"

"Six weeks from now, I will be Tore Haakon, star football player for the Hawley Hawks of Hawley College in Ohio."

I snorted. "You may wanna start by calling it soccer."

Tore rolled his eyes. "Semantics."

"Not to Americans," Greg pointed out. "They'll be mighty confused when you start talking about being a midfielder in football, as that is not a known position in American football."

I studied Tore. "You wouldn't make a bad quarterback, actually. You've got the build for it."

"Sure, and if they actually kicked the ball instead of throwing it, I might stand a chance." Tore threw up his hands. "Why on earth would they call it football when they aren't even allowed to kick the ball?"

I wasn't about to debate that with him since I didn't see the logic either.

"It's not even a proper ball, is it?" Greg said. "Their football. It's more of a sphere than a ball, really."

"An egg," Nils declared solemnly. "They play with a leather egg."

"Speaking of eggs," I said, "anyone hungry? The kitchen staff made those sandwiches you love so much, Greg."

"The ones with carpaccio and truffle mayonnaise on that wholewheat Dutch bread?" Greg perked up like a meerkat spotting something interesting. "Why didn't you say so earlier?"

I grinned. "Because I enjoy watching you pretend to be too posh to ask for them."

"I'm not too posh for anything," Greg protested, but he was already getting up. "I simply have refined taste."

"Right." I stood as well, stretching until my back cracked. "That's why the press had pictures of you eating McDonald's in your Bentley last month."

"That was a moment of weakness." Greg sniffed. "And those photos were clearly doctored."

The mention of doctored photos made my stomach clench, but I forced a laugh. That was what we did, after all. Made jokes, kept it light, pretended the constant scrutiny didn't wear us down like water on rock. "At least yours was actually eating McDonald's. Not some fabricated—"

"Floris." Nils's quiet voice cut through my darkening thoughts. "Massachusetts. Fresh start. Remember?"

I took a deep breath of garden air. He was right. In a few weeks, I'd be a regular student. No press following my every move. No need to watch every word, every gesture. No one recording me with their phones, waiting for me to mess up again.

"Yeah." I managed a genuine smile this time. "Though I still can't believe we're actually doing this."

"Not me." Greg slowly sat down again, the thought of a sandwich apparently forgotten. "The King won't allow it."

The King being the King of the United Kingdom, aka Greg's uncle.

"Maybe when Floris and I have a positive experience, he'll relent," Tore offered.

"Maybe." Greg didn't sound convinced, and I couldn't blame him. His life was far more scrutinized than that of any of us due to the British press that followed him like bloodhounds on a hunt. The last few months had not been easy for me, what with the scandal and all, but up until then, I'd had it relatively easy. The Dutch media was relaxed and tended to stick to the rules the royal family had agreed on with them, which meant the kids —my older brother plus my cousins and me—were off limits. Usually. Unless we did something stupid when visiting our best friend in the UK... like I had done.

Dammit, why could I not let it go? It had been three months by now, but it kept playing through my head, kept popping into my brain, kept resurfacing at the most inopportune times. Laurens, my brother, had assured me over and over it would take time. He meant well, but he was the golden boy in the eyes of the media, the guy who could do no wrong. Easy for him to say I should let it go.

"It may help to find a specific program you want to do rather than make a generalized request," Nils suggested. "You're studying International Relations, right?"

Greg nodded.

"So find some college or university that's specialized in that or that offers some highly acclaimed special program. Maybe that will help."

Not a bad idea, actually.

Greg seemed to consider it. "It's worth a try. Thanks."

"At least you know what you want to do," I said, finishing my beer. "The Dutch press is still waiting for me to find my 'purpose.' Apparently, becoming a civil engineer isn't it."

"Hey, you're Dutch. Water management is practically in your DNA," Nils pointed out.

"I know, but they probably expected something more... princely. You know, like international diplomacy or humanitarian work."

"Water management *is* humanitarian work," Tore said. "Ask New Orleans or, I don't know, Bangladesh."

A comfortable silence fell over our group. The sun was setting now, painting the old castle walls in shades of amber and gold. In a few weeks, I'd be trading this familiar view for a dorm room in Worcester, Massachusetts. The thought was both terrifying and exhilarating.

"Promise me one thing," Greg said suddenly, his voice serious. "If the press does find you, call us. Don't try to handle it alone."

I swallowed hard, remembering those first horrific weeks after the video surfaced. "I promise. But they won't find me. I'm going to be regular college student Floris who happens to be really into water management and terrible American beer."

"And maybe find someone special?" Tore waggled his eyebrows suggestively.

I threw my empty beer bottle at him. "Not everyone needs to find the love of their life in college. I'm going there to study, not to hook up."

"Sure," all three of them said in unison, and we burst out laughing.

"Besides," I added, "who'd want to date someone who can't even legally buy them a drink?"

"Ah yes, because that's the first thing people look for in a partner." Greg's voice dripped sarcasm. "The ability to purchase alcohol."

"All the more reason to keep things simple in Massachusetts. Study. Make normal friends. Maybe join some clubs that don't involve anything more scandalous than a heated debate about structural engineering."

"Sounds thrilling," Tore deadpanned. "You'll be the talk of the town. 'Dutch Student Really into Concrete.'"

"Better than 'Royal Romeo Ruins Reputation,'" I shot back, then immediately regretted it when their faces fell.

Greg leaned forward, his expression serious. "Look, mate, you did nothing wrong. That wanker should've come forward and told the truth."

"And risk his career? His reputation?" I shook my head. "No, it was better this way. Let people think what they want about me. I can take it."

"You shouldn't have to," Nils said quietly.

I stood up, suddenly restless. "Well, that's what being royal is about, isn't it? Taking it. Looking perfect. Never complaining." I forced a smile. "But hey, for one blessed year, I get to be Floris. No titles, no expectations, no press. Just me and my weird obsession with water management systems."

"And terrible American beer," Tore added helpfully.

"And terrible American beer," I agreed, grateful for the return to lighter territory. "Which, if the movies are correct, will be served in copious amounts in red cups at those infamous frat parties."

"That's the spirit," Tore said. "Who knows? Maybe you'll even join a fraternity."

A fraternity? Now there was a thought I hadn't considered. That whole Greek life, as the Americans called it, was rather foreign to me. Sure, we had fraternities at Dutch universities, but the American ones seemed to be at a whole other level. Something else I was eager to find out for myself.

Greg stood again. "Now, about those sandwiches..."

1

FLORIS

The things I did to prove a point.

I'd expected Massachusetts to be pleasant in the summer, like those idyllic New England postcards with their perfect, white churches and autumn leaves. The reality? Satan himself would've needed a cold shower.

Vernon Technical College looked as impressive in real life as it had in that fancy brochure they'd sent me, offering a fascinating mix of gothic-style buildings and modern, glass structures sprawled across gently rolling hills. My dormitory, Smelter Hall, stood like a proud sentinel among them, all Gothic arches and weathered stone that wouldn't have looked out of place in one of the older universities back home, like Leiden.

But the stately appearance had been deceiving. The ancient building clearly predated air conditioning and possibly the invention of comfort itself. Maybe back in 1910, they didn't believe one should be able to breathe in order to learn?

What a difference from the classic Dutch summer I'd left behind back home: windy, wet, and with a temperature hovering around eighteen degrees Celsius, woefully chilly for mid-August. A happy medium between the two would've been great. Which reminded me, I needed to figure out how to measure temperature in Fahrenheit. There was a formula that I had learned in physics back in high school, but that felt like ages ago. Eighteen degrees was... somewhere in the mid-sixties, maybe?

Sweat trickled down my spine as I hauled my two overstuffed suitcases—because apparently, I couldn't pack light to save my life—up yet another flight of stairs. The stairwell felt like a sauna designed by someone who'd never experienced joy. Through the tall, multi-paned windows, I caught glimpses of the pristine campus green, where other students lounged in the shade of century-old oaks, looking far more comfortable than I felt right now.

My polo shirt, which had started the day as a perfectly respectable piece of clothing, now clung to my back like a clingy ex who couldn't take a hint. When I stopped for a quick breather, the wrought-iron railing beneath my palm was hot enough to fry an egg, making me wonder if perhaps I should've listened to my father's advice about hiring movers. But no, I'd wanted the full college experience, hadn't I? Besides, I wasn't moving in with furniture or other big things. Just two suitcases and one oversized backpack.

I was seriously starting to regret my royal declaration of "I'll do everything myself, like any other student!" That had seemed noble and democratic when I'd announced it back home in the Netherlands. Before I'd discovered my room was on the third floor. Before I realized this architectural masterpiece had been designed by someone who thought elevators were for the weak. Before my harsh confrontation with the hell-like temperatures here.

"Oh, for fuck's sake," I muttered as I nearly dropped a suitcase on my foot. At this point, death by luggage was starting to look like an attractive alternative to climbing one more step.

Fuck me sideways with a windmill. At least back home, everything was flat.

I staggered up the last few steps to the third floor, my legs burning in protest. Note to self: three flights of stairs while lugging two seriously overweight suitcases? Not my brightest moment. They had spinner wheels, I had told myself. Fat lotta good that did me when I had to carry them.

The long corridor stretched before me like something out of *The Shining*, identical wooden doors marching along both sides. Room 314 waited halfway down, my home for the next year. Only a few more steps.

I took a deep breath, shifted my backpack, and knocked before using my key. The door swung open to reveal my new kingdom—all twenty square meters of it—and my roommate, who was already there. Orson Ritchey from New Orleans, according to the housing info. Twenty-four years old and in the first year of his master's degree in civil engineering. The Dean had placed me with an older student on purpose, he'd mentioned, perhaps worried the undergraduates would have a bad influence on me? Maybe he'd read some stories about me, the so-called Party Prince.

Orson stood at the window, tall and lean, with a riot of wild, brown curls that caught the sunlight streaming in. When he turned, his sharp features and intelligent, brown eyes behind wire-rimmed glasses stood out. He assessed me with the kind of focused intensity usually reserved for complicated mathematical equations. I fought the urge to check if my shirt was on backwards or if I'd grown a second head. Maybe he was judging me for being such a sweaty disaster?

"Hi," I said, dropping my suitcases and plastering on my

most winning smile. The same smile that had charmed count-less dignitaries and gotten me out of trouble more times than I could count. "I'm Floris. Your new roommate."

He crossed the room in three steps. "Orson."

His handshake was firm and precise, like everything else about him seemed to be. Major points for that. I'd suffered through enough limp handshakes at royal functions to last several lifetimes. Those always felt like holding a particularly unenthusiastic wet fish.

He gestured to the empty bed on the right side of the room. "That's yours."

I dragged my suitcases over, grateful to finally set them down. The room was smaller than I'd expected, with two narrow beds, two desks, and built-in closets. Orson's side was already meticulously organized: books arranged by size on his desk, his pencils and pens neatly lined up, and a small fan positioned perfectly in the window.

I winced. If he expected the same kind of neatness from me, he was in for a nasty shock. But right now, I had other news to share with him that was more pressing. While I had zero desire to announce my real identity to the whole campus, I did want to come clean to my roommate. He was bound to find out anyway when living with me, and I'd rather have him hear it from me.

"Listen," I said, wiping sweat from my forehead, "I should probably tell you something before we get settled in. The info you got about me said I was an exchange student from the Netherlands, but I'm actually—"

"A prince." He crossed his arms. "I got a call from the Dean's office yesterday, telling me that your last name wasn't van Orange but—"

"Van Oranje Nassau," I said softly, figuring he was stumbling over the pronunciation. "I'm sorry. I didn't know they would call you before I had a chance to explain myself."

"I was wondering why they'd placed me with an undergraduate, but it made sense when I found out about your identity."

"Yeah, I figured they were hoping a graduate student would have a positive influence on me?"

He quirked an eyebrow. "Do you need one? A positive influence, I mean?"

I firmly shook my head. "Nope, I'm good."

"But if you're a prince, what on earth are you doing here?"

"Getting an education, like you. I'm in my third year of university back in the Netherlands, and I'm doing this year at Vernon as part of an exchange program to finish my bachelor's degree in civil engineering."

"Because you need that for what, exactly?"

I sighed. "I'm fifth in line for the throne, Orson. I will never be king, and trust me, I'm delighted about that. But I am expected to do something with my life, to contribute to society in some meaningful way, so that's what I'm doing."

"I googled you."

I winced. Nothing good could come from seeing what the press wrote about me. Ask me how I knew. "Most of it are lies."

"I sure hope so because otherwise, we're gonna have a problem."

I held up my hands placatingly. "No problems, I swear. I want to study and fly under the radar. Other than you and the Dean, no one knows my real identity. All my papers say Floris van Oranje."

He studied me for a few beats more, then slowly nodded. "As long as you don't expect special treatment. I'm here to study, not babysit royalty."

"Trust me, that's the last thing I want," I assured him,

running a hand through my sweat-dampened hair. "I'm here to study and experience a somewhat normal college life. No royal fanfare, no special treatment. Hell, I'd prefer if you forgot about the whole prince thing entirely."

Orson's posture relaxed slightly, though his analytical gaze remained. "That's... surprisingly reasonable."

"Well, I do expect you to bow every time I enter the room..." I grinned, unable to resist teasing him a little. When his eyes widened in alarm, I quickly added, "I'm kidding. Seriously, I hate all that formal stuff. We have a saying in Dutch, which translated, goes, 'Just act normal and you'll be crazy enough.' The Dutch don't tolerate people who think they're above everyone else. Even our Prime Minister rides his bike to work."

Orson blinked. "That's interesting."

"Anyway, all this to say that I don't want any special treatment."

"Good, because I don't have time for that." I caught the ghost of a smile. "And don't expect me to be your tour guide. Or your party buddy. I have a strict study schedule, and I plan to stick to it."

"Duly noted." Of course, that was like offering a red rag to a bull because now I wanted to crack that disciplined exterior. There was something intriguing about my serious roommate, something that made me want to see what lay beneath all that careful control. Plus, he was seriously cute in an adorkable way.

His gaze flickered over my face, then to my suitcases. "You carried those up yourself?" There was a note of surprise in his voice, though his expression remained neutral.

"Yeah, I wanted the full college experience." I wheezed out a laugh, still trying to catch my breath. "Though I'm seriously regretting that decision now. I didn't expect the stairs to be quite so..."

"Brutal?" The corner of his mouth twitched. "Welcome to Smelter Hall, where every day is leg day."

"At least I won't need a gym membership." I collapsed onto my bare mattress. The springs creaked in protest, and I winced. "Please tell me the beds aren't always this loud."

The noise was concerning for more reasons than one. Hooking up would be a nightmare with these squeaky springs announcing every movement to the entire floor. Not that scoring a hookup was my first priority, but still. At some point, I would like to get some.

"They are." Orson returned to organizing his space, his movements precise and methodical as he arranged textbooks on his desk. "I brought a memory foam topper. It helps with both the noise and the medieval torture device they call a mattress."

I'd definitely have to order one of those. "Does Amazon deliver here?"

"Sure. Just don't order one in the next few days. They won't be able to get here during move-in week." He paused, those intelligent, brown eyes studying me again. "You may want to get a fan, too. The heat index is supposed to hit a hundred degrees tomorrow."

A hundred degrees? What was that in Celsius? Oh, wait, wasn't one hundred body temperature? So that would mean around thirty-seven Celsius.

"Sweet baby Jesus." I sat up, eyeing his fan with naked envy. "And here I thought the Netherlands was bad during our one week of summer."

That earned me another almost-smile, gone so quickly, I might have imagined it. "You really aren't what I expected."

"Let me guess, you pictured some spoiled brat who'd show up with an entourage and demand a red carpet?" When he didn't deny it, I laughed. "Sorry to disappoint. Though I do have excellent taste in clothes, if that helps maintain the image."

"I'll try to contain my excitement."

Dry as the Sahara, that one. But there was something oddly charming about his deadpan delivery.

I stood, grimacing at my sweat-soaked shirt. "I think I may grab a quick shower. I promise I'm usually more presentable, but these stairs have thoroughly humbled me."

"Bathroom's down the hall to the right." He gestured vaguely without looking up from his precise arrangement of notebooks. "Though fair warning, the water pressure's questionable at best."

"Builds character, right? That seems to be a theme here. Between the stairs, the mattress, and now questionable water pressure, my character should be stellar by the end of the year."

"At least you have a sense of humor about it." Orson's tone was dry, but there was something almost approving in it. He'd moved on to making his bed with a military precision any drill sergeant would be proud of.

I threw one of my suitcases on the bed and opened it. After some rummaging, I found my toiletries bag and a change of clothes. Thank fuck I had brought some mini bottles of shampoo and shower gel to tide me over until I could stop by a supermarket.

"Life's too short not to laugh at yourself occasionally." I headed for the door, then paused. "Hey, quick question. Any good places to grab coffee around here? I'm going to need industrial quantities to survive unpacking."

"The campus coffee shop's decent. It's in the student center." He adjusted his glasses, considering. "But if you want the good stuff, there's this place called Acoustic Java about ten minutes away. They roast their own beans."

"A man who knows his coffee. I knew we'd find common ground." I flashed him another grin before heading out.

As I walked down the hall, a smile played on my lips. I was stupidly excited about this year, even with the medieval mattress and Satan's sauna masquerading as a dorm.

At my request, the Dutch press had not been informed I would be studying abroad, which meant I could live in relative anonymity here. Granted, Dutch reporters were nowhere near as bad as the British tabloid press, but they could still be a nuisance, especially when one wanted privacy.

College was supposed to be about discovering yourself, about experimenting, about making mistakes and learning from them. But when your mistakes were shared with the whole world, little mishaps could become sensational headlines in a heartbeat. I'd been there and done that once. Never again.

No, I would treasure every moment of peace and quiet until, inevitably, the press would find out where I was. But hopefully, that would take them a while since my father had agreed he would not voluntarily tell anyone where I was.

In the meantime, I would embrace life as an American college student, including having a roommate. Orson fascinated me—in an uptight, absolutely-needs-to-loosen-up kind of way.

Challenge accepted.

2

ORSON

The cafeteria buzzed with the kind of chaotic energy that made my skin crawl. This was my fifth year at VTC, but I still hadn't gotten used to the constant noise, the throngs of bodies, the overwhelming smell of greasy food. New Orleans could be crazy busy, but the vibe was different, somehow, and it didn't get to me.

My laptop screen glowed with the problem set I'd been working on after finishing my dinner, but the numbers kept swimming before my eyes. They were off, somehow. I'd done the equations, but something didn't add up. The final numbers were nowhere near what I would've expected them to be. I'd already double-checked my calculations, but I had clearly missed something. Something that could mean the difference between a structure that stood and one that failed. In the real world, that could mean the difference between life and death. Just like one wrong step on that roof during Katrina...

I pushed that thought away, but it clung like the humid New Orleans air had that day. It had been twenty years by now, but the people who had said the pain would get less over time had lied. I missed him as much as I had as a kid, though maybe in different ways.

Fuck, I needed to focus on this problem. Professor Gibbons wouldn't be impressed if I didn't ace this, and I wanted her recommendation for when I graduated to get into a top engineering firm. It wasn't due for another two weeks, but still.

"You got this," I muttered to myself, a habit Mom always teased me about. But I needed to get this right. Civil engineering wasn't about passing classes for me or about getting a degree. It was about making sure no other four-year-old would have to watch their father disappear beneath rising waters. Every equation I solved, every structure I designed, was another step toward that goal.

Dad had been an engineer too. Would he be proud of me now, hunched over differential equations while other students actually enjoyed their college experience? Or would he want me to learn to live a little, like Mom kept suggesting? I rubbed my tired eyes beneath my glasses. It didn't matter. I couldn't afford distractions. Not when there was so much at stake.

I forced my attention back to the screen, but movement in my peripheral vision made me look up. Floris towered over my table, a tray laden with food in his hands and an easy smile on his face. After almost two weeks of living together, I'd noticed he wore that smile like armor: charming and practiced but rarely reaching his eyes.

Still, there was something magnetic about Floris, the way he carried himself with casual grace despite his imposing height, how his green eyes sparkled with good humor even when he complained about the "medieval" accommodations, the easy charm that rolled off him in waves and made you instantly like him.

"Mind if I join you?" he asked, already pulling out a chair. "Every other table looks like a freshman mixer, and I'm too old to explain what a cassette tape is."

I snorted. "It's a free country."

"So I keep hearing." He set down his tray and studied its contents with the kind of dismay usually reserved for discovering the milk was spoiled. "I still can't wrap my head around what passes for a balanced meal here. In Europe, this would be considered a cry for help."

Looking at his tray, I couldn't hold back my grin. He'd managed to collect what looked like one of everything: a slice of pizza, a burger, some fries, a scoop of pasta, and some sad-looking vegetables.

"Welcome to real college dining," I said, enjoying his horror. "You learn to survive on what's here, or your appetite gets creative fast."

"Creative?" Floris poked at his burger with a fork like he expected it to stab him back. "In the Netherlands, we prefer vegetables that haven't been waterboarded into submission. These look like they've confessed to crimes they didn't commit."

I laughed despite myself. His deadpan delivery combined with his slight Dutch accent made everything ten times funnier. "The salads are pretty decent here, but anything else can be sucked through a straw. What can I say, America is not known for its cuisine."

"You know what else I've noticed?" Floris said, and I closed my laptop. My study plans could wait; his commentary was too entertaining to miss.

"What?"

"Your portion sizes. They're massive. This burger is roughly the size of my head. Is this meant to feed me for the semester, or am I supposed to share it with the entire table?"

"That's nothing. Wait until you see Thanksgiving dinner. We basically eat until we hate ourselves, take a nap, then eat some more."

Floris's eyes widened. "You mean the turkey and the..." He waved his hand vaguely. "The orange stuff?"

"Sweet potato casserole. With marshmallow topping. And yeah, but that's only part of it. My mom makes this cornbread dressing that'll change your life." The memory of Mom's cooking made my chest ache a little. "Though nothing beats her gumbo."

"Gumbo? That's the famous soup from New Orleans, right?"

"Calling gumbo soup is like calling the Rhine a creek. It's more like..." I searched for words that would do justice to Mom's gumbo. "It's history in a pot. Every family has their own recipe, passed down through generations. Mom learned hers from my grandmother, who learned it from her mother. The secret's in the roux; if you don't near-burn it, you're not doing it right."

"Burn it?" Floris looked genuinely intrigued now, abandoning his assault on the burger. "On purpose?"

"Almost-burn it," I corrected. "It needs to be dark brown, like chocolate. Takes forever, standing there stirring flour and oil until your arm feels like it's gonna fall off. But that's what gives gumbo its depth."

"That sounds intriguing."

"What are some classic Dutch dishes?"

Floris shifted in his seat. "The Netherlands aren't known for haute cuisine either. Most fancy restaurants back home serve French food since the majority of our classic dishes are basically farmer's food. Take *stamppot*, for example. It literally means mashed dish, and it's mashed potatoes with vegetables mixed in, usually served with bacon bits, smoked sausage, and sometimes, gravy or butter."

"Mashed potatoes mixed with vegetables? Like what?"

"Depends on the version. Carrots, sauerkraut, or even broccoli. My favorite is kale." He grinned at my expression. "I know, I know. Americans think kale is this fancy superfood, but in the Netherlands, it's traditional winter food. Poor people's food, really. Though now it's having this weird renaissance because suddenly, everyone has discovered it's healthy."

I had trouble looking away, his enthusiasm infectious. The careful mask he usually wore had slipped, revealing something more genuine underneath. His eyes lit up when he talked about home, and his hands moved expressively as he described Dutch comfort food.

"Sounds pretty hearty," I said, trying to imagine it. "We've got something similar in New Orleans: dirty rice. Though we add more spice."

"I would kill for some spices. Everything here so far has been completely bland." Floris took a brave bite of the vegetables. His expression cycled through several emotions before settling on resignation. "Well," he said after swallowing, "let's hope the vitamins haven't been cooked to death."

"That's the spirit. Lower your standards enough and everything becomes edible."

"You're a terrible ambassador for American food culture, you know that?"

I shrugged. "Wait until you try Taco Bell at 2 a.m. That's when the real cultural education begins."

His green eyes sparkled with amusement. "Is that a threat or a promise?"

"Depends on how desperate for food you get during finals week."

I watched as he cut another precise bite of his burger, somehow managing to make even cafeteria food look elegant. His movements were graceful and practiced, probably from years of state dinners and formal events. Even here, surrounded by students wolfing down their food, he maintained perfect posture and proper table manners. It was kind of fascinating, actually, how he could make even this look dignified.

Then again, I hadn't seen one bad picture of him online yet. And yes, I had looked some more, this time ignoring the obvious trashy websites that kept showing this video of him that I had a hard time reconciling with what I'd seen of him so far, and focusing on official pictures of him, in which he looked so damn handsome.

Not that I was *looking*. Sure, I'd accepted my own sexuality years ago and had no issues with being gay, but dating and relationships were distractions I couldn't afford. My goals were too important to risk getting sidetracked by attraction, no matter how gracefully the guy ate terrible cafeteria food.

"You're staring," he said with a wide grin. His eyes crinkled at the corners when he really smiled. Not that practiced, princely smile he usually wore, but something more genuine.

Heat crept up my neck. "Sorry. I was..." I scrambled for an explanation that wouldn't sound weird. "...thinking about how different our food cultures are."

"Nice save." His eyes sparkled with amusement. "Though I bet we could find some common ground. Both our cultures have a thing for fried food, for instance. You should try *bitterballen* sometimes. They're these crispy little balls filled with beef ragout."

"Sounds better than whatever this is supposed to be." I gestured at the mystery meat on my own tray. "Though I'm confident nothing beats New Orleans beignets."

"Bet you my *stroopwafels* could give them a run for their money."

"Your what now?"

"*Stroopwafels*. Two thin waffle cookies with caramel syrup in between." His face lit up. "Actually, I have some in our room. It turns out Walmart here sells them, which made me very happy. Want to try one later?"

The offer caught me off guard. I usually avoided getting too friendly with roommates. It complicated things, created expectations I couldn't meet while maintaining my focus on studies. But something about Floris made it hard to keep my usual distance.

"Sure," I heard myself say. "Thanks."

His genuine smile, so different from his usual polished one, made something flutter in my chest. I quickly looked back at my laptop, reminding myself why I was here. Civil engineering. Preventing disasters. Making Dad proud. I couldn't afford distractions, even tall, charming Dutch ones with kind eyes and intriguing food.

But one cookie wouldn't hurt, right?

"So what else do you miss?" I asked. "Food-wise, I mean."

"Proper bread." He sighed dramatically. "Dark, dense bread that doesn't taste like sugar. And *hagelslag*."

He sounded like he was choking with two harsh g-sounds. "What now?"

"Chocolate sprinkles. But not like the ones here. Ours are different. We eat them on bread for breakfast."

I stared at him. "You eat sprinkles. For breakfast."

"On wholewheat bread with butter!" he defended, as if that made it more reasonable. "Don't judge until you've tried it. Though I suppose it does sound a bit ridiculous when I say it out loud."

"Says the guy who questioned our portion sizes and how unhealthy our food was," I teased. "At least we don't eat dessert toppings for breakfast."

His laughter was surprisingly warm and real, nothing like

the polite chuckles I usually heard from him. "Fair point. Though I maintain that your vegetables are still guilty of war crimes. Plus, you eat donuts for breakfast. Those have got to be worse than *hagelslag*."

We were quiet for a while as he ate.

"So," Floris said finally, pushing his tray away, "what are you working on?"

I tensed slightly. "An assignment for Advanced Structural Analysis. Professor Gibbons likes to give us assignments right out of the gate."

"Ah." He nodded sagely. "That explains why you look like the numbers personally offended you."

"They might have." I glared at my laptop. "There's this one problem that's being particularly stubborn. We have to calculate the load-bearing capacity of a bridge, but the numbers feel off."

"Want another set of eyes? Maybe I can offer a fresh perspective?" When I hesitated, he added, "No pressure. Just offering."

I studied him for a moment. Most people didn't volunteer to look at engineering problems for fun, but then again, Floris had surprised me more than once already. Like finding him watching that documentary about climate change yesterday evening. That had been about the last thing I had expected of him. "The Party Prince", the European tabloids called him, but so far, I saw little evidence of him partying.

"Sure. Why not?"

I flipped my laptop open and he moved his chair around to my side of the table, suddenly close enough that I could smell his cologne: something subtle and expensive that made me think of crisp, autumn mornings. His shoulder brushed mine as he leaned in to look at my screen. For a minute or so, he said nothing as he read through the problem and studied the numbers on the screen.

"Where is the bridge located?" he asked.

As soon as he asked it, the missing part popped into my brain like a jack-in-the-box. "Environmental loads. I didn't properly account for those. It's located near San Francisco."

"Earthquakes." He nodded. "Plus probably changes in temperature? Not sure how cold it gets there during the winter."

"The wind is a factor too. They even had a tornado warning recently, so I'd have to take that into account as well. I did the standard environmental load, but in this case, it should be much lower considering the circumstances. Thank you."

"You did the work yourself. All I did was ask a question." He smiled, and this close, I could see the faint freckles scattered across his nose. "Well, since I've saved you from a mathematical crisis, want to try those *stroopwafels* now?"

I glanced at my watch and realized with a start that we'd been talking for almost an hour. This had been… nice. Easy, in a way conversations rarely were for me. "I should finish this first."

"Right, of course." The mask slipped back into place, but not completely. There was still warmth in his eyes as he gathered his mostly untouched food. "Thanks for the cultural exchange. Even if your country's idea of cuisine is deeply concerning."

"Save me a cookie," I said quickly, somehow uneasy with the hint of disappointment on his face.

His smile was back. "Will do. See you in a little bit?"

I nodded.

His long legs ate up the ground as he walked away, my eyes glued to his back. Should I have said yes? But if I had, he would've lured me into more conversations and then I would've had to scramble to finish this project.

I needed to focus. I had goals. Important ones. Getting distracted by my roommate's infectious laugh and the way his whole face transformed when he talked about something he loved wasn't part of the plan. Even if he did look unfairly good in that blue henley that brought out the green in his eyes. Even if those jeans clung to his round ass and made it pop.

Nope. Not going there.

Maybe there was more to my roommate than met the eye, but I couldn't afford to find out.

3

FLORIS

I stared at my phone, willing the numbers to change. Who in their right mind scheduled classes this early? Back home, nothing started before nine, a perfectly civilized hour that didn't require sacrificing sleep or sanity. But here I was, two weeks into my American college experience, contemplating if showing up to class in pajamas would be too much of a cultural faux pas.

Then again, Americans didn't really seem to care much about things like that. I'd seen people grab coffee while clearly still in their sleepwear. Maybe I was assimilating with more ease than I had thought?

Nah, I was still processing surprises every day, unexpected cultural customs and fascinating habits that baffled me. Sure, I'd visited the States before, but those had been carefully orchestrated royal visits with reasonable schedules and minimal interaction with actual American daily life or, for lack of a better word, ordinary Americans.

TV shows and movies hadn't prepared me for the reality of American college culture either. Where were the frat parties and the Greek life they had promised me? So far, the wildest thing

I'd witnessed was someone double-fisting energy drinks during a late-night study session.

My theory was that Vernon Tech attracted a different crowd than those party schools I'd seen in films. These students actually seemed serious about their education—a fact that would probably shock the tabloids if they ever found me here. It didn't really match their image of me. It was a major reason why I had picked VTC and not some easy party college.

What had surprised me most, though, was how friendly everyone was. Complete strangers said, "Hi," on campus, which would've earned you concerned looks at best and a few choice curse words at worst in Amsterdam. The cashier at the campus store had asked how my day was going, and she'd actually seemed interested in the answer. Back home, small talk was reserved for people you knew, and even then, it was more about complaining about the weather than genuine conversation.

Speaking of weather, the humidity here was doing ungodly things to my hair. No wonder Americans were obsessed with air conditioning. Without it, we'd all probably melt into puddles of sweat and regret. The Dutch might complain about rain, but at least we didn't have to deal with air that felt like breathing through a wet blanket.

Unable to avoid the inevitable any longer, I finally slid out of bed. Orson was already up and had been for a while, judging by the pristine state of his side of the room. Even his bed was made with those precise hospital corners that made my messily bundled sheets look like modern art gone wrong. He was probably out to get some coffee or something, his one vice as far as I could tell.

Yawning and stumbling around in pre-coffee haze, I gathered my shower supplies, then grabbed my brand-new, bright red flip-flops. I'd never been a flip-flop guy but they were a necessity here, so I found a pair for ten bucks at Target. Four generations of ancestors were beaming with pride for being that frugal.

I stumbled to the bathroom, which was at the end of the hallway, hoping a shower stall would be available. The shared facilities were another thing I was still getting used to. Back home, I'd had my own bathroom, obviously... and someone who had cleaned it for me. Here, I had to dodge half-naked guys in various states of wakefulness if I wanted to brush my teeth.

I kept my eyes firmly fixed ahead as I navigated the morning traffic of towel-clad students. Being openly gay meant I had to be extra careful. One wrong glance, one lingering look, and I'd be that creepy gay dude perving on straight guys in the bathroom.

And these guys might not know my royal status, but if they ever found out, I didn't want any cause for rumors. The tabloids would have a field day with that one: *Gay Prince Causes Scandal in American College Showers.*

No, thanks. I'd learned my lesson about public spaces and unwanted attention. These days, I treated communal bathrooms like a museum of classical statues: appreciate the artistry in theory, but don't touch and definitely don't stare at their junk.

The bathroom was already steamy when I entered, the ancient pipes groaning like tortured souls. Three of the four shower stalls were occupied, their occupants hidden behind thin, plastic curtains that had seen better days. The fourth one—my target—had a puddle forming underneath it that suggested the drain was having an existential crisis.

Perfect. Just perfect.

I picked my way across the wet floor, trying not to think about what might be living in that puddle. The shower curtain stuck to my arm as I stepped in, and I suppressed a shudder. Back home, I'd never appreciated the luxury of a clean, private bathroom. Now? I'd trade my favorite pair of shoes for one shower without wearing flip-flops.

The water pressure was its usual pathetic self, more of a suggestion than an actual stream. I tilted my head back, letting the lukewarm spray hit my face while trying to ignore the off-key butchering of a Taylor Swift song coming from two stalls down. At least someone was having a good morning.

The water suddenly turned ice cold, yanking me from my thoughts with a yelp that was entirely undignified for someone of my station. Another charming quirk of ancient plumbing. In the summer, it wasn't that bad, but in the winter, an involuntary ice bath like that would be a nasty shock to my system.

When I got back to our room, Orson was at his desk, studying, his posture perfect even as he sat at his desk. How did he do that? I always ended up slouching like a melting snowman. A cup of steaming coffee was right next to him, and my mouth watered as the smell hit me. I swallowed.

"Morning."

"Morning." Orson looked up from his textbook. "I brought you coffee too."

"Oh my god, thank you. You're amazing." I eagerly reached for the cup he'd put on my desk.

He swallowed, his eyes traveling lower. "Don't you want to get dressed first? The coffee will be too hot to drink anyway."

I looked down at myself. Right. I was wearing only boxer briefs. "Good thinking."

With regret, I put the coffee back down, then rummaged through my closet until I'd found a pair of clean shorts. Hmm, I also needed a shirt. Had I put away my laundry yesterday? No. The clean pile was... somewhere.

"Your clean clothes are on your chair," Orson said.

I turned around and found him staring at me. Was he annoyed with me? He looked a bit... tense. "Huh?"

"The ones you left in the dryer last night? I brought them up when I got mine."

"You're a saint." I dug through the pile, trying not to scatter socks everywhere. "Though I swear I meant to get them myself."

"Before or after they became communal property?" His tone was dry but not unkind. "You left them there for three hours."

"Sorry." I winced, finally locating an acceptable shirt. "I got caught up watching a documentary about the Dutch Delta Works and lost track of time. Completely forgot about them."

"The what works?"

"Delta Works. It's this massive system of dams, sluices, locks, dikes, levees, and storm surge barriers." I pulled the shirt over my head. "They started building it after this huge flood in 1953 that killed almost two thousand people. It's why I want to be a civil engineer, actually. Water management is kind of our thing in the Netherlands."

When I emerged from the shirt, Orson was watching me with an odd expression. "I didn't know it had a name. The Dutch system, I mean. I knew you guys had a way of keeping the water out, but not that it had a name. Or that it was built after a flooding."

"Yeah, it's pretty impressive. The American Society of Civil Engineers named it one of the Seven Wonders of the Modern World." I started gathering my books, trying to remember if I'd done the reading for today's class. "We have this saying in Dutch: 'God created the world, but the Dutch created the Netherlands.' About a third of our country is below sea level, you know."

"Really?" Now I had his full attention. "How does that even work?"

"Lots of pumps. And dikes. And constant maintenance." I

grinned, warming to the topic despite my morning fog. "We've been fighting the water for centuries. It's basically our national hobby at this point, right after complaining about the weather."

"But how do you keep the water from seeping in?" Orson's brow furrowed in that way it did when he was working through a complex problem. "The pressure must be immense."

"That's where the engineering comes in. We've got these things called polders. They're basically reclaimed land surrounded by dikes. Inside each polder, there's a complex network of canals and pumping stations that constantly remove water." I put my backpack down and grabbed my phone, pulling up some pictures I'd taken back home. "See these windmills? They weren't for show. Originally, they powered the pumps that kept the land dry."

Orson leaned in. "And now?"

"Electric pumps, mostly. Though we keep the windmills maintained. They're our back-up system if the power fails." I swiped to another picture. "This is the Oosterscheldekering. It's my favorite part of the Delta Works."

"Why's that?"

"Because it's a perfect balance of engineering and ecology. They originally planned to dam up the entire estuary, but environmentalists pointed out it would most likely destroy the ecosystem. So instead, they built this storm surge barrier that lets water flow through normally but can close when needed. That meant the ecosystem wasn't impacted, thus saving many species, including our beloved mussels." I realized I was rambling and felt heat creep up my neck. "Sorry, I get a bit excited about this stuff."

"Don't apologize." My breath caught as Orson leaned closer, his shoulder brushing mine as he studied the picture on my phone. The contact sent a shiver down my spine that had nothing to do with the fan blasting air at me. This close, I could smell the faint scent of his shampoo: something clean and citrusy. "It's refreshing to meet someone else who understands why this matters."

I was just going to pretend I wasn't impacted by his presence at all. I could do that, right? "This is the Maeslantkering, another part of the Delta Works. Those arms are about as long as the Eiffel Tower is tall."

"Holy shit," he breathed, and I couldn't help but grin at his obvious fascination. "And it moves?"

"Yep. When there's a storm surge, they swing shut to protect Rotterdam's harbor. The whole thing is automated, with computers monitoring the water levels and weather conditions." I paused, remembering something. "Actually, after Katrina, some American engineers came to study our system and we sent Dutch engineers to New Orleans to advise."

The mention of Katrina made Orson tense beside me. Was that a sore topic for him? He must've been old enough to experience it. Had it been traumatic? Not something I wanted to ask him about now, but I filed it away for future reference.

"Unfortunately, little of it was implemented," Orson said, his face tight.

"I'm sure it was complicated. The Mississippi Delta is very different from the situation in my country."

Orson let out a heavy sigh, one that seemed charged with a lot more than mere frustration. "It wasn't that. It was about the cost and politics, and ultimately, about the decision that money mattered more than people's lives... and preventing another Katrina."

The bitterness in his voice caught me off guard. This wasn't academic interest; this was personal. I wanted to ask more, but something in his expression warned me off. Instead, I checked my phone again and groaned. "Speaking of preventing disasters, I should probably head to class before I'm late. Again." I stuffed my books into my backpack. "Thanks for rescuing my laundry, by the way. I'll try to be more responsible next time."

"No problem." He was already back to his textbook, that moment of vulnerability gone like it had never happened.

I grabbed my coffee, accidentally knocking over a pile of books I'd left precariously balanced on my desk. They crashed to the floor with a sound like thunder.

Orson jumped. "Jesus Christ!"

"Sorry, sorry!" I scrambled to pick them up. "I'll organize these properly later, I promise."

His sigh was equal parts exasperation and resignation. "You said that yesterday. And the day before."

"I mean it this time?" I tried my most winning smile, the one that usually got me out of trouble.

"Your chaos is migrating," he pointed out, gesturing to where one of my hoodies had somehow ended up on his perfectly made bed. "I'm starting to think you're actually a very tall tornado disguised as a person."

Heat crept up my neck. "I'll fix it. Really. As soon as I'm done with classes today."

"Sure." His tone suggested he didn't believe me, and honestly? Fair enough. "Though you might want to do something about your hair first."

"What's wrong with my hair?" I patted it cautiously, then caught my reflection in my phone screen. "Oh, fuck me."

The humidity had turned my usually manageable waves into something that looked like I'd stuck my finger in an electrical socket. No wonder Orson had given me an amused look. I made a futile attempt to tame it with my fingers, but it sprang right back up like some sort of demented jack-in-the-box.

I sighed deeply. "This is my life now. I'll just tell everyone it's a bold fashion statement."

That earned me a snort from Orson. "You could try using product."

"I did right when I got out of the shower. The humidity ate it." I shouldered my backpack, accepting defeat. "The weather here is personally offended by my hair's existence. I'm convinced of it."

"Welcome to New England. Where the weather's made up and the seasons don't matter."

"Did you make a joke?" I gasped in mock horror. "Quick, someone check if hell's frozen over."

"I contain multitudes." His deadpan delivery was perfect, but I caught the slight quirk at the corner of his mouth. "Now go be late for class."

"Yes, sir." I threw him a mock salute and headed for the door, then paused. "Hey, want to grab coffee later? That place you mentioned, Acoustic Java?"

The question surprised both of us, I think. I hadn't planned to ask, but something about our conversation about water management and his reaction to Katrina made me want to know more. Plus, he actually seemed interested in engineering beyond passing classes, which was refreshing.

Orson hesitated, his expression doing that thing where he seemed to be calculating all possible outcomes before making a decision. "I have a study group at four."

"Before, then? Come on, you can explain more about American water management systems to me. I'll even buy you one of those fancy drinks with too many words in the name."

"I have to study."

"You always have to study." The words came out before I

could stop them. "I mean, everyone needs breaks, right? Even engineering students."

Orson sighed, looking away. "Maybe. It depends on how much progress I've made by then."

That wasn't a no, and I clung to that hope. "Awesome, see you then."

I rushed out the door, speed-walking across campus. The late-August sun was already blazing, promising another day of sticky heat. Students sprawled on the grass, enjoying the last days of summer, while others hurried to class like me.

I couldn't help smiling, despite being late and probably looking like I'd been dragged backward through a hedge. This was exactly what I'd wanted: to be another student rushing to class, no press following my every move. Just me, my wrinkled shirt—I really should've hung up that laundry—and the promise of caffeine after class.

Though I could probably use some help with the organization thing. Maybe Orson would teach me his ways if I bribed him with more Dutch snacks...

My mind wandered back to Orson's reaction to my messy habits. He wasn't wrong; I was a tornado in human form compared to his meticulous organization. But there was something endearing about how he pretended to be annoyed while still bringing up my laundry, getting me coffee, and reminding me about class times.

My phone buzzed as I slid into my seat in the lecture hall, barely making it before class started. A message from Greg lit up my screen:

GREG

Survived peasant life so far? Or has the lack of servants broken you?

I snorted, earning a few looks from nearby students.

ME

Still alive. Though American plumbing is trying
to kill me. Also, did you know they start class at
8 AM? That has to violate some human rights
convention.

GREG

The horror. Shall I send a diplomatic rescue
mission?

ME

Nah, I'm good. Actually enjoying being normal
for once. Though my roommate probably thinks
I'm a disaster.

GREG

But is he wrong?

ME

Rude. I'm perfectly capable of taking care of
myself.

I paused, thinking of the chaos currently occupying my side
of the room, then added:

ME

Mostly.

GREG

Sure, Your Highness. Whatever helps you sleep
on your peasant mattress.

The professor started talking before I could respond with an
appropriately witty comeback. I tucked my phone away, trying to
focus on stochastic differential equations instead of Greg's
teasing or my roommate's perfectly organized desk.

Speaking of Orson, I needed to get my mess under control
before he snapped and murdered me in my sleep. Though

knowing him, he'd probably clean up the crime scene afterward and neatly sort my remains, labeling each bone.

The thought made me smile. For someone so serious, he had a surprisingly sharp sense of humor when he let his guard down. Now if only I could figure out how to make that happen more often...

4

ORSON

The Vernon Tech library surrounded me like a cathedral of learning, all polished wood and towering shelves that disappeared into shadowy heights. Light streamed through tall, arched windows, highlighting dust motes that danced in the air. The quiet murmur of students and the subtle creaking of old wood created that particular library atmosphere that usually calmed me, but today, even that couldn't ease my frustration.

I stared at my laptop screen until the words blurred together, the feedback from Professor Chen burning into my retinas.

While your technical analysis is sound, the project management approach lacks practical consideration of real-world variables...

Real-world variables. Because I knew nothing about those.

My hands clenched into fists under the table. I'd spent hours on this assignment, triple-checking every calculation, reviewing every detail. But somehow, I'd still missed something crucial. The weight of disappointment settled heavy in my chest, mixing with that familiar guilt. How could I ever hope to succeed in the real world when I couldn't even do it in a college-level assignment?

Project management was a required course, and though I hated it, I could see the crucial importance of it. It sucked that I was so bad at it.

"There you are!"

I jumped at Floris's voice, nearly knocking over my coffee. He dropped into the chair across from me with his usual grace, all long limbs and easy smile. Today, he wore a soft-looking, navy T-shirt that made his green eyes even more striking. Not that I was noticing things like that.

"I've been looking everywhere for you," he said. "You missed dinner."

I clicked away from the feedback. "Not hungry."

"Liar. You've been here since your last class ended. That's..." He checked his phone. "Five hours ago."

"I'm fine."

"Sure." His tone made it clear he didn't believe me. "That's why you're trying to murder your laptop with your stare."

I sighed, pushing my glasses up to rub my tired eyes. "Don't you have somewhere else to be?"

"Nope." He popped the "p" sound, settling in like he planned to stay awhile. "Want to tell me what's wrong?"

"Nothing's wrong."

"Right." He leaned forward, those green eyes far too perceptive. "And I'm the King of England."

The absurdity of that statement, coming from an actual prince, almost made me smile. Almost. "It's..." I hesitated, but something in his expression made me continue. "Got some feedback on my project management assignment. It wasn't great."

"Define 'wasn't great.'"

When I showed him the screen, his eyebrows shot up.

"That's what has you looking like someone killed your puppy? These are good comments."

"Good?" I scoffed. "She said it lacks practical consideration of real-world variables."

"Yeah, but your technical analysis was sound. So you're missing some parts, big deal. It's not like she wants you to rewrite the whole thing. Let me read it."

Before I could protest, he'd moved his chair around to my side of the table. He leaned in to read, and I caught a whiff of that subtle cologne he wore. It was as distracting as everything else about him. For all the focus I prided myself on, I had a hard time ignoring him, especially when we were in our room. He drew my eyes like a magnet.

"Ah," he said after a few minutes. "I see what she means."

"What?"

"You've covered all the technical risks perfectly, but you haven't considered the human element enough." His finger traced down the screen. "Like here. You've accounted for material failures and structural stress, but what about worker safety? Communication breakdowns? Cultural differences between teams?"

I blinked. "How do you know about project management?"

He snorted. "My whole life has been nothing but project management, though maybe not quite as technical as this. But management does come naturally to me."

"Right." I'd almost forgotten who he was, which was probably exactly what he wanted. "I guess royal duties involve a lot of coordination."

"You have no idea." His voice held a hint of something darker, but it vanished quickly. "Look, you've got all the technical aspects nailed, but projects don't exist in a vacuum. People are messy. They miscommunicate, they have bad days, they make assumptions."

I frowned at the screen. "But those are variables I can't control."

"Exactly." His eyes lit up with understanding. "That's what scares you, isn't it? The unpredictable human element?"

The observation hit too close to home. I shifted uncomfortably in my chair. "I prefer working with numbers. They don't lie. They don't make mistakes."

"No, but people do. And people are who we're building for." His voice was gentle but firm. "The most brilliant engineering solution in the world won't work if the people implementing it don't understand it, if cultural differences create communication barriers, or if budget constraints force shortcuts."

I wanted to argue, but he had a point. "So what would you suggest?"

"Add a section about stakeholder management. Communication protocols. Cultural considerations if you're working with international teams." His fingers flew across the keyboard as he made notes for me. "Training requirements, safety protocols, contingency plans for human error."

The suggestions were actually... good. Really good.

"You've done this before."

He laughed softly. "I've seen my share of projects go sideways because someone forgot to account for the human factor. Did you know we once had a visiting dignitary almost cause an international incident because no one told him we eat our famous herring raw?"

I blinked. "Like sushi, raw?"

"Like, served with diced onions and holding it by the tail, then lowering it into your mouth, raw."

My eyes widened. "Excuse me? That doesn't sound appetizing in the least."

He leaned in. "It's disgusting. But don't ever tell anyone I said that. They'd revoke my Dutch citizenship for blasphemy like that."

Despite myself, I smiled. "No, they wouldn't."

He winked at me. "You don't know that. We take our raw herring very seriously." He grinned, then turned serious again. "My point is, technical excellence is crucial, but it's not everything. The best engineers are the ones who understand that they're building for people."

His words struck something in me: a truth I'd been avoiding. I'd focused so hard on the technical aspects because they were safe, predictable. Unlike people. Unlike that day on the roof when human decisions had meant the difference between life and death.

"It's hard for me. These kinds of courses. And I want to get it right."

"I know." His voice was surprisingly gentle. "But maybe perfect isn't always possible. Maybe sometimes, good enough, with room for human factors, is better than technical perfection that doesn't account for reality."

I looked at him then, really looked at him. Gone was the carefree prince persona he usually wore. Instead, I saw someone who understood more than he let on, who carried his own weight of expectations and fears.

"Want to help me revise this?" I asked before I could think better of it.

His smile lit up his whole face. "Thought you'd never ask."

For the next hour, Floris helped me restructure my project plan, adding layers I hadn't even considered. He had an uncanny knack for spotting potential human complications, probably from years of navigating royal protocols and diplomatic relations. It was eye-opening.

"See here?" He pointed at a section about resource allocation. "You need to consider language barriers, different time zones if you're working internationally, even religious or holiday schedules in different countries. Like the Fourth of July here."

"Or Mardi Gras back home."

"Oh?" His eyes lit up with interest. "I've heard of Mardi Gras. It's like a parade, right?"

"It's hard to explain. Beautiful and chaotic and probably something you have to experience to understand. The whole city transforms. People throw beads from floats, there's music everywhere, and everyone eats king cake until they're sick."

"King cake?" He perked up. "Finally, a cake fit for my station."

"Not that kind of king." I found myself smiling despite my earlier mood. "It's named for the three kings who visited baby Jesus. There's a plastic baby hidden inside, and if you get it in your slice, you have to buy the next cake."

"You hide plastic babies in cake?" He looked genuinely horrified. "That seems highly unsafe, not to mention a tad creepy."

"Says the guy who eats raw fish by dangling it over his mouth."

"Touché." He laughed, then gestured back at my screen. "Speaking of cultural differences, that's exactly the kind of thing you need to consider in project management. What seems normal to you might be bizarre to someone else."

He had a point. I added a section about cultural awareness and communication protocols, surprised by how naturally the words flowed now that I had a different perspective. "This was really helpful. Thanks."

"Any time." His smile was warm, genuine in a way his usual

polished one wasn't. "Though I do accept payment in the form of coffee or those beignets you keep talking about."

"Deal." The word was out before I could stop it. "I mean, if you want. Not that you have to—"

"Orson." He cut off my rambling with gentle amusement. "I want to. Besides, someone needs to teach you that there's life outside this library."

"I have a life," I protested weakly.

"Really? When's the last time you did something for fun?"

I opened my mouth, then closed it. When was the last time? Between classes, studying, and my self-imposed pressure to excel, I couldn't remember.

"That's what I thought." His voice held no judgment, only understanding. "Look, I'm not saying you need to go wild. But it's okay to take a break sometimes. To let yourself breathe."

Something in his tone made me look up. His green eyes were serious now, holding none of their usual mischief. For a moment, I saw past the charming prince exterior to someone who might understand more than I'd given him credit for.

"I don't know how to find that balance. Or even where to start."

"You can start by agreeing to explore Worcester with me this weekend."

I immediately opened my mouth to protest. "I can't." When he simply quirked an eyebrow, I cringed. "I have to... study?"

"Do you? Or do you tell yourself you have to because it's easier?"

Fuck, he was seeing so much more than I thought... than I liked. "I don't know."

"What do you want to do once you have your master's?"

"Find a job as a civil engineer and get the experience I need to ultimately help my city or other areas that are in danger zones for extreme flooding."

"And then?"

I frowned. "What do you mean?"

"When will you have time to make friends? To date or hook up? To find someone you want to share your life with?"

The question caught me off guard. "Dating isn't really a priority right now."

"Because you're focusing on your studies, or because you're afraid?"

"I'm not afraid," I said automatically, but the words felt hollow even to me. "I don't have time for distractions."

"Is that what relationships are to you? Distractions?"

I shifted uncomfortably in my chair. "Look, not everyone needs to date in college. Some of us have more important things to focus on."

"Like saving the world through perfect engineering?" His tone was gentle, taking any sting out of the words. "You know, it's possible to do both. To work toward your goals and still have a personal life."

"Maybe for some people." I started gathering my things, suddenly needing to escape this conversation. "But I can't afford to lose focus. Not when..."

I stopped myself, but Floris leaned forward, his eyes intent on my face. "Not when what?"

"Nothing." I shoved my laptop into my bag with more force than necessary. "Thanks for the help with the project plan."

"Orson." His hand caught my wrist, stopping my frantic packing. His touch was warm, sending an unexpected shiver up my arm.

"What?"

"If you googled me, you know I'm gay. Openly gay."

What did that have to do with anything? "Yes."

"All I'm saying is that you can talk to me. I'm a safe space."

It took me a few seconds to work out what he meant. "I'm not in the closet. I mean, I'm gay, but I'm out. Well, to those that need to know, anyway, like my mom and my sister."

His brows furrowed. "But you're not out on campus?"

I shifted in my seat, avoiding his eyes. "It's not a secret or something. I just don't date. Or..." I swallowed, "...hook up."

"Why not?" His voice was soft, understanding.

God, where did I even begin with explaining that? I started packing up again, needing to move, to do something with my hands. "I can't..."

"Can't what? Live?"

His words stopped me cold.

"Because that's what you're doing, you know. Not living. You're merely existing."

The truth in his words hit like a physical blow. "You don't understand."

"Don't I?" Something flickered across his face—pain, maybe, or regret. "You think I don't know what it's like to be paralyzed by the fear of making the wrong choice? To feel like every decision could have catastrophic consequences?"

I stared at him, really seeing him, beyond the charming smile and easy grace. He was someone who understood more than I'd realized. A man who carried his own weight of expectations and fears. "That video," I said slowly. "That's why you're here, isn't it? To escape?"

The grainy video had been easy to find once I'd googled him. Floris pressed against some guy outside a London club, their faces close. The headlines had screamed about assault, about the Dutch prince forcing himself on someone. But watching it, something hadn't added up. The way the other guy's hands had gripped Floris's shirt, pulling him closer rather than pushing away. How the clip cut off right as the other man leaned in. The editing had been deliberate, manipulative. And Floris's silence afterward, refusing to defend himself despite the media frenzy, spoke volumes about his character.

Floris's expression shuttered so fast, it was like watching a door slam. "That's not—" He stopped, ran a hand through his hair. "It's complicated."

"Because you couldn't defend yourself without outing someone else." The words came out before I could stop them. When his head snapped up, I added quickly, "I did more research. Found some Dutch articles that seemed more balanced than the British tabloids."

He was quiet for a long moment, his fingers tracing patterns on the wooden table. "You know what the worst part was?" His voice was barely above a whisper. "Everyone assumed I'd done something wrong. That I'd forced myself on him. And I couldn't say anything without making it worse for him."

The pain in his voice made my chest tight. "That must've been hard."

"Yeah." He gave a hollow laugh. "But hey, at least it taught me a valuable lesson about trust and public spaces." His smile was bitter. "And about how quickly people will believe the worst of you."

I knew something about that, about having people make assumptions, about carrying the weight of others' expectations and judgments. Though in my case, it was more about living up to my father's sacrifice, proving I was worth saving.

"Is that why you're so careful here? Why you don't want people to know who you are?"

"Partly." He shrugged, but I could see the tension in his shoulders. "I want one year where I can mess up without it making international headlines. Where I can be me. Without the crown, without the expectations. Without having to be perfect all the time."

The longing in his voice resonated with something deep inside me. How many times had I wished for the same thing? To be free of the guilt, the pressure, the constant need to prove myself? "I get it. Not the royal part, obviously. But the pressure to be perfect? The fear of messing up? Yeah, I get that."

Our eyes met across the table, and I saw recognition there, a shared understanding that went beyond words. Here was someone else who knew what it was like to live under the weight of expectations, albeit for very different reasons.

"We're quite a pair, aren't we?" His smile was softer now, more genuine.

"I'm not—" I started to protest, but he cut me off with a look.

He leaned forward, those green eyes intense. "So here's what we're going to do. This weekend, we're going to explore Worcester. No studying, no responsibilities. Two guys checking out their new city."

"It's not new to me."

"It is if you've never made the effort to do some sightseeing."

"I can't—"

"You can. The world won't end if you take one day off." His voice softened. "Trust me, I'm something of an expert on balancing duty and personal life. Or at least, I'm learning to be."

I should say no. I had reading to do, problems to solve, a perfect GPA to maintain. But something in his expression made me hesitate. Maybe he was right. Maybe I did need to learn how to live a little.

I took a deep breath. "Okay."

5

FLORIS

Worcester's downtown spread before us. Historic brick buildings stood shoulder to shoulder with modern, glass structures, all bathed in the golden light of a September morning. The Commons buzzed with weekend activity, food trucks lining the periphery while students and locals sprawled on the grass, soaking up what might be one of the last warm days before fall truly set in.

"I can't believe you actually came with me," I said to Orson as we walked, still half-expecting him to suddenly remember an urgent study session and bolt. He looked different outside of our dorm room—more relaxed somehow, though still carrying himself with that careful precision that seemed as much a part of him as his wild curls.

And, much to my surprise, he was carrying a camera. A very nice one, even.

"I said I would, didn't I?" He adjusted his glasses, a habit I'd noticed he had when feeling defensive. "Besides, you wouldn't stop texting me reminders this morning when I was at the library."

"I sent exactly three texts."

"In the span of ten minutes."

"I was being thorough." I grinned at his eye roll. "Come on, even you have to admit this beats staring at textbooks all day."

"I plead the fifth."

Not wanting to annoy him, I gestured at his Nikon. "I didn't know you liked photography."

He let out a little laugh. "I do. It's a hobby of mine, but I don't do it as often as I should."

"Should? Isn't a hobby something you do because you want to? Because you love it?"

He opened his mouth, then closed it again, a frown marring his features. "You're right. I don't use my camera as often as I would like."

I bumped his shoulder. "Then I'm glad you brought it today."

The morning air carried the scent of coffee from nearby cafés mixed with something sweet, probably from the waffle truck that had caught my eye. My stomach growled, reminding me I'd skipped breakfast in my excitement to start our exploration.

"You're hungry," Orson observed.

"I'm always hungry. It's my natural state of being." I nodded toward the waffle truck. "Want to split one? They smell amazing."

He hesitated, that familiar calculation playing across his features. "I can get my own—"

"Nope, my treat. Consider it payment for helping me with that calculus problem on Monday." I was already heading for the truck, knowing he'd follow. "Besides, I need a neutral party to tell me if these measure up to proper Belgian waffles."

"You're Dutch, not Belgian."

"Yes, but I've had enough Belgian waffles to be a qualified judge. It's practically a requirement of European royalty."

"You're ridiculous," Orson said, but he followed me to the truck anyway.

Once we had our waffles, we found a bench near the Commons' central fountain, where the spray provided some relief from the late-summer heat. Orson took a few pictures before he put his camera down and focused on his waffle.

The waffles were actually decent: crispy on the outside, fluffy inside, and drowning in maple syrup. The syrup wasn't something I was used to, as we didn't have it back home, but I did like it. It was slightly nutty and while sweeter than I was used to, still yummy.

"Verdict?" Orson asked as I took another bite.

I made a show of considering, chewing thoughtfully. "Not bad. The texture's good, though they're sweeter than European ones. Belgian waffles are more about the dough than the toppings."

"You really are a waffle snob."

"I prefer waffle connoisseur."

I watched as he carefully cut his portion into precise bites. Even when eating street food, he maintained that methodical approach.

"You know you can pick it up, right? That's kind of the point of street food."

He shot me a look. "That's rich, coming from a guy who eats a hamburger with a knife and fork. Also, some of us prefer not wearing our breakfast."

"Where's the fun in that?" I deliberately took a huge bite, letting syrup drip down my chin. His expression of horror was worth the sticky mess.

"You're actually five years old."

"Six, thank you very much." I wiped my face with a napkin, grinning. "So, what do you want to see first? Mechanics Hall is supposed to be amazing, or we could check out that art museum—"

"You researched tourist attractions?"

The surprise in his voice made me pause. "I always research places I'm visiting. It's kind of ingrained at this point, like a part of royal training. Know your destination, understand its history, don't accidentally offend the locals..."

"That's considerate."

His words warmed something inside me. "It's habit by now, though I have to admit, Worcester has more interesting history than I expected. Did you know this city was a major stop on the Underground Railroad?"

"I did, actually." Orson's eyes lit up with genuine interest. "There are still houses standing from that era, with hidden rooms and escape tunnels. The Salisbury House downtown has some of the original architecture preserved."

"Want to check it out?" I suggested, hoping to maintain that spark of enthusiasm. "It's not far from here."

He hesitated, and I could practically see him weighing the educational value against his study schedule. "I suppose it would be relevant to my architectural history course."

"That's the spirit! Justify fun with academics." I stood, offering him a hand up. "Come on, I'll even let you tell me about load-bearing walls and whatever else catches your engineering eye."

He ignored my hand but rose anyway, his lips twitching with what might have been a suppressed smile. "You have no idea what you're getting into. I can talk about historical construction methods for hours."

"Try me." I fell into step beside him as we headed down the

street. "I once listened to a two-hour lecture on proper fork placement at state dinners. I think I can handle you."

As we walked, Orson began to relax, pointing out architectural details I would've missed—the way certain buildings used different brick patterns for stability, how window placements revealed their original purposes. His voice took on a different quality when he talked about architecture, losing that careful restraint.

"See how the corners are reinforced?" He gestured to an old bank building that he'd taken at least a dozen pictures of. "That's called quoining. It's both functional and decorative."

"Like your personality," I teased. "Practical on the outside, but secretly artistic."

He shot me a look. "You're comparing me to a building?"

"If the load-bearing wall fits..."

"That doesn't even make sense."

"Sure it does. You're sturdy, reliable, carefully constructed..." I trailed off, realizing I might be revealing too much about how much attention I'd been paying to him. "And apparently, I need to stop before this metaphor completely collapses."

To my surprise, he laughed. A real laugh, not one of his usual quiet exhales. The sound made something flutter in my chest.

"You're impossible," he said, but there was fondness in his voice.

"Thank you." I bowed slightly, drawing another almost-laugh from him. "I do try."

We turned down a side street, where the buildings grew older, their brick facades telling stories of centuries past. The sidewalk narrowed, forcing us to walk closer together. His arm brushed mine occasionally, each contact sending little sparks across my skin that I tried very hard to ignore.

This was dangerous territory. Orson was my roommate, and more importantly, he was someone who saw me as Floris—not the prince, not the tabloid target, but the real me. I couldn't risk complicating that with attraction, no matter how much I wanted to make him laugh again.

But damn, he made it hard when he looked like this—relaxed, passionate about something he loved, those brown eyes bright behind his glasses and that wild hair catching the sunlight...

"Are you even listening?" His voice broke through my thoughts.

"Of course." I hadn't been, but I recovered quickly. "You were talking about... bricks?"

He rolled his eyes. "The structural importance of proper mortar composition in historical restoration, actually."

"Right, that's totally what I meant to say."

"Sure it was." But he was smiling slightly, and I counted that as a win.

As we continued our walk, I found myself watching him more than the architecture. The way he gestured when explaining something complex, how his whole face lit up when he spotted an interesting structural detail, how he allowed himself to enjoy our surroundings. This was a different Orson than the one who spent hours hunched over textbooks in our room, and I wanted to know more about him.

"That building there," Orson said, pointing to an imposing structure with elaborate stonework, "is Mechanics Hall. It was built in 1857 for the Worcester County Mechanics Association."

I whistled softly as he took a picture. "The acoustics in there must be amazing." When he gave me a surprised look, I shrugged. "What? I know things. Plus, it was in my research. They host classical concerts there, right?"

"Among other things. The architecture is incredible, a perfect example of Renaissance Revival style." His eyes traced the building's facade with obvious appreciation. "Look at those window arches, and the way they handled the cornices..."

It was hard to look at the building rather than his face. The way his eyes lit up when he talked about architecture was captivating. It struck me that maybe civil engineering wasn't his true passion. He seemed far more passionate about the art and history of buildings than about the mere structural aspects of them.

"Come on," I said, nodding toward the building's entrance. "Let's see if we can look inside. Maybe they'll let us check out that famous concert hall."

"They do tours sometimes, but I don't know if—"

"Leave it to me." I grinned, already heading for the door. "I have ways of making doors open."

"Please tell me you're not going to pull the prince card."

"Wouldn't dream of it. I'm naturally charming."

He snorted. "And so modest too."

"Modesty is overrated. Besides," I threw him a wink over my shoulder, "you haven't seen me in action yet."

As it turned out, charm wasn't necessary. The hall was open for a pre-concert setup, and a friendly elderly volunteer named Margaret was more than happy to show us around. She reminded me a bit of my grandmother, if my grandmother wore sensible shoes instead of designer heels and carried a ring of keys instead of the weight of royal protocol.

"Now, the acoustics in here are so perfect," Margaret explained as we entered the main hall, "that they say you can hear a pin drop from anywhere in the room."

The space took my breath away. Soaring columns stretched toward an elaborately decorated ceiling, while afternoon light filtered through tall windows, casting warm patterns across rows of wooden seats. The air held that particular stillness unique to concert halls, a waiting silence that seemed to vibrate with possibility.

But what really caught my attention was Orson's face. He stood in the center aisle, head tilted back to study the architectural details, completely lost in the moment. His usual careful mask had slipped entirely, replaced by an expression of pure wonder that made my heart do complicated things.

"The ceiling was hand-painted," Margaret continued, but I barely heard her. I was too busy watching how Orson's eyes traced every detail, how his fingers twitched like he wanted to touch the ornate woodwork, how his whole body seemed to lean toward the history surrounding us.

This wasn't academic interest. This was passion; raw and real and riveting to witness.

"The restoration work must have been incredible," he said softly, almost to himself. "Look at how they preserved the original plasterwork while incorporating modern safety features..."

"Oh, you know about restoration?" Margaret perked up. "We have some fascinating documentation about the process. Would you like to see?"

Before I could blink, we were being led to a small office filled with architectural drawings and historical photographs. Orson looked like he'd discovered a buried treasure, carefully examining each document while Margaret detailed the painstaking work that had gone into preserving the hall's original features.

I hung back, content to watch. He was in his element here, asking intelligent questions about techniques I'd never heard of, his eyes bright with genuine enthusiasm.

"The way they balanced historical accuracy with modern requirements is fascinating," he was saying, gesturing to a particularly detailed drawing. "How they integrated the new support structure while preserving the original aesthetic."

"You should've seen the debates about that," Margaret chuckled. "Some wanted to completely modernize, others wouldn't hear of changing a single detail. In the end, we found a middle ground."

"That's what makes great restoration work," Orson said, his voice warm with conviction. "Finding that perfect balance between preserving history and ensuring safety and functionality for the future."

I couldn't help myself. "Sounds like you've found your calling."

His head snapped up, that familiar tension returning to his shoulders. "It's interesting from an engineering perspective."

"Is it?" I kept my voice gentle. "Because you look happier talking about restoration than I've ever seen you discussing modern engineering projects."

Margaret looked between us, then tactfully excused herself to "check on something," leaving us alone among the blueprints and photographs.

"It doesn't matter," Orson said quietly, carefully replacing the drawing he'd been studying. "Civil engineering is what I need to do."

"Need to do, or want to do?"

His jaw tightened. "They're the same thing."

"Are they?" I stepped closer, close enough to see the tension in his face. "Because from where I'm standing, it looks like you're forcing yourself onto a path that doesn't make you happy."

"You don't understand." His voice was barely above a whisper. "I have to... I need to make it mean something."

"Make what mean something?"

But he was already shutting down, that wall sliding back into place. "We should go. You probably have other places you want to see."

I wanted to push, to make him talk to me, but I recognized that look. I'd worn it myself often enough, that careful mask that said some topics were off limits, some wounds too raw to probe.

"Alright," I said instead. "But Orson? For what it's worth, I think you'd make an amazing architectural restoration specialist. The way you light up when you talk about it... That's not nothing."

He didn't respond, but something flickered across his face—longing, maybe, or regret. Then he was moving past me toward the door, his shoulders set in that familiar rigid line.

I followed him out, nodding goodbye to Margaret as we passed. The late-afternoon sun hit us like a physical thing after the dim interior, and I blinked against the sudden brightness.

"That was interesting, right?" I asked, desperate to get back in Orson's good graces. I'd pushed too hard, too fast. Not the first time I'd made that mistake, but somehow, this one mattered.

He hesitated, and for a moment, I thought he'd refuse and instead, retreat back to the safety of our dorm and his textbooks. But then his shoulders relaxed slightly. "It was very interesting."

It wasn't much, but it was something. A crack in the wall, maybe, or at least a window to peek through. I'd take it.

But maybe when it came to Orson, I'd take whatever he was willing to give.

6

ORSON

We walked in silence for a few blocks, my mind still churning from our conversation at Mechanics Hall. Floris's words had hit too close to home, exposing doubts I usually kept buried under equations and problem sets. The worst part was that he wasn't entirely wrong. The way I'd felt in that concert hall, surrounded by history and craftsmanship...

But I couldn't think about that. I had a plan, a purpose. Dad had died making sure I lived. I couldn't waste that sacrifice chasing some romantic notion about old buildings.

"You're doing it again," Floris said, his voice cutting through my spiral.

"Doing what?"

"That thing where you get lost in your head and look like you're solving differential equations." He bumped my shoulder gently. "Come on, that coffee shop you've been raving about is around the corner. I'll buy you something with enough caffeine to draw you out of your head."

I wanted to be annoyed at how easily he read me, but there

was something disarming about his casual concern. "I don't need—"

"Let me guess, you don't need caffeine because you run on pure determination and mathematical formulas?"

Despite myself, I smiled. "Something like that."

The coffee shop appeared ahead, a narrow storefront wedged between two larger buildings. The smell of freshly roasted coffee beans hit us as soon as we opened the door, and I felt some of my tension ease. This place had become my sanctuary during study breaks, though I'd never mentioned that to Floris.

Inside, exposed brick walls and worn, wooden floors gave the space a cozy feel. Edison bulbs hung from the ceiling in artistic clusters, casting warm light over mismatched furniture and local artwork. The afternoon crowd had thinned, leaving several comfortable spots open.

"This is nice," Floris said, looking around with genuine interest. "Very... Worcester."

"What does that even mean?"

"You know, historic but trying to be hip about it." He grinned. "Like you."

I rolled my eyes, but warmth crept up my neck. "Order your coffee, you idiot."

"One venti caramel macchiato with extra whip and—" Floris started.

"They don't do Starbucks sizes here," I cut in, unable to hide my amusement. "And please don't ask for anything with whipped cream. The baristas are coffee purists."

"Ah." He studied the chalkboard menu with exaggerated concentration. "So I should probably avoid asking for anything with 'Frappuccino' in the name?"

"Unless you want to watch them die inside."

The barista—a guy with impressive tattoo sleeves and a carefully waxed mustache—waited with barely concealed judgment as Floris considered his options.

"In that case, I'll have whatever he usually gets," Floris said finally, gesturing to me. "Since he clearly knows his way around here."

"Cold brew, black," I told the barista. "And he'll have the same."

Floris's eyebrows shot up. "That's intense."

"Trust me." I led him to my favorite corner, where worn, leather armchairs faced each other across a scarred, wooden table. "Their cold brew is different. Smooth, not bitter."

He settled into one of the chairs, his long legs stretched out in front of him. "You come here a lot?"

"It's quiet. Good for studying." And for escaping when our room felt too small, when his presence became too distracting. Not that I was going to tell him that part.

"Of course it is." His tone was gently teasing. "Heaven forbid you do something for enjoyment."

I was saved from responding by the arrival of our drinks. Floris took a cautious sip, then his eyes widened.

"Okay, you were right. This is actually good."

"Try not to sound so surprised."

Floris laughed, and something inside me tightened at the sound. "You know what this reminds me of? There's this tiny coffee shop in Amsterdam, hidden in some back alley where few tourists ever venture. They roast their own beans too, and the owner is this grumpy old man who refuses to serve anything but black coffee. No sugar, no milk, definitely no whipped cream."

"Sounds perfect."

"You would think that." His eyes crinkled at the corners when he smiled. "Maybe I'll take you there someday."

The casual offer caught me off guard. "To Amsterdam?"

"Why not? You could see the Delta Works in person. Plus, all those historic buildings you pretend not to be fascinated by..."

I shifted uncomfortably. "Floris—"

"I know, I know. We don't talk about your secret love affair with historical architecture." He held up his hands in surrender. "We'll change the topic, I promise."

"Thanks." I took a long sip of coffee to avoid meeting his eyes. The cold brew was perfect as always, smooth and strong without being bitter. Like Floris himself, I thought, then immediately tried to un-think it. "What was it like, growing up in the public eye?"

Floris was quiet for a moment, his fingers tracing patterns on his coffee cup. The afternoon light filtering through the windows caught the green in his eyes, making them almost luminescent.

"Complicated," he said finally. "Everything you do, every choice you make, is scrutinized. It's like living in a fishbowl where the fish are expected to perform on command."

I waited, sensing there was more.

"You know what's weird?" He leaned forward slightly. "The hardest part isn't the big stuff, like the formal events, the speeches, the official duties. Those were manageable for me since the king is my uncle and not my father. My cousins have it much harder in that aspect. But even then, it's the small things. Like not being able to have a bad day in public, or knowing that if you trip or say something stupid, it'll probably end up on social media."

"I can't even imagine. How old were you when you realized you weren't like everyone else?" I asked Floris.

"Four or five, maybe?" Floris took another sip of his coffee, his expression thoughtful. "There was this moment in kindergarten that stands out. I'd made this absolute disaster of an art project with glue and glitter everywhere. The teacher started to tell me it was okay, that not everyone could be good at art, but then she caught herself. Suddenly, my mess was 'very creative' and 'showing real potential.'" He made air quotes with his fingers. "That's when I first noticed adults treated me differently. Not the kids. They were too young to realize, and that lasted until midway through elementary school. And after that, most kids were determined to make sure I wouldn't feel special, so they sure as hell never gave me preferential treatment. The Dutch are pretty good at that, keeping your ego in check. But the adults, that was a different story. And once I was eighteen, the agreement the royal family had with the press about not harassing the kids no longer applied since I was now a legal adult, so that brought massive press interest."

"That must be exhausting. Always being watched, waiting for the next headline."

"It is. But you get used to it. You learn to be careful." He traced the rim of his coffee cup. "Though sometimes, being careful isn't enough."

The resigned acceptance in his voice bothered me more than it should have. "Is that why you're so good at wearing masks?"

His head snapped up. "What do you mean?"

"You have different versions of yourself. The charming prince, the carefree student, the serious engineer. But sometimes..." I hesitated, wondering if I was overstepping. "Sometimes, I catch glimpses of someone else. Someone who feels more real."

Floris was quiet for a long moment, studying me with those intense, green eyes. "You're more observant than I gave you credit for."

"Engineering brain. We're trained to notice patterns."

"Is that what I am? A pattern to analyze?"

There was something in his voice I couldn't quite read. "No, you're..." I searched for the right words. "You're more like one of those historic buildings. Complex layers under a carefully maintained facade."

His laugh was surprised and genuine. "You're comparing me to architecture? After you came at me for saying you were similar to a building?"

Heat crept up my neck. "Maybe?"

"You know, most people try poetry or music for metaphors. But you go straight for load-bearing walls and structural integrity."

"Shut up," I muttered, but I was smiling despite myself.

"No, no, I like it." His eyes sparkled with amusement. "Tell me more about my complex layers. Do I have good bones? Strong foundation?"

"I take it back. You're more like that waffle truck: all flash and questionable substance."

Floris's dramatic gasp drew looks from nearby tables. "I am wounded. Mortally wounded. After I bought you coffee and everything."

"You'll survive."

"Will I? Or will I crumble like poorly maintained masonry?"

I laughed. The sound surprised even me. "You're hilarious."

His smile faded. "I've learned to be entertaining, since that's what people seemed to expect. I mean, I'm not forcing it, don't get me wrong. But it did grow out of necessity originally. You learn pretty quickly that there's the real you and the public you, and those aren't always the same person."

Something in his voice resonated with me—that sense of performing, of trying to live up to expectations. Though in my case, it was one person's expectations. My own. "Is that why you're here? To find out who the real you is?"

His green eyes met mine, startlingly direct. "Partly. But mostly I'm here because I'm tired of being careful all the time. Of second-guessing every word, every action." Floris paused, then added quietly, "Of being perfect. I can make normal mistakes here, like leaving my laundry in the dryer too long or getting lost on campus." His lips curved into a smile. "Nobody knows who I am, so nobody's watching, waiting for me to mess up."

"Except me," I pointed out.

His laugh was surprisingly warm. "Yeah, but you're different. You don't care about the prince thing."

"Should I?"

"God, no." He took another sip of coffee. "It's refreshing. Most people either treat me like I'm made of glass or try to use me to get something. And then there's a few who treat me like shit to make sure I'm not getting arrogant. You treat me like I'm..."

"A disaster who can't remember to get his laundry?"

"I was going to say 'normal' but yeah, that works too." His eyes sparkled with amusement. "Though I'll have you know, I'm getting better at the laundry thing."

"You left your socks in the dryer again yesterday."

"Details." He waved dismissively. "The point is, it's nice having someone who sees past all the royal stuff. Who sees... me."

Something in his voice made me look up, and our eyes met across the table. For a moment, neither of us spoke, and I felt that dangerous flutter in my chest again. I cleared my throat. "Even if 'you' is someone who thinks chocolate sprinkles are a legitimate breakfast food?"

"*Hagelslag*," he corrected. "And don't knock it till you've tried it. Besides, you Americans put marshmallows on sweet potatoes and call it a vegetable dish. You have no room to judge."

"That's different."

"How?"

"It just is." I couldn't help smiling at his exaggerated eye roll. "At least we don't eat raw fish by dangling it over our mouths."

"You're never going to let that go, are you?"

"Nope."

He laughed again, and I watched the way his whole face lit up when he was genuinely amused. It was different from his public smile—warmer, more real. I was starting to catalog these differences, noting when the mask slipped and the real Floris showed through. That was probably dangerous.

I cleared my throat. "In the Netherlands, do you usually have security?"

"God, no." He looked at me in horror. "You mean like the Secret Service? With earpieces and those scary, dark suits that probably come with a lifetime subscription to *Resting Murder Face Monthly*?"

I snorted. He was so funny. "Yeah."

"No, and if they offered it to me, I'd refuse faster than my brother turns down carbs. I understand why it's needed for my uncle and his direct family, but no, thank you. That's such an invasion of privacy that I'd never score a hookup ever again. Can you imagine?" He pretended to do a dramatic whisper into an imaginary earpiece. "'Target is making bedroom eyes at subject in blue shirt. Permission to engage in flirting? Over.' Yeah, that's a mood killer right there."

I almost spat my coffee out and needed a moment to control myself enough to swallow. "Can you refrain from being so funny when I'm trying to drink coffee?"

Floris grinned. "No promises. Your reactions are too entertaining." He leaned back in his chair, studying me. "You know, you should laugh more often. It suits you."

Heat crept up my neck, and I busied myself with my coffee to hide my reaction. "So, no security, but there must be other restrictions? Rules?"

"Some." He shrugged. "Don't embarrass the family, try not to cause international incidents, that sort of thing. Though according to certain British tabloids, I'm not very good at following those."

The bitterness in his voice made me look up. "That video—"

"Let's not." He cut me off, but gently. "Today's been good. I'd rather not ruin it by diving into that particular mess. I shouldn't have brought it up again."

I nodded, understanding the need to keep some wounds private.

We sat in comfortable silence for a while, sipping our coffee. Outside, people hurried past the windows, caught up in their own lives, completely unaware they were walking past actual royalty.

"Sometimes, I forget," I said.

"Forget what?"

"Who you are. I mean, not *you* you, but..." I gestured vaguely, trying to find the right words. "*Prince* you."

His smile was soft, genuine. "Good. That's exactly what I want." He paused, then added, "Though I hope you remember enough not to be shocked when the British tabloids eventually figure out where I am and show up with their cameras and creative interpretation of facts."

"Will they?"

"Eventually. They always do." He sighed, running a hand

through his hair. "But hopefully not for a while. I'd like to enjoy this—" he gestured between us "—while it lasts."

Something warm unfurled inside me at his words. "This?"

"You know, having a friend who sees me. Who calls me out on my bullshit and doesn't treat me like I'm made of glass." He met my eyes. "It's nice."

"Even when I lecture you about laundry etiquette?"

"Especially then." His eyes crinkled at the corners. "Though I maintain that the dryer is plotting against me. It eats socks on purpose."

"Sure it does." I couldn't help smiling. "It's all part of an elaborate conspiracy by American appliances to undermine European royalty."

"Finally, someone who understands!" He threw up his hands dramatically. "Next, you'll tell me you've noticed how the washing machines are secretly allied with the vending machines to create chaos."

"You're ridiculous."

"You like it."

And God help me, I did. That was becoming a problem.

7

FLORIS

Rule number one of being gay is that you don't look at other guys in the locker room or shower. Or in your dorm room, when you accidentally walk in on your roommate getting changed, as fate would have it. Orson immediately turned his back to me, treating me to a view of his rather spectacular ass. *Look away*, I told myself firmly. *Dammit, Floris, look away.*

Only when Orson pulled up his tight boxer briefs—not really much of an improvement on his previous state since they perfectly outlined said ass—did I manage to drag my eyes off him. Jesus, if he saw me staring at him like this, he'd immediately ask for another roommate. He might be gay, but that didn't mean I could stare. That I should stare.

I forced myself to turn around, fumbling with my own clothes as I tried to ignore the rustling sounds behind me. My face felt hot, and not from the humid September air seeping through our ancient windows.

"Sorry," I managed, proud that my voice sounded almost normal. "I should've knocked."

"It's your room too," Orson said, his voice muffled like he was pulling on a shirt. Thank god. Or maybe not thank god, because now I had the image of his lean back seared into my brain, all smooth skin and subtle muscle that spoke of someone who took care of himself without being showy about it.

To distract myself, I started changing too, though my hands felt clumsy on my buttons. The fact that I could feel his presence behind me made everything ten times more complicated. Not that he would watch. Orson was too proper, too focused on his studies to notice things like his disaster of a roommate trying not to spontaneously combust from attraction.

"I'm heading to the Eagles game," I said, desperate to fill the charged silence. "Want to come?"

"Can't. Need to study."

Of course he did. I pulled my newly purchased Vernon Eagles jersey over my head, then risked a glance over my shoulder. Orson was fully dressed now, though those jeans really weren't much better than the boxer briefs had been. They still showed every line of his body. His very, very attractive body.

I swallowed. "You sure? It might be fun."

"I have a problem set due Monday."

"It's Friday."

"Exactly. I need the whole weekend to get it perfect."

I bit back a sigh. "Right. Well, if you change your mind..."

But he was already settling at his desk, effectively ending the conversation. I grabbed my phone and wallet, trying not to feel disappointed. This attraction was dangerous anyway. The last thing I needed was to develop feelings for my roommate, especially one who viewed anything fun as a distraction from his studies.

Still, as I headed out the door, I couldn't shake the image of lean muscle and smooth skin, or the way my heart had practically stopped when I'd walked in on him. I needed to stop this. Nip this in the bud. Force myself to quit entertaining even the slightest hope for something more because nothing could come from this.

We were oil and water, as opposite as two people could possibly be. The only things we had in common were our studies and being gay. And maybe our sense of humor. And we did seem to like the same kind of documentaries, but that was not enough to build anything serious on.

Not that I was looking for anything serious. I was way too young for that. A hookup would be awesome, but not with Orson. He wasn't the type, as he'd said so himself, and besides, he was my roommate. It would muddy the waters and lead to complications I didn't want. Like losing him as a roommate. As a friend. And I couldn't bear that thought so no, I just had to get my shit together and learn to share a space with someone I... liked. Was attracted to. Whatever.

The game should be a good distraction. I knew little about American football other than what a touchdown was, but that was fine, I'd been assured.

"We're not going for the game," Brett, the guy who had invited me to join him and his friends, had assured me. "The team sucks anyway. It's just a fun atmosphere."

And he wasn't wrong. Throngs of people dressed in Vernon colors headed toward the football stadium. The energy was infectious—students decked out in blue and gold, faces painted, carrying signs and foam fingers. Music blasted from somewhere ahead, mixing with laughter and excited chatter. This was exactly what I needed: noise, chaos, anything to drown out thoughts of my half-naked roommate.

"Floris!" Brett waved from a group near the stadium entrance. "Over here!"

I threaded my way through the crowd, grateful for the distraction. Brett was part of my calculus study group, and he seemed genuinely friendly.

"Nice jersey," he said as I approached. "Though fair warning: wearing Eagles merch means you're committed to disappointment."

"I'm Dutch. We're used to our teams letting us down in crucial moments." When they looked confused, I added, "Soccer. Or football, as the civilized world calls it."

That earned me some laughs. Brett introduced me to his friends—names I immediately forgot because my brain was still stuck on Orson's back muscles. *Get it together, van Oranje.*

"So," a girl whose name might have been Ashley said, "you've never seen American football before?"

"Only in movies." I followed them toward the stands. "Though I'm pretty sure *Remember the Titans* wasn't an accurate representation of typical game strategy."

"God, I wish," Brett laughed. "Our team's more like *Forget the Score.*"

The stadium was smaller than I had expected, but the atmosphere was electric. Students packed the stands, the air thick with excitement and the smell of popcorn and hot dogs. We found spots near the middle, and I tried to focus on Brett's explanation of basic rules instead of wondering what Orson was doing. Was he really studying, or was he just avoiding social situations? And why did I care so much?

I wanted to spend more time with him, but every time I asked him to do something, he turned me down. Even after our outing to Worcester, which had been so nice. Was there nothing I could think of that he'd be willing to do with me? Maybe I needed to try a little harder... without ever venturing into the territory of not taking no for an answer.

"Earth to Floris?" Brett waved a hand in front of my face. "You zoned out there."

"Sorry." I forced a smile. "Just trying to understand why you call it football when you barely use your feet."

That launched a heated debate about sports terminology that carried us through the pre-game warm-up.

The game itself was... interesting. By halftime, I understood why Brett had said we weren't here for the actual football. The Eagles were living up to their reputation for creative ways to lose, currently down by four touchdowns. But the crowd's energy remained high, fueled by what I suspected was more than just school spirit, if the subtle passing of flasks was any indication.

"See?" Brett nudged my arm, gesturing at our flailing quarterback. "What did I tell you? Pure comedy gold."

I laughed, but my mind drifted to Orson again. He would probably have something fascinating to say about the physics of a badly thrown football, complete with calculations of trajectory and force. The thought made me smile despite myself.

"Okay, spill." Ashley dropped into the seat next to me. "Who are you thinking about?"

"What? No one." I said it too quickly, and she grinned.

"Please. You've had that dreamy look all night. So who is he?"

"There's no *he*." I focused on the field, where our team was finding new and creative ways to fumble. "I'm trying to figure out how many ways one can drop the ball in a game, literally and figuratively."

"Uh-huh." She didn't sound convinced. "That's why you keep checking your phone every five minutes?"

Had I been doing that? Shit. I forced my hands to stay still in my lap. "I'm checking the time."

"Right. Because watching paint dry—I mean, Eagles football—is so riveting, you need constant time updates."

I couldn't help grinning. "You're kind of terrifying, you know that?"

"So I've been told." She bumped my shoulder. "Come on, who's the guy? Promise I won't tell."

I sighed, debating how much to say. "It's complicated."

"Isn't it always?" Her voice softened. "Let me guess. He's straight?"

"No, actually. But he's..." I searched for words that wouldn't give too much away. "He's very focused on his studies. Not interested in dating or anything else that might distract him."

"Ah." She nodded sagely. "One of those. We get a lot of them here."

"He's not just one of anything," I said before I could stop myself. "He's..." *Brilliant. Fascinating. Frustrating. Gorgeous when he gets excited about something he loves.* None of which I could say out loud. "Complicated," I finished lamely.

She grinned. "Sounds... complicated." When I rolled my eyes at her, she chuckled. "I'll get off your ass now, I promise."

"Thanks," I muttered, though I couldn't help smiling. Ashley reminded me a bit of my cousin Juliana—too perceptive for my own good.

The marching band took the field for halftime, their formations about as coordinated as our team's offense had been. But there was something charming about their enthusiasm, even as they nearly collided during what I assumed was supposed to be an arrow formation.

My phone buzzed in my pocket. I tried not to look too eager

as I pulled it out, but my heart did a stupid little skip when I saw Orson's name.

> **ORSON**
>
> Did they score yet?

> **ME**
>
> Define "they"

> Because if you mean the other team, then yes. Multiple times.

> If you mean us... well...

> **ORSON**
>
> That bad?

> **ME**
>
> Let's just say I've seen more coordination in a kindergarten football game. Though the crowd's still having fun. You could still come join us...

I held my breath, waiting for his response, aware of Ashley's knowing look beside me.

> **ORSON**
>
> Can't. Still working. But thanks for the updates.

My fingers hovered over the keyboard. I wanted to push, to tell him the problem set would still be there tomorrow, that he deserved a break. But I remembered how he'd tensed when I'd suggested the same thing earlier.

> **ME**
>
> No problem. Good luck with the studying.

I slipped my phone back in my pocket, ignoring Ashley's raised eyebrow.

"That was him, I assume? You lit up like a Christmas tree when he texted. Maybe he's not as uninterested as you think."

I snorted. "Trust me, he's made it very clear that even friendship would be a distraction from his goals."

"Could be he needs a good distraction."

I wasn't counting on it.

When the game ended—the Eagles had somehow, by sheer luck, managed to get one touchdown in—Brett leaned over to me. "Wanna come hang out in my dorm? It's our post-game tradition."

"Sounds good."

Anything to not have to face Orson yet. Not before I had myself in check again.

Brett's dorm room was packed with people, music competing with excited chatter as everyone relived the game's most spectacular failures. Someone had strung up cheap LED lights that cast everything in a blue glow, making it feel almost like a club. If clubs smelled like pizza and had motivational posters on the walls.

"So what's the verdict?" Brett handed me a Coke. "American football: yay or nay?"

"The game itself? Confusing. The atmosphere?" I grinned. "Pretty amazing, actually. Though I still don't understand why you call it football."

"Because 'organized chaos with occasional running' doesn't roll off the tongue as well."

I laughed, settling onto the floor since every other surface was occupied. The carpet was questionable at best, but I'd survived worse. Probably. "Fair enough. Though I have to ask— why support a team that consistently loses?"

"Character building." Brett dropped down beside me. "Plus,

imagine how epic it'll be when we finally win something important. The parties will be legendary."

"Optimistic of you."

"Hey, my mom always says hope springs eternal." Brett grinned. "Though in the Eagles' case, hope mostly springs into fumbles and missed passes."

I laughed, but my phone buzzing in my pocket distracted me. Another text from Orson.

> **ORSON**
>
> Made good progress. Going to bed soon. Don't wake me when you come in?

Something fluttered inside my belly at the fact that he'd thought to tell me.

> **ME**
>
> I'll be ninja-quiet. Promise.

* * *

Ninja-quiet was what I had in mind when I finally made it back to my room around two in the morning. The party had proven to be more fun than I had expected, and I felt like I'd made some new friends. And best of all, it had kept my mind off Orson. Mostly.

I opened the door to our room quietly. Orson had put some WD-40 on the hinges the other day, so it had stopped squeaking. The only sounds now were Orson's soft snores, and they made me smile.

I probably should take off my shoes first so my footsteps would be quiet, and so I toed them off, gently pushing them aside. Brushing my teeth would have to be skipped. I didn't want to head to the bathroom and back for that. That was sure to wake Orson up. Instead, I quietly undressed. Surely in this case, Orson would forgive me for throwing my clothes on my desk chair. It wasn't like I could see enough to put them anywhere else.

Dressed in just my boxer briefs, I tiptoed toward my bed… only to trip over my shoes, stumbling forward with all the grace of a drunk giraffe. I crashed right into Orson's bed, all but falling on top of him.

"Wha—?" Orson bolted, his hair a wild mess and his eyes wide behind his glasses. Wait, why was he wearing his glasses in bed?

"Shit, sorry!" I whispered, though whispering seemed pointless now. "I was trying not to wake you."

"Wasn't sleeping," he mumbled, rubbing his eyes. "Was waiting."

I pushed myself on one elbow, our faces only inches apart. I could just see enough with a glimpse of moonlight peeking in from between the curtains. "Waiting? For what?"

"You." He blinked owlishly at me. "Wanted to make sure you got back okay. It got so late, and…"

Warmth filled me. "You were worried about me?"

"No." He adjusted his glasses, a sure tell that he was lying. "Just… Campus isn't always safe at night, and you're never back this late. Wanted to make sure you hadn't gotten yourself into trouble."

"Right." I couldn't help smiling. "So you stayed up wearing your glasses in bed because you weren't worried at all."

He scowled, but there was no heat in it. "Shut up. I was reading."

"Of course you were." I straightened up, immediately

missing his warmth. "Well, I'm back safe and sound. No need to worry—I mean, no need to not worry anymore."

Even in the dim light, I could see his cheeks flush. "Whatever. Just... go to bed."

But as I reluctantly removed myself from his bed and climbed into my own, I couldn't wipe the smile off my face. He'd waited up for me. Maybe I wasn't the only one feeling this... whatever this was.

Though that thought was probably more dangerous than any late-night campus walk could ever be.

8

ORSON

The bass from the frat house speakers vibrated through my bones as we approached, and I already regretted letting Floris talk me into this. Halloween parties weren't my thing. Too many people, too much chaos, too many opportunities for things to go wrong.

But he'd looked so excited when he'd asked, those green eyes lighting up as he described the "quintessential American college experience" we needed to have. He'd been almost giddy to discover that VTC did, in fact, have frat parties. The fact that I'd survived three years here without ever attending one was apparently not convincing proof it wasn't all that quintessential.

It was getting harder and harder to say no every time Floris invited me to do something. My almost consistent rejections didn't seem to deter him from asking again, which somehow made me feel guilty.

Plus, I liked spending time with him. He was funny and kind, caring and smart, and he had this aura about him, this charm that drew me to him like a damn moth to a flame. And he was so, so freaking hot. Sharing a room with him had become the sweetest kind of torture.

"You okay?" Floris asked beside me, his hand brushing my arm. He was dressed as Han Solo, because of course he was. The costume suited him perfectly—that casual confidence, the way he carried himself like he owned any room he walked into. Meanwhile, I'd cobbled together what passed for a Luke Skywalker outfit, mainly because Floris had insisted we needed matching costumes and I'd been too flustered by his enthusiasm to argue.

"Fine," I lied, adjusting my glasses. "I'm processing."

His smile was knowing. "We don't have to stay long. Just long enough to say we did it, yeah?"

The fact that he was already offering an escape route brought such warmth inside. Two months ago, I would've sworn the "Party Prince" wouldn't understand my discomfort with crowds. But Floris had proven to be full of surprises.

Inside, the party was exactly what I'd expected—too loud, too crowded, and definitely violating several fire codes. Red cups littered every surface, and the air was thick with the smell of cheap beer and cheaper cologne. Fake cobwebs draped the ceiling, and someone had arranged plastic skeletons in questionable poses throughout the room.

Floris's face lit up as he took it all in. "This is brilliant! Look at that skeleton doing a keg stand!"

I couldn't help smiling at his enthusiasm. Everything about American college life seemed to delight him, from the dining hall's mysterious "meatloaf surprise" to the ancient washing machines that ate socks. His joy was infectious, making even this chaos seem almost bearable.

"Prince Charming!" A voice called out, and I turned to see a guy from Floris's calculus study group approaching. Mike? Mark? Something with an M. "You made it!"

"Matt!" Floris's grin widened. Of course he remembered everyone's name. "Nice costume!"

Matt was dressed as what I assumed was supposed to be a zombie frat boy, though he mostly looked like someone who'd lost a fight with a make-up kit. "Thanks! You guys want drinks? We've got this stuff called 'witch's brew' that'll knock your socks off."

I opened my mouth to decline, but Floris beat me to it. "Maybe later. We just got here, want to look around first."

Matt nodded, already distracted by someone else calling his name. "Cool, cool. Catch you later!"

As he disappeared into the crowd, I gave Floris a look. "Prince Charming?"

He shrugged, a slight flush coloring his cheeks. "They decided I look like Disney royalty. I didn't correct them."

I snorted. If they only knew.

"Come on," Floris said, gently guiding me through the throngs of people. "Let's find somewhere less crowded."

We ended up in a slightly quieter corner near a window, where the cool, October air provided some relief from the press of bodies. Floris seemed to know half the people there, greeting everyone with that easy charm that made him so popular. But I noticed he never left my side, always staying close enough that his presence felt like a buffer between me and the chaos.

"You're good at this," I observed as he finished chatting with yet another classmate whose name he somehow remembered.

"At what?"

"Making people feel seen. Important." I gestured vaguely at the room. "Everyone loves you."

His smile faltered slightly. "They love the version of me they see. It's not quite the same thing."

I hated that I had inadvertently brought up something that bothered him. "I'll go grab us some drinks. What's your poison?"

He hesitated. "Better make it a soda. A Coke, please. And no, Pepsi is not okay. If they serve Pepsi, water will do."

I snorted. Of course he was a Coke snob. "Why no beer? Campus police rarely intervene at these parties from what I hear."

"Can't risk it. If I get photographed and my identity leaks, it may cause problems for my family."

He gave me another one of those sad smiles, and it shocked me how much I was willing to do to make it disappear again. I'd find him a Coke if I had to grab it from someone's personal fridge myself. "One Coke coming up."

As it turned out, no drastic measures were needed as I found countless cans of Coke in a massive cooler. Thanks to the buckets of ice dumped in there, they were even cold. I grabbed one for myself as well. I'd need the caffeine to get me through this. No alcohol for me, thank you very much. I didn't like how it made me feel. Too loose, too reckless, too uncontrolled.

When I came back, carrying the two cans, I found Floris in a quiet corner with another guy standing very close to him. He had his hand on Floris's shoulder, but as I came to a sudden stop and watched, it traveled lower, morphing into a... a caress. Who the hell was that and what was he doing? Should I interrupt? Maybe Floris was into him and I should give them some privacy?

In the end, my curiosity won. I needed to know who this guy was. Sliding a few steps to the right, I was able to see his face. He looked familiar. Wasn't he in my project management class? Bit of an obnoxious guy with an annoyingly high-pitched voice that sounded very fake. James. Yeah, that was his name, James.

He was slightly unsteady, wavering back and forth, and his eyes were glassy. How drunk was he? My money was on straight-up intoxicated. Was Floris into that?

He was now brushing Floris's cheek with his right finger, leaning in even closer. Maybe it was time to walk away and give them their privacy. Up until now, I'd been focused on James, but now I took a good look at Floris... and froze.

Floris's expression made my chest tight—a flash of genuine anxiety beneath his careful mask. Something was wrong. He wasn't smiling, wasn't his usual confident self. His whole body was tense, coiled as a spring, and he looked like a cornered animal, desperate to get away.

He didn't want this.

But why was he not simply sending James packing? I'd never seen Floris lost for words. Surely a few of his well-timed remarks would end this.

He was scared.

The realization hit me with the force of a gale. He was panicking. He was trying to be polite, to avoid causing a scene, but this asshole wasn't taking the hint. This must've stirred up bad memories from that incident in the UK, from that video, and now he was panicking.

I had to help him.

"Come on, don't be like that." James trailed his hand down Floris's chest. "One dance? I promise I'll make it worth your while."

Before I could think too hard about it, I stepped forward. "Actually, he's here with me."

Both of them turned to look at me, James with annoyance and Floris with surprise.

"I'm his boyfriend," I added firmly, putting the drinks down on a table and moving closer to Floris. "So maybe back off?"

Understanding dawned in Floris's eyes, and he immediately played along, leaning into me slightly. "Sorry, James. I'm already taken."

James looked between us, clearly trying to process this through his alcohol-fogged brain. "But you're..."

I quirked an eyebrow. "The matching costumes aren't enough to convince you?"

James blinked as if registering our characters for the first time. "Yeah, but he's—"

"Not interested," I finished for him, surprising myself with how steady my voice sounded. "Now, if you'll excuse us?"

I took Floris's hand, ignoring the way my heart jumped at the contact, and led him away from the increasingly awkward situation. We didn't stop until we reached the back porch, where the cool, night air helped calm down my temper. My mom always said it took a lot to ignite it but once it did, it burned hot.

"Thank you," Floris said quietly, still holding my hand. "You didn't have to do that."

"Yes, I did." I reluctantly let go of his hand, already missing its warmth. "You looked uncomfortable."

"I was." He leaned against the porch railing, moonlight catching the green in his eyes. "Usually, I'm better at handling those situations, but after... Well, you know. The video. I get nervous about causing scenes now."

The admission made my chest ache. "You shouldn't have to handle them at all. No means no, drunk or not."

His smile was soft, genuine in a way his public ones rarely were. "My hero."

"Shut up." But I was smiling too, unable to help myself. "I was being a friend."

"A very convincing boyfriend, you mean." His eyes sparkled

with amusement. "The way you stepped in all protective and commanding? Oscar-worthy performance."

Heat crept up my neck. "It was the first thing I could think of."

"Well, it worked perfectly." Then, before I could process what was happening, he leaned in and pressed a quick kiss to my cheek. "Thank you, Orson. Really."

The spot where his lips had touched my skin burned like a brand. "You're welcome," I managed, hoping the darkness hid my blush.

We stood in comfortable silence for a while, watching the stars peek through scattered clouds. The music from inside was muted out here, and the October air carried the damp, earthy scent of wet leaves. My cheek still tingled where his lips had touched it, and I tried very hard not to think about how natural it had felt to call myself his boyfriend, to hold his hand.

"Want to head back?" Floris asked. "I'm done with this party. We could grab some hot chocolate from the vending machine, maybe watch a movie?"

The offer was tempting, more tempting than it should have been. "Yeah," I said, trying to ignore how much I liked the sound of "we" in his voice. "That sounds good."

As we walked back across campus, Floris stayed close, our shoulders occasionally brushing. The contact sent little sparks through me each time, and I was hyper-aware of his presence.

"You know," he said after a while, "you're pretty good at the whole knight in shining armor thing."

I snorted. "Says the actual prince."

"Hey, some of us prefer to be the damsel in distress occasionally." His tone was light, but there was something underneath it. "It's nice, having someone willing to step in like that."

The vulnerability in his voice made my chest tight. "Any time."

"Careful, I might hold you to that."

"I mean it." The words came out more intense than I'd intended. "You shouldn't have to deal with that kind of situation alone."

Floris was quiet for a moment, and when I glanced at him, his expression was thoughtful. "You'll make some lucky guy an amazing boyfriend one day."

The simple honesty in his voice made me glow on the inside. Dangerous territory, I reminded myself. I had goals, responsibilities. I couldn't afford to get distracted by how the moonlight caught his eyes or how his hand kept brushing mine as we walked.

But maybe, just for tonight, I could let myself enjoy this moment. After all, what harm could one cup of hot chocolate do?

"Race you to the vending machines?" Floris suggested, his eyes sparkling with mischief.

I laughed. "In these costumes?"

"Why not? Let Worcester see Luke Skywalker and Han Solo sprinting through the Commons. Give them something to talk about."

And before I could protest, he was off, his long legs eating up the ground. I hesitated for only a moment before following, my own laughter joining his in the cool October night.

For once, I didn't think about my father's sacrifice or my carefully planned future. I ran, chasing the sound of Floris's laughter and ignoring the truth that took root in my heart.

Because I was definitely in trouble. Big, big trouble.

9

FLORIS

Orson always had a study group on Wednesday afternoons, so I had set up a FaceTime call with Greg, Nils, and Tore so we could talk in private. I settled on my bed, propping my phone against my laptop as Greg's face filled the screen, soon joined by Nils and Tore in their separate windows.

"Finally escaped your roommate, then?" Greg's posh accent came through clearly.

As if I would ever want to deliberately escape Orson's presence. I wasn't looking too deep into the why of that feeling, though.

"He's at his study group," I said, adjusting my position. "How's everyone doing?"

"Bloody brilliant," Tore said. "I'm loving college life. Though that asshole Farron is still being a dick."

Nils frowned. "Farron?"

"The star defender on his football team," I helpfully supplied. "You know, the one Tore can't stop talking about for more than five minutes?"

"Shut up, Floris," Tore growled, but his cheeks reddened.

"What? I'm providing context for our forgetful hockey prince here." I grinned innocently at the camera.

Nils's eyes lit up. "Ah, right. That one."

I focused on Tore again. "What did the walking attitude problem do this time?"

"He keeps challenging my plays during practice. Like yesterday? I had this perfect set-up for a goal, but Mr. Know-It-All starts yelling that I'm not following proper formation." Tore's face flushed with frustration, his jaw clenching. "Then he has the nerve to demonstrate the 'correct' way, which was exactly what I was doing in the first place!"

"Sounds like someone's trying to get your attention," Greg teased.

"Yeah, my attention to punch him. He deliberately shoulders past me in the locker room too. Who does that?"

"Someone who desperately wants to feel your muscles?" I suggested, waggling my eyebrows. "I mean, there are easier ways to cop a feel, but maybe he's shy."

"I swear to god, Floris, when I see you next—"

"You'll thank me for my incredible insight into the human heart? Why, you're welcome!"

"Shut your face," Tore snapped, and I held up my hands in a mock surrender. The way Tore's eyes lit up when he talked about Farron, even if it was to complain, told me everything I needed to know about his true feelings for him. But I valued my life too much to point out just how many times he'd mentioned Farron in our last three calls.

"Speaking of attention," Nils said, his face brightening, "I got some news. Remember that assistant hockey coach position I mentioned? At the college near Buffalo in upstate New York?"

"Yeah?" I leaned closer to my screen. "The one where you'd have to brave the American winter? Are you sure you don't want to apply somewhere tropical instead? I hear Hawaii has ice rinks."

Nils rolled his eyes. "They've invited me for an interview next week. Through Zoom, obviously, but that didn't seem to be an issue for them."

Since Nils was older than us by a few years, attending college as a student wasn't an option for him. The good news was that he had a degree in sports and experience as a hockey coach, not to mention he'd played hockey for years at a competitive level. He'd be perfect for this job.

"That's amazing, Nils!" Greg said and Nils's smile widened even more. "You'll do brilliantly. I know you will."

"God, I hope so. It's the first college that has shown serious interest so far. Well, I'm not counting the two that offered me a salary that was below what we would pay interns."

"I have every confidence you'll get the job," I said. "Though I still can't believe you're choosing to live somewhere that gets more snow than Sweden."

"Some of us actually like winter sports, you wimp," Nils shot back with a grin.

"Oh, I love snow. I just thought you would've been sick and tired of it by now."

Nils seemed to consider it. "Nah, not even close. I love the cold."

"Well, Buffalo should be a good fit, then. From what I understand, they get a buttload of snow each winter. So as the Americans would say, fingers crossed."

Greg frowned. "You don't say the same in Dutch?"

I shook my head. "No, we call it *duimen*, which means thumbing. As in, I'll be thumbing for you. Which is what the Germans call it as well, though their expression is that they'll press their thumbs for you."

"That's fascinating." Tore leaned forward. "In Norwegian, we say *fingrene krysset*, which is also fingers crossed, but I know in Swedish, it's *hålla tummarna*, which is holding your thumbs, translated literally. Why does one language mention all fingers and others only thumbs?"

I grinned. "Maybe because the Dutch, Germans, and Norwegians are only moderately wishing you luck, whereas the Brits, Americans, and Swedish are fully on your side? Though I have to say, if you're really committed to someone's success, you should probably cross your toes too. Go big or go home, right?"

"Only you would turn well-wishes into a competition," Greg said with a laugh.

"Hey, I'm just saying, if we're going to wish Nils luck, we might as well use all available digits. I'm personally willing to cross my eyes too, but that might make this video call a bit challenging."

"When exactly is the interview?" Tore asked Nils.

"Next Thursday. I'm nervous as hell, but—"

Nils was cut off by the sound of my door opening.

I turned to see Orson walking in, his backpack slung over one shoulder and wearing that soft, green sweater that made his eyes look like molten chocolate. My heart did that weird flutter thing it had started doing lately whenever he appeared.

He stopped short when he saw me on the call. "Oh, sorry," he said, already backing toward the door. "My study group was canceled, but I can come back later."

"No!" The word came out louder than I intended. "I mean, stay. Actually..." I glanced at my friends on screen, who were watching with varying degrees of curiosity. "Would you like to meet some of my friends?"

Orson hesitated, shifting his weight from one foot to the

other. I could see the uncertainty in his eyes, but also his desire not to make things awkward. "I wouldn't want to intrude."

"You wouldn't be," I assured him, patting the space next to me on the bed. "Come on."

Was I imagining the slight pink tinge to his cheeks as he sat down and settled beside me, his thigh barely brushing against mine? The contact sent a familiar warmth through my body that I tried desperately to ignore.

"Everyone, this is my roommate, Orson," I said to the screen. "Orson, meet Greg, Nils, and Tore."

"Hello," Orson said, giving an awkward little wave that was somehow both dorky and adorable.

"Mate, Floris has told us so much about you," Greg said warmly. "All good things, I promise."

"All lies, I'm sure," Orson said with a self-deprecating smile that made me want to list every wonderful thing about him.

"Actually," Nils chimed in, "he mentioned you're the only reason he's passing calculus."

I elbowed Orson gently. "See? I give credit where credit's due."

"Speaking of credit," Tore said, "Floris tells us you're into photography? Got any embarrassing shots of him we can use for blackmail?"

"Oh god," I groaned, but Orson's laugh next to me made it worth it.

"Sorry to disappoint, but Floris is annoyingly photogenic," Orson said. "Even when he's face-planted in a pile of leaves."

"That was one time!" I protested, remembering how I had slipped on wet leaves that day and had landed rather inelegantly. Orson had taken some pictures before helping me up. "And I thought we'd agreed to never mention that again."

Orson tapped his chin. "Funny, that's not how I remember it. My recollection is that you begged me to forget it ever happened and that I told you I wasn't sure if I could do that. I made no promises."

That had the others in stitches, of course, even more when I pouted.

"You're all terrible people," I declared. "I don't know why I'm friends with any of you."

"Because we're charming and delightful," Greg said with a grin that had charmed countless tabloid photographers.

The conversation flowed easily after that, with Orson fitting into our dynamic as naturally as if he'd always been there. My friends asked him questions about his photography, his classes, his family, and he answered everything with that quiet confidence I'd come to associate with him. He and Greg got into an animated discussion about modern versus classic architecture, while Tore kept trying to get Orson to share more embarrassing stories about me.

"There has to be something," Tore insisted. "You're living with our resident disaster gay prince. Has he tried to microwave metal yet?"

"That was one time," I protested, "and I maintain that container didn't clearly state it had a metal handle. Plus, I was twelve, okay?"

"He did wash his red socks with a white shirt again last week," Orson offered, his eyes twinkling. "Then declared his now-pink shirt to be the new fashion color this fall."

"Betrayal!" I clutched my chest dramatically. "And here I was, about to nominate you for roommate of the year."

When Greg mentioned something about his sister Charlotte's latest charity event, I caught the slight widening of Orson's eyes, the barely perceptible straightening of his shoulders, but he didn't say anything. I watched him carefully, wondering if he was connecting the dots.

When we finally ended the call forty minutes later, Orson was quiet for a moment, still sitting close enough that I could feel the warmth radiating from his body.

"So," he said slowly, "that was Prince Gregory... Right?"

"You recognized him?"

"Kind of hard not to. He's only been on every major news outlet since birth." Orson turned to look at me, his expression unreadable. "And the others?"

I sighed, running a hand through my hair. "Yeah. They're also princes. Nils is from Sweden, Tore from Norway."

"Oh god." Orson buried his face in his hands. "I talked about architecture with the prince of England."

"Technically, he's not the prince of... Never mind," I said quickly when Orson's face tightened. "I know they're all royals like me, but they're my friends and they've had my back for as long as I can remember. It's not easy finding true friends in my world."

"I can't believe I told a bunch of princes about that time you got stuck in the revolving door at the library," he groaned.

"Hey, that door was definitely malfunctioning," I defended myself. "And besides, they've seen me do way worse. Ask Tore about the time we tried to convince the palace guards I could speak to ducks."

He let out a sigh. "I wish I had known. I would've shut up. God, I probably sounded like an idiot."

"Hey." I touched his arm gently, trying to ignore how my fingers tingled at the contact. "You were perfect. They loved you."

"You're only saying that to make me feel better."

"I'm saying it because it's true." I smiled, remembering one of my favorite movies. "Have you ever seen *Notting Hill*, with Julia Roberts and Hugh Grant?"

"Yeah, why?"

"Do you remember that moment where Julia's character, Anna Scott, is giving that speech in the bookstore? About being just a girl?"

He nodded.

"That's kind of what it's like for us. We may be princes, but underneath, we're just guys, standing in front of others, asking them to..." I trailed off, realizing too late what I was quoting, and heat rushed to my face.

Orson's warm, brown eyes met mine, something soft and undefined passing between us. The air felt thick suddenly, charged with possibility. My heart hammered against my ribs.

"Thanks for including me," Orson said quietly, breaking the moment. But his smile held a warmth that made my stomach flip.

I watched him get up and head to his desk, presumably to study, and tried to calm my racing heart. What was happening between us? Was this proof that whatever it was, he was feeling it too? I had no idea, but was I brave enough to find out? The thought of ruining our friendship terrified me, but the way my body reacted to his presence, the way my heart lifted at his smile...

Maybe some risks were worth taking. I just had to figure out if this was one of them.

And maybe stop quoting romantic comedies before I completely exposed myself.

Though knowing my luck, I'd probably end up recreating the entire pottery scene from *Ghost* before I managed to actually tell him how I felt.

10

ORSON

I'd been at my desk for hours, working through problem sets and triple-checking my calculations. The familiar routine usually calmed me, but today something felt off, like that peculiar stillness before a storm that every New Orleans native learns to recognize. That heavy, electric feeling where the air pressed against your skin like a wet blanket, and even the birds go quiet, as if holding their breath. The kind of atmospheric tension that made the hair on your arms stand up and had you checking the sky, muscle memory from too many summers spent watching for that telltale green tinge in the clouds.

But why was I feeling like this?

Floris was out at some campus event he'd tried to drag me to, something about international students and cultural exchange. The room felt different without his constant motion and cheerful chatter. Quieter, but not necessarily in a good way. I'd gotten used to his presence, his ability to pull me out of my own head when I started spiraling into perfectionist territory.

It amazed me how quickly he'd become such an essential part of my daily routine. Mere months ago, I'd dreaded having a new roommate, and even more after meeting him, since he seemed so carefree and disorganized. But Floris had this way of making everything brighter, whether he was explaining Dutch water management with surprising passion or teasing me about my "excessive" organization habits. He slipped coffee onto my desk during late-night study sessions, dragged me out for actual meals instead of protein bars, and somehow knew exactly when I needed to be pulled away from my books before I drove myself crazy. The friendship that had developed between us felt like finding an unexpected solution to a complex equation: surprising but perfectly logical once you saw all the variables.

The phone's vibration startled me out of my concentration. I rarely got calls. Mom preferred texting, and Tia was usually too busy as a freshman in college to check in with me regularly. The New Orleans area code made my stomach clench.

"Hello?"

"Orson? It's Principal Matthews."

My heart stuttered. Principal Matthews had been Dad's friend, had given Mom her job after... after Dad had died. He wouldn't call unless—

"What's wrong?"

"Your mother collapsed during third period. They're taking her to University Medical Center."

The words hit like physical blows. *Collapsed. Hospital.* The room tilted sideways, and I gripped my desk hard enough to hurt. "Is she okay?"

"They think it might've been a heart attack. I called Tia and she's already on her way to the hospital. Orson, if it was a heart attack..."

I swallowed thickly. "She may need surgery."

"Yes. I know this is awfully inconvenient for you, but you need to come home. Your mom and sister need you."

"Yes, of course. I'll figure something out." The words came automatically while my mind raced. Flights. I needed to check flights. But last-minute tickets were expensive, and the emergency fund Mom insisted I maintained wouldn't be enough.

"Glad to hear that. Tia was very distraught, so Mrs. Bowman, Tia's counselor from senior year, is with her at the hospital now. She has offered to stay with her until you're here or your mom is released. Is that okay with you?"

Why was he asking me? I wasn't... Fuck, I *was* the adult now. With my mom unable to make these decisions and Tia being so young emotionally speaking, I had to make the call. "Yes. Thank you so much. I will... I'll get there as soon as I can."

I ended the call, my hands shaking so badly, I nearly dropped the phone. *Mom. Hospital. Heart attack.* The words swirled in my head, each one carrying echoes of that day on the roof, of water rising and choices that couldn't be unmade.

Not again. I couldn't lose someone else. Not like this. Not when I was too far away to help.

The door opened, and Floris walked in, his usual energy filling our small room. He stopped short when he saw my face.

"What's wrong?"

"My mom..." The words stuck in my throat. Saying them would make it real. "She collapsed at school. They think it was a heart attack."

Floris dropped his bag and was beside me in two strides. "Is she at the hospital?"

I nodded, my hands still shaking. "In New Orleans. My sister's there, but she's only twenty and has some developmental delays. She can't handle this. I need to..." I ran a hand through my hair, trying to focus. "I need to book a flight. I need to go home."

"Let me help." His voice was steady, grounding. "I can call my travel planner—"

"No." The word came out sharper than I intended. "I can't... I don't need..."

"Orson." His hand landed on my shoulder, warm and solid. "Let me do this. Please."

I looked up at him then, really looked. His green eyes were serious, none of his usual playfulness present, only genuine concern and a steadiness I desperately needed right now.

"I can't pay you back right away," I said finally, hating how my voice shook. "Flights are expensive, and the emergency fund—"

"Stop." His grip on my shoulder tightened slightly. "Money isn't an issue. What matters is getting you to your family."

"But—"

"No buts. I'm calling my travel planner right now." He was already pulling out his phone. "Give me your passport so I have your info."

"I... I don't have a passport."

"Your driver's license, then."

Right. I had that. I handed him my whole wallet.

"Okay. Pack what you need. I'll make sure you're on the first flight home."

I wanted to argue, to insist I could handle this myself, but the room was starting to spin and my hands wouldn't stop shaking. *Mom. Hospital. Heart attack.* The words kept cycling through my head, each rotation bringing fresh waves of panic.

"Breathe," Floris said softly, and I realized I'd been holding my breath. "We'll get you there as soon as we can. Focus on packing, okay?"

I nodded, grateful for the direction. This, I could do. Pack. Simple steps. Logical sequence. One thing at a time.

In the background, Floris had switched to Dutch. It was such a harsh language, like he was choking.

When I had packed my bag, he finished his call. "Let's go."

"You got me a flight?"

He nodded. "You're all set. I'll drive you to the airport."

"How... what..." I struggled to form coherent questions as Floris grabbed my bag and steered me toward the door. "From Logan? You're driving me to Boston?"

"No. I arranged for a private charter from Worcester Regional Airport. It's leaving as soon as you get there, so we need to hurry." His hand was steady on my elbow, guiding me down the stairs I usually took two at a time. "The pilot is already filing the flight plan and running the pre-flight checks."

Private charter. The words penetrated my fog of panic. "Floris, I can't—"

"You can and you will." His voice was firm but gentle. "Let me do this for you. Please."

Something in his tone made me look at him. His eyes were intense, almost pleading. "Why?"

"Because you're my friend, and your family needs you." He led me to his car, opening the passenger door. "And because I can help. It's that simple."

Nothing was ever that simple. But my phone buzzed with a text from Tia—it *had* been a heart attack, and Mom was in surgery now, needing a bypass—and suddenly, I couldn't argue anymore. I needed to get there.

The drive to the airport was a blur. Floris handled everything, speaking quietly to airport personnel who seemed to materialize out of nowhere to escort us through security and onto the tarmac. A sleek private jet waited there, its engines already humming.

"I'll let your professors know what's happening," Floris said as we reached the stairs to the plane. "Don't worry about anything here, okay? Focus on your family."

I nodded, not trusting my voice. Then, before I could think better of it, I pulled him into a fierce hug. "Thank you," I whispered.

His arms came around me, strong and steady. "Text me when you land?"

"Yeah." I pulled back, trying to ignore how right it had felt in his arms. "I will."

The flight was surreal. I'd never been on a private plane before, and in any other circumstance, I might've been fascinated by the luxury surrounding me. But all I could think about was Mom, lying in a hospital bed while I was trapped in the air, useless.

The flight attendant kept offering me drinks and snacks but my stomach was too knotted to even consider food. I kept checking my phone, even though I knew it wouldn't work at this altitude. What if something happened while I was in the air? What if...

No. I couldn't think like that. Mom was strong. She'd raised two kids alone, worked full time, kept us all together after Dad... She wouldn't leave us. She couldn't.

But the memory of that day on the roof kept creeping back, the way the water had risen so fast, how quickly everything had changed. One minute, life was normal. The next...

My phone buzzed the moment we landed, making me jump.

TIA

She's out of surgery. Doctor says it went well.
Where are you?

My hands shook as I typed back.

Just landed. On my way.

I hadn't even thought about how to get to the hospital from the airport, but I didn't have to. A uniformed driver was waiting for me, holding up an iPad with my name on it. Floris had arranged a car for me, and my heart filled with gratitude all over again. The black, sleek car was another luxury that would've embarrassed me if I'd had the capacity to feel anything beyond desperate urgency. The driver seemed to sense my state, breaking several speed limits as we headed toward the hospital.

New Orleans rushed past the windows, familiar and strange at once. The heavy air hit me as soon as I stepped out of the car, that distinctive mix of humidity and history that always meant home. But right now, even that felt wrong, twisted by worry and fear.

I found Tia in the cardiac ICU waiting room, curled up in an uncomfortable-looking chair with Mrs. Bowman beside her. My sister looked so young, her face pale and drawn, and something inside me cracked at the sight.

"Orson!" She launched herself at me, and I caught her in a tight hug. She was shaking, or maybe I was. Maybe we both were.

Whether it was because she'd been a preemie, because she'd been sick a lot as a child, or simply because she was born that way, Tia was sweet and lovely, but very young for her age. She'd been held back twice, and even now, Mom had hesitated letting her attend the local community college.

"How is she?" I asked into her hair, not ready to let go yet.

"Stable." Tia's voice was muffled against my shirt. "They did a triple bypass. The doctor said she'll need to be here for about a week, and then..." She pulled back, wiping her eyes. "How did you get here so fast? I thought it would take you hours to get a flight, maybe till tomorrow."

"My roommate helped." That felt like such an inadequate description of what Floris had done, but I couldn't find the right words to explain how he'd swept in and taken control when I was falling apart. "Can we see her?"

Tia nodded. "They said family can visit for five minutes every hour. She's still pretty out of it from the anesthesia, but…"

"But she's alive," I finished, and my voice cracked on the last word.

My sister grabbed my hand, squeezing hard. "She's alive."

Mrs. Bowman touched my arm gently. "Now that you're here, I should head home. But call if you need anything, okay?"

I managed to thank her, grateful for how she'd stayed with Tia during those terrifying hours when I was too far away to help. Then a nurse appeared to tell us we could see Mom.

Nothing could've prepared me for how she looked, so small and pale against the white hospital sheets, surrounded by beeping machines and tubes. But her hand was warm when I took it, and her chest rose and fell in steady rhythm.

"I love you," I whispered, not sure if she could hear me through the sedation. "We're here, Mom. We've got you."

Tia's hand found mine again, and we stood there together, watching our mother breathe, each beep of the heart monitor a reminder that we hadn't lost her. Not today. Not like this.

My phone buzzed in my pocket with a text from Floris.

FLORIS

Landed safely?

ME

Yes. She's out of surgery. Stable.

FLORIS

Thank god. Take care of yourself too, okay? Let
me know if you need anything.

ME

I will. Thank you again. For everything.

FLORIS

Don't mention it.

A warmth spread through me. I didn't deserve this kindness, this friendship that asked nothing in return. But god, I was grateful for it.

"Your roommate?" Tia asked, noticing my expression.

"Yeah." I squeezed her hand. "He's... He's a good friend."

That felt like the biggest understatement ever, but it would have to do for now. I had more important things to focus on, like making sure history didn't repeat itself, like keeping our family together, like being the person Dad would've wanted me to be.

Mom stirred slightly, her fingers twitching in mine, and I held on tight.

We'd get through this. We had to.

11

FLORIS

The New Orleans airport was smaller than I'd expected, though still bustling with pre-Thanksgiving travelers. Like me. I adjusted my backpack, scanning the crowd for Orson's familiar, wild curls. He'd insisted on picking me up himself, despite my protests that I could easily get an Uber or a car service.

"Floris!"

I turned at his voice, and there he was, looking more relaxed than I had expected. The New Orleans humidity had turned his curls even wilder than usual, and his brown eyes were bright behind his glasses. Something inside me unfurled at the sight of him. The dorm room had been way too empty without him there.

"Hey." I pulled him into a quick hug before I could overthink it. "Thanks for picking me up."

"Of course." He stepped back, adjusting his glasses in that endearing way he had when feeling slightly flustered. "Though I still can't believe you flew commercial."

I grinned. "I'm trying to blend in, remember? Nothing says 'I'm actually a prince' quite like showing up in a private jet.

Besides, if the Dutch press ever found out I'd flown private, they would have my ass. We're supposed to act normal, remember?"

"Right, because your designer luggage is so subtle." He nodded at my Louis Vuitton carry-on.

"It's practical!"

"It probably costs more than my laptop."

"That's..." I couldn't actually argue with that. "Not the point. Besides, you're the one who invited me for Thanksgiving. The least I could do is try to be somewhat normal about getting here."

His expression softened. "You didn't have to come. I know you had other options."

"Hey." I caught his arm, making him look at me. "I wanted to come. After everything you've been through lately..." I trailed off, remembering how worried he'd been about his mom. "How is she doing?"

"Better." Relief filled his voice. "The doctors cleared her to host Thanksgiving, as long as she takes it easy. Which is why you're here, actually. Mom insisted on having you over after I told her how you helped me get home that day."

Warmth bloomed in my chest. "I didn't do anything special."

"You got me a private plane in less than an hour."

"All I did was make good use of the privileges I have because of my background." I shouldered my bag, following him toward the exit. "Anyone in my position would've done the same."

He bumped my shoulder. "Maybe, but you were there, and that's not something I'll ever forget."

Sweet gratitude filled me. "Well, wait until you see what I brought as a hostess gift. Nothing says, 'thank you for having me' quite like three-hundred-year-old wine from the royal cellars."

Orson stopped dead in his tracks. "Please tell me you're joking."

"Of course I am." I laughed at his horrified expression. "I brought a lovely gift basket with some classic Dutch goodies, including some traditional holiday cookies. Though I did consider bringing the crown jewels. They make excellent conversation pieces at dinner parties."

"You're impossible." But he was grinning now, shaking his head.

"That's why you like me." I waggled my eyebrows at him.

The humidity hit like a wall as we stepped outside, immediately making my hair curl. Back in Massachusetts, the humidity had made place for a cold, dry air that made my skin itch and my hands crack. "Oh wow. You weren't kidding about the weather here."

"Welcome to New Orleans." His smile was fond. "Where the air is thick enough to chew and your hair has its own agenda."

"I can feel my styling products giving up already." I ran a hand through my increasingly unruly hair. "How do you deal with this?"

"Bold of you to assume I deal with it at all." He gestured to his own curls, which seemed to have expanded in the brief time we'd been outside. "I've accepted my fate as a human dandelion."

I laughed, following him to his car, an older model Toyota that had definitely seen better days. "A very handsome dandelion, though."

The words slipped out before I could stop them. Orson's ears turned pink, but he ignored the comment otherwise and opened the trunk for my bag.

"Mom's excited to meet you," he said as we pulled out of the parking lot, clearly changing the subject. "Though I should warn you, she's probably going to try to feed you until you burst."

"I look forward to it."

American highways all looked the same—not that that was any different back home. But Orson navigated them with ease, confident behind the wheel.

"How's Tia doing?" I asked.

His expression softened at the mention of his sister. "Better now that Mom's home. She was pretty scared for a while there."

"Understandable." I'd gotten to know Tia a bit through Orson's stories and the occasional video call. She seemed like a sweet girl, eager to please if somewhat naïve for her age. Precious, that was the best word to describe her. "And you? How are you holding up?"

He was quiet for a moment, focusing on navigating through traffic. "I'm okay. It was rough, at first. But Mom's following all the doctor's orders, and her prognosis is good." He glanced at me briefly. "Thanks again for making it possible for me to get here so quickly that day. I don't know what I would've done if—"

"Hey." I cut him off gently. "You don't need to keep thanking me. That's what friends are for, right?"

His smile was small but genuine. "Right."

The city proper came into view, a mix of historical architecture and modern buildings that somehow worked together in a way that spoke of resilience and renewal. I could see why Orson loved it, despite everything that had happened here. I watched the unfamiliar landscape roll past—palm trees and sprawling oaks draped with Spanish moss, everything so different from the New England fall we'd left behind.

"I can't wait to show you the French Quarter," he said, some of his usual enthusiasm returning. "The architecture is incredible, with a unique blend of French, Spanish, and Caribbean influences. Plus, there's this café that makes the best beignets you've ever tasted."

"Better than *stroopwafels*?"

"Way better."

"Them's fighting words," I teased, loving how animated he got when talking about his city. Plus, I was proud to show off the expression I had learned days prior. "But I'll reserve judgment until I try them."

We turned onto a quiet street lined with modest houses, each with its own character. Some were painted in bright colors, others were more neutral but had wraparound porches, all with a distinct charm. Orson pulled up in front of a pale yellow two-story with a white trim and small front garden that looked well-loved.

"Home sweet home," he said, putting the car in park. "It's not much, but—"

"It's perfect." And it was. The house had personality, warmth—not something I took for granted despite having grown up in a place that could be described as having grandeur. "Very you."

He gave me an odd look. "What does that mean?"

"Practical but with hidden charm. Like those built-in book-shelves I can see through the window: functional but pretty to look at too."

"You're doing it again."

"What?"

"Comparing me to architecture." But he was smiling as he grabbed my bag from the trunk. "Come on, let's get you settled before Mom sends out a search party."

The front door opened before we reached it, revealing a girl with Orson's wild curls and sharp features. She bounded down the steps and threw herself at her brother, who caught her one-armed while somehow managing not to drop my bag.

"You're late," she accused, then turned to me with a bright smile. "Hi! I'm Tia. Thanks for letting my brother borrow your private jet."

"Tia," Orson groaned, but I laughed.

"Technically, it wasn't mine. And I'm Floris. It's nice to finally meet you in person."

"Come in, come in!" A woman's voice called from inside. "You're letting all the air conditioning out!"

Orson's mom stood in the doorway, one hand on her hip. She was smaller than I'd expected, with laugh lines around her eyes and that same determined set to her jaw that Orson got when tackling particularly challenging problems. There was some color in her cheeks, thank god, though she looked tired.

"Mrs. Ritchey," I started formally, but she waved me off.

"Diana, please. And get in here so I can hug you properly."

Before I could respond, I found myself enveloped in a warm embrace that smelled of vanilla and something spicy. The hug was firm but gentle, motherly in a way that made my throat tight with how much I missed my own mom suddenly.

"Thank you," she whispered, just for me to hear. "For getting my son home that day."

"I—" I started, but she pulled back, holding me at arm's length to study my face.

"You're too skinny," she declared. "Don't they feed you at that fancy college?"

"Mom," Orson protested, but there was fond exasperation in his voice. "He just got here."

"And he's going to eat proper food while he's here." She patted my cheek. "I've got gumbo simmering, and there's bread pudding for dessert."

My stomach growled right on cue, making everyone laugh. "That sounds amazing."

"Good answer." She turned to Orson. "Show him where he's staying, then bring him back down. The gumbo needs about twenty more minutes anyway."

The inside of the house was as charming as the exterior—hardwood floors worn smooth by years of footsteps, walls painted in warm colors and decorated with family photos. I followed Orson upstairs, trying not to be too obvious about studying the pictures. There was one of a much younger Orson holding baby Tia, his wild curls even more unruly than now. Another showed him with a man who must have been his father, both grinning at the camera with identical dimples.

"You can have my room," Orson said, pushing open a door. "I'll take the couch."

"I can't kick you out of your room—"

"You're not kicking me out. I'm offering." He set my bag down. "Besides, Mom would kill me if I made a guest sleep on the couch."

I looked around the room, taking in the details. Bookshelves lined one wall, filled with engineering texts and what looked like historical architecture books. A desk sat under the window, everything arranged with Orson's characteristic precision. The walls were a soft blue that reminded me of the sky after a storm.

"Bathroom's across the hall. I'll let you get settled."

"Orson." I caught his arm before he could leave. "Thank you. For inviting me."

Something flickered in his eyes. Warmth maybe, or understanding. "Thank you for coming."

We stood there for a moment, my hand still on his arm, and I found myself studying the gold flecks in his brown eyes, the way his curls fell across his forehead. The urge to brush them back was almost overwhelming.

"Boys!" Diana's voice floated up the stairs. "Gumbo's ready!"

The moment broke. Orson stepped back, adjusting his glasses. "We should..."

"Yeah." I followed him downstairs, trying to ignore the lingering warmth where my hand had touched his arm.

The kitchen was warm and fragrant, steam rising from a large pot on the stove. Diana stood stirring it while Tia set the table, moving with the easy familiarity of a long-established routine.

"Perfect timing," Diana said, ladling the gumbo into bowls. "Floris, honey, you sit here next to Orson. Have you ever had gumbo before?"

"No, ma'am." I settled into the indicated chair, watching as she placed a bowl in front of me. It smelled incredible, though I couldn't place any of the spices.

"None of that 'ma'am' business. It's Diana." She sat across from me, her movements careful but steady. "Now, the secret to good gumbo is—"

"Mom," Orson interrupted gently. "Let him try it first before you give away all your cooking secrets."

I took a spoonful, and the flavors exploded across my tongue —complex, spicy but not overwhelming, with depths I couldn't even begin to identify. "This is amazing."

Diana beamed. "The trick is—"

"The roux," I finished, remembering what Orson had told me. "You have to almost burn it."

Her eyebrows shot up. "You know about roux?"

"Orson told me." I took another spoonful, savoring the flavors. "He said it's what gives gumbo its depth."

"Did he now?" She looked at her son with something like surprise. "I didn't know you paid that much attention to my cooking."

Orson's ears turned pink. "I pay attention to everything."

"Except when to take breaks from studying," Tia piped up. "Or when someone's flirting with him."

"Tia!" Orson choked on his water while I tried very hard not to react to that particular observation.

Diana's eyes darted between us, a knowing smile playing at her lips. "So, Floris, tell me about your studies. Orson says you're interested in water management?"

I latched onto the change of subject gratefully, launching into an explanation of Dutch water management systems and my interest in civil engineering. As I talked, Diana's eyes kept drifting to Orson, watching his reactions with that particular maternal insight that seemed to see right through carefully constructed walls.

"You know," she said during a lull in conversation, "we had some Dutch engineers come down after Katrina. They had some interesting ideas about improving our flood defenses."

Orson tensed beside me so I kept my voice casual. "The Delta Works inspired a lot of flood management systems world-wide. Though every situation is unique, of course. What works in the Netherlands might not be practical here."

"True." She stirred her gumbo thoughtfully. "But sometimes, outside perspective can be valuable. Help us see things differently."

Something about the way she said it made me think she wasn't talking about engineering. I glanced at Orson, who was studying his bowl with unusual intensity.

"Different perspectives are always valuable," I agreed carefully. "Though local knowledge is crucial too. You can't impose solutions without understanding the specific challenges and history of a place."

Diana's smile widened slightly. "Very diplomatic. Your royal training shows."

I nearly dropped my spoon. "You know?"

"Of course I know." She looked amused. "I'm a teacher. I

know how to use Google, and when Orson mentioned you arranged for a private charter, I was curious about who you were. Not many people have access to that kind of wealth or privilege."

"Mom," Orson started, but she waved him off.

"Oh, relax. I'm not going to tell anyone. Though I have to say, you're not quite what I expected from a prince."

"Thank you, I think?"

"It is a compliment," she assured me. "Now, who wants seconds?"

12

ORSON

I woke up with that frenetic energy of a Christmas morning, and that despite having slept on our lumpy couch. A week of that and I wouldn't be able to walk, but I'd bear it with a smile on my face if that was the price for having Floris here.

I'd missed him. Funny how that worked. I hadn't expected to miss his constant chatter, his terrible jokes, even the chaos he brought to every space he occupied. But I had. It had felt like someone had dimmed the lights, though come to think of it, that was probably because of all the stress around Mom and not so much Floris. That seemed a far more likely explanation.

But the fact was that I had missed him. Now he was here for a whole week, and I couldn't stop smiling, couldn't quite believe he'd chosen to spend his Thanksgiving break with us instead of choosing one of the undoubtedly far more exotic options he'd had. He'd mentioned an invite to go scuba diving in the Caribbean, and yet he was here.

It had meant a lot to Mom too, I could tell. He'd loved her gumbo, always a surefire way to get my mom's approval, but she genuinely liked him. She'd loved the gift basket he'd brought her, which had included a refrigerator magnet with cute little wooden shoes, a gorgeous colander with pictures of tulips, and oven mitts in that classic white-and-blue pattern the Netherlands were famous for. Delft Blue, Floris had called it.

We'd talked for a long time yesterday, all four of us, and he'd drawn even Tia into our conversations. She now stared at him with little hearts in her eyes, despite knowing he was gay.

I couldn't blame them for liking him. What was not to like? He was the best friend I could've ever wished for, and I was stupidly excited to show him my city.

After a simple breakfast—I warned Floris to leave room for snacks—we headed out. The French Quarter was alive with its usual mix of tourists and locals, music spilling from doorways and mingling with the sounds of horse-drawn carriages on cobblestone streets. I watched Floris take it all in, his eyes wide as he studied the wrought-iron balconies and colorful facades. The morning sun caught his hair, turning it almost golden, and I forced myself to look away.

"This is incredible." Floris craned his neck to study a particularly ornate balcony. His fingers twitched like he wanted to touch the intricate ironwork, an urge I was well familiar with. "It feels like I'm somewhere else entirely. It's hard to believe this exists in the same country as Worcester, that they're both in the US."

"We certainly like to think we're special," I said with a grin. "And we have the language to prove it. Creole is nothing like you've ever heard."

Floris turned to me, frowning. "I thought it was bastard French, for lack of a better word."

I shook my head. "It's a mix of French, African languages, Spanish, and Native American words that all came together in its own complete language system with unique grammar and pronunciation. Like, in French you'd say *je vais* for 'I go,' but in Creole, it becomes *mo té allé*. Mom's family spoke it at home when she was growing up, and even though we don't use it much in our house, you can still hear it all over certain neighborhoods, especially when the older folks get together."

"Oh wow, I never knew. But you understand it?"

I wiggled my hand. "Enough to get by if needed, but I'm not fluent in it."

We continued our walk, making our way down Royal Street.

"How did all this survive Katrina?" Floris asked. "The French Quarter, I mean. The water must have been brutal on these old buildings."

My chest tightened at the question. "This part of the city is actually on higher ground, so it didn't flood." I paused, swallowing past the sudden thickness in my throat. "The water went other places instead."

Something in my tone must've alerted him because Floris turned to study my face. "I'm sorry. I shouldn't have asked."

"It's okay." I took a deep breath. "I should learn to talk about it."

He reached for my hand and held it for a moment. "Maybe, but when you're ready. Not because I keep pushing you with questions."

"It's okay."

He let go of my hand again, and I felt strangely bereft.

"So, where are these famous beignets you keep promising me?" he asked, and I appreciated his forced change of topic.

"Café du Monde is just ahead." I led him toward the familiar green and white awning. "Fair warning: you're going to get powdered sugar everywhere. It's basically a requirement."

"Food that requires wearing it? That doesn't sound like you at all."

Leave it to Floris to get me out of my head.

The café was busy as always, but we managed to snag a table near the edge where we could watch the street life. Floris's face when he took his first bite of a beignet was almost comical, his eyes widening as the hot, fluffy pastry practically melted in his mouth.

"Okay," he said after swallowing, "I concede. These might actually be better than *stroopwafels*. Infinitely messier, but wow, they're yummy."

"I'll take that as high praise." I watched as he tried to eat the next one more carefully, failing to avoid the shower of powdered sugar. A white streak appeared on his nose. He looked so freaking adorable.

"You've got…" I gestured to my own nose.

He wiped at it, managing to spread more sugar across his face. "Better?"

"Worse, actually." Without thinking, I reached across the table with a napkin, gently wiping the sugar away. His skin was warm under my touch, and our eyes met for a moment that felt charged with something I wasn't ready to name.

I pulled back quickly, heat creeping up my neck. "There. Now you look less like you lost a fight with a powdered donut."

"My hero." His smile was soft, almost fond. "So, what else do I need to see while I'm here?"

The question brought back that familiar weight, the one that always came with thinking about my dad, about what had happened, about how I had failed him. But this was Floris. He'd chartered a private plane to get me home when Mom was sick. He'd become so much more than a roommate or friend. He was someone I trusted, even if that trust terrified me sometimes.

"There's something I want to show you," I heard myself say. "But it's not exactly a tourist spot."

He must've heard something in my voice because his expression turned serious. He reached across the table, his hand landing on mine for a moment. The touch was brief but grounding, giving me courage. "I'd love to see it... and listen to your story."

He knew. It didn't surprise me, and that, too, was a comfort. "Thank you."

We walked in comfortable silence, leaving the bustle of the French Quarter behind. The streets became more residential, houses showing varying stages of repair and renewal. Some areas still bore the scars of Katrina, even after all these years— water lines visible on buildings, empty lots where homes once stood. Floris seemed to sense I couldn't talk and he continued to walk quietly beside me, taking it all in. His hand brushed against mine from time to time, and I loved that casual reminder that I was not alone.

Finally, we reached the house. My old house. It looked different now. It was renovated, painted a different color, someone else's home. But I could still see it as it was that day, water rising faster than anyone had predicted.

"This is where we lived," I said quietly, "when Katrina hit."

Floris moved closer, his shoulder brushing mine in silent support. He didn't speak, just waited.

"What's your first memory?" I asked him. "The first one you can remember?"

He smiled. "Sledding down a mountain in Austria with my uncle Friso, who is now king, and my cousins. I had just turned five. We were on a family trip there, and we were high up in the mountains, where there was snow even in the summer. My father didn't like it one bit, as he's afraid of heights, but my uncle lived for that shit. We didn't bring a sled, of course, but he found a thick trash bag and used that. And off we went, me between his legs and him holding on tight to me as we whooshed down the mountain. Best thing ever, which is why it must've burned itself into my memory." Then his smile faded. "But I'm gonna take a wild guess and say yours isn't quite so positive."

I shook my head. "I was four. Old enough to remember, not old enough to understand. Tia was only a few months old, and she was sick with pneumonia." The words came slow, each one heavy. "She was a preemie, born at twenty-nine weeks with underdeveloped lungs, and she had bronchopulmonary dysplasia, a lung illness. That's why my parents were so hesitant to evacuate. Putting Tia in a shelter full of other kids would've put her at high risk. And we thought we were safe here. The forecasts kept changing. First, they said the storm would turn, then that the levees would hold. By the time we realized how bad it was going to be, it was too late to evacuate."

I could feel Floris's eyes on me, but I kept my gaze on the house. "The water rose so fast. Dad got us onto the roof. He carried Tia up first, then came back for me. Mom had managed to get up by herself and was holding Tia. But I was scared, trying to climb too quickly. I slipped." I swallowed heavily, the scar on my shin aching. "Cut myself pretty bad on the edge of the roof. Dad had to climb all the way back down to push me up."

The memory was vivid: the howling wind, the rising water, my father's strong hands lifting me. "He managed to push me up onto the roof, but then the current was too strong. He couldn't hold on anymore. Mom tried to reach him, but..."

My voice cracked. Floris's hand found mine, warm and steady, grounding me in the present.

"I watched him disappear under the water." The words felt like they were being torn from somewhere deep inside me. "He died saving me. And sometimes I wonder... if I hadn't slipped, if

I hadn't been so clumsy, he wouldn't have had to come back for me..."

"Stop." Floris's voice was gentle but firm. "You can't think like that."

"Can't I?" I turned to look at him finally, seeing nothing but understanding in his green eyes. "He was an engineer, Floris. He could've done so much good, helped so many people. Instead, he died saving one scared kid who couldn't even climb a roof properly."

"A four-year-old kid, who must've been terrified. A kid who grew up to want to prevent other families from going through the same thing." His hand squeezed mine. "Who's brilliant and dedicated and working so hard to make a difference."

"But what if it's not enough?" The question that had haunted me for years finally spilled out. "What if I can't live up to his sacrifice?"

"Oh, Orson." Before I could react, Floris pulled me into a tight hug. I stiffened for a moment, then melted into it, letting his warmth seep into all the cold places inside me. "You don't have to earn the right to be alive."

"But he died saving me." The words felt like they were being torn from somewhere deep inside. "He could've stayed on the roof with Tia, but he came back for me. And now..."

"Now you feel like you have to live up to that sacrifice." Floris squeezed my hand. "Like you have to be perfect to justify his choice."

I looked up then, meeting his eyes. "How did you...?"

"Because I understand what it's like to feel the weight of someone else's expectations. To think you have to be perfect to be worthy of what they gave up for you." His thumb traced circles on my palm, sending shivers up my arm. "But Orson, your dad didn't save you so you could spend your life trying to prove you deserved it. He saved you because he loved you. Any parent worth a damn would choose their kid's life over their own. That's the whole essence of being a parent, isn't it?"

"The last thing he said was, 'It'll be okay, buddy.'" I swallowed hard. "And I've tried. God, I've tried so hard to be worthy of what he did."

"Orson." Floris's voice was impossibly gentle. "You were four years old. You didn't need to be worthy. You were his son. That was enough."

"But I have to make it mean something," I whispered into his shoulder. "His death has to have a purpose."

"It did." Floris pulled back enough to look at me, his hands warm on my shoulders. "It meant you lived. You grew up. You became this amazing person who cares so deeply about helping others. That's more than enough."

I blinked hard against sudden tears. "I miss him. And I'm scared of losing anyone else. When Mom collapsed, all I could think was 'not again.'"

"I know." His voice was soft, understanding. "Is that why you push yourself so hard? Why you won't let yourself have anything beyond your studies?"

The question hit too close to home. "I can't afford distractions. If I mess up, if I make the wrong choice..."

"Then you learn from it and try again." His hands moved to frame my face, forcing me to meet his eyes. "You're allowed to *live*, Orson. To make mistakes. To want things beyond honoring your father's memory. But for what it's worth, I think your dad would be proud of you. Not because you're perfect, but because you're you. Because you care so much about helping others that you're willing to give up your own dreams to do it."

I stiffened. "What do you mean?"

"I've seen how you light up when you talk about historical architecture and restoration. That's your passion, not modern civil engineering." He leaned forward slightly. "But you're pushing yourself into a different path because you think that's what you need to do to honor your dad's sacrifice."

"I... That's not..." But the protest died in my throat because he was right. Of course he was right. "Civil engineering saves lives."

"So does preserving historical buildings properly. Making sure they're structurally sound while maintaining their character." His voice was gentle but firm. "You don't have to save lives the way he did or how you think you should. Sometimes, the best way to honor someone's memory is to live authentically, to be true to who you are."

I stared at him, this prince who somehow saw right through all my carefully constructed walls. "When did you get so wise?"

His smile was soft, real. "I'm full of surprises. Also, probably the sugar high from those beignets. They were seriously amazing."

I laughed despite myself, and something in my chest loosened slightly. Leave it to Floris to lighten the mood with a joke.

"Want to see more of the Quarter?" I offered. "There's this amazing historical house museum that shows the original Spanish colonial architecture..."

His face lit up. "Lead the way."

As we walked through the familiar streets, Floris asked intelligent questions about the architecture, genuinely interested in the historical details I usually kept to myself. And if our shoulders brushed more often than strictly necessary, well, that was because of the crowded sidewalks.

The words he had spoken settled somewhere deep inside

me, warm and healing. Maybe he was right. Maybe being alive, being me, was enough.

Maybe.

13

FLORIS

Orson's bed was only marginally more comfortable than my creaky mattress in our dorm room, but it smelled like him, so I had still slept like a baby. Hell, I'd even slept in somewhat, not waking up till nine.

Thanksgiving preparations were already underway downstairs. I could hear Diana humming as she worked in the kitchen, the occasional clatter of pots and pans punctuating her melody. The sounds and smells wafting up were enough to make my stomach growl loud enough to qualify as its own musical accompaniment.

I'd offered to help the day before, but she'd shooed me away with a fond, "You're our guest, honey." Though I suspected it had more to do with protecting her kitchen from my questionable culinary skills than actual hospitality. Orson had probably warned her about the microwave incident and my general proneness to clumsiness. In my defense, how was I supposed to know that aluminum foil and microwaves were mortal enemies? That wasn't covered in my royal education, though maybe it should have been, right between "proper tea-sipping etiquette" and "how to wave without looking like you're swatting flies."

Now I stared at my reflection in the bathroom mirror, toothbrush hanging from my mouth as I tried to tame my increasingly wild curls. The New Orleans humidity was doing things to my hair that defied both gravity and common sense. At this rate, I'd need a royal decree to get it to lay flat. Maybe I could claim diplomatic immunity from bad hair days? Was that a thing? Note to self: consult with the Dutch ambassador about adding that to international treaties.

Not that it seemed to matter to Orson. Granted, his hair was even wilder than mine, but it only added to his charm. My mind drifted back to the previous day, to Orson standing in front of his old house, to the raw vulnerability in his voice as he shared his story. The weight he'd been carrying all these years, that desperate need to prove himself worthy of his father's sacrifice, explained so much about him. His obsessive studying, his reluctance to take risks or allow himself any joy beyond academic achievement, his fanatical attention to detail.

My chest ached for how young he'd been, only four years old, watching his father disappear beneath the rising waters. No wonder he triple-checked everything, planned for every contingency, always wanted to be in control. He'd learned too early how quickly life could change, how one moment could alter everything.

And yet despite that trauma, or maybe because of it, he'd grown into someone incredible. He was brilliant and caring and so much stronger than he knew. The way his eyes had lit up when we'd toured that historical house museum afterwards, his whole face transformed as he explained the architectural details... That was the real Orson, the one he kept buried beneath duty and guilt.

I wanted to see more of that Orson. I wanted to be the one who helped him rediscover joy, who showed him he deserved happiness beyond honoring his father's memory. The urge to kiss him had been almost overwhelming when he'd gotten excited about those original Spanish colonial features, his hands gesturing animatedly as he explained their historical significance.

But would telling him how I felt add more pressure? The last thing I wanted was to become another complication in his carefully ordered life. We had built a beautiful friendship, one that meant so much to me. Was I willing to risk all that?

Plus, there was the whole prince thing to consider. Any relationship with me would eventually mean public scrutiny, and Orson had been through enough trauma without adding tabloid headlines to the mix.

Still, the way he'd looked at me sometimes yesterday, those lingering glances when he thought I wasn't paying attention... I wasn't imagining the spark between us. He felt it too, even if he hadn't said anything. Maybe...

No. For now, being his friend was enough. Had to be enough. He needed someone in his corner who expected nothing from him except being himself. I could be...

The bathroom door opened suddenly, and there was Orson, wearing nothing but boxer briefs that left very little to the imagination. He froze when he saw me, those intelligent, brown eyes widening behind his glasses. His lean, toned body caught me off guard. I'd seen him like this before, of course. Hard not to when we were roommates. But somehow, his beauty had never hit me as hard as it did now.

His chest was smooth and pale, with a light dusting of freckles across his shoulders that made my fingers itch to trace them. The morning light filtering through the small bathroom window caught his wild curls, turning them almost copper, even more chaotic than usual from sleep. A thin scar on his right shin caught my eye, a reminder of the story he'd told me about climbing onto that roof during Katrina.

Heat rushed to my face as I realized I was equally under-dressed, standing there in my boxer briefs. His gaze flickered over me briefly before snapping back to my face, a blush creeping up his neck. Those slim, elegant hands of his gripped the doorframe like he needed the support, and I couldn't blame him. The air between us felt suddenly thick with possibility.

"Sorry!" He started to back out, but his foot caught on the bath mat. I reached out instinctively to steady him, my hand landing on his bare shoulder. The contact sent electricity through my fingertips.

Time seemed to slow. We were standing too close, close enough that I could see the gold flecks in his brown eyes, count the freckles scattered across his nose. His skin was warm under my palm, and I couldn't make myself let go.

"Hi," I managed, my voice embarrassingly rough.

"Hi." His eyes dropped to my mouth for a fraction of a second, then snapped back up. "I should—"

I kissed him.

Later, I wouldn't be able to say exactly what made me do it. Maybe it was the way the morning light caught his eyes, or how vulnerable he looked with his sleep-mussed hair and bare skin. Maybe it was that I'd wanted to for so long that I couldn't hold back anymore.

The kiss was gentle at first, hesitant, giving him every chance to pull away. But then Orson made this soft sound in the back of his throat and kissed me back, and my world narrowed to the feel of his lips against mine, the warmth of his skin under my hands.

His fingers tangled in my hair as he deepened the kiss, and everything else fell away: my carefully constructed reasons why this was a bad idea, my fears about complicating our friendship, my worries whether he felt the same way, all of it gone in the rush of finally, finally knowing how he tasted.

Then, as suddenly as it began, it was over. Orson jerked back like he'd been burned, his eyes wide behind his glasses. "I... I can't..."

Before I could say anything, he was gone, practically running back to his room. The door closed with a soft click that somehow hurt more than if he'd slammed it.

I stood there, my heart pounding, lips still tingling from the kiss. What had I done? I'd promised myself I wouldn't push, wouldn't risk our friendship, and now...

"Floris?" Diana's voice floated up from downstairs. "Breakfast is ready if you want some!"

"Coming!" I called back, grateful my voice sounded steadier than I felt.

I quickly threw on some clothes, trying to calm my racing thoughts. When I heard Orson's door open and his footsteps on the stairs, I waited a few minutes before following. I needed time to compose myself, to put on that mask of casual charm I'd perfected over years of public appearances.

But god, the memory of his lips against mine, the way he'd kissed me back before panic set in...

No. I couldn't think about that now. Not when I had to face him and his family over breakfast, pretending everything was normal.

As if things would ever be normal again.

When I finally made it downstairs, the kitchen was alive with Thanksgiving preparations. Diana stood at the stove, stirring something that smelled amazing while giving instructions to

Tia, who was chopping vegetables with impressive precision. Orson sat at the table, fully dressed now in jeans and a dark blue T-shirt, determinedly not looking at me.

"There you are!" Diana turned from the stove, wielding a wooden spoon like a conductor's baton. "Help yourself to coffee and toast. We've got a busy day ahead."

I managed what I hoped was a normal smile, avoiding Orson's general direction as I poured myself coffee. The mug trembled slightly in my hand, and I gripped it tighter. I gave myself a firm talking to. *Get it together. You're literally trained for awkward social situations.*

"What can I do to help?" I asked as I munched on the toast, desperate for something to occupy myself with besides replaying that kiss in my head.

"Actually," Diana said, "I need someone to run to the store. I forgot to buy cranberry sauce, and apparently, my homemade one won't do." She shot a fond look at Tia, who was making a face. "Would you mind? You boys can go together."

My heart stuttered. Orson's head snapped up, panic flashing across his face before he carefully schooled his expression.

"I can go alone," I offered quickly. "Just give me directions—"

"Nonsense." Diana waved the spoon dismissively. "The stores will be crazy today. You'll need someone who knows the way to survive."

I caught Orson's eye accidentally, and for a moment, I saw my own panic reflected there. But he just nodded stiffly and stood. "Let me grab my keys."

The drive to the store was possibly the most awkward seven minutes of my life, and that included the time where I had to explain to the King of England why his favorite horse was wearing my underwear on its head. In my defense, I had been nine and Greg had totally dared me.

Orson gripped the steering wheel like he expected it to make a break for freedom, his knuckles white. I stared out the window, trying to ignore how the confined space of the car made it impossible not to be aware of his presence, of the lingering taste of him on my lips.

The streets were busy as expected, other last-minute shoppers presumably on similar missions. Each stop light felt like an eternity, the silence between us growing heavier with each passing moment.

"Orson—" I started, at the same time as he said, "Listen—"

We both stopped. I gestured for him to continue, but he shook his head, jaw tight.

"About what happened..." I tried again.

"Don't." His voice was strained. "Please. I can't..."

"Can't what?" The words came out sharper than I intended. "Can't talk about it? Can't acknowledge that you kissed me back?"

He flinched like I'd struck him. "It was a mistake."

That hurt more than it should have. "Was it? Because from where I was standing, which was very close to you in the bathroom, it didn't feel like a mistake."

"Floris." My name sounded like it was being torn from somewhere deep inside him. "I can't do this. I can't deal with another complication, another distraction."

"Is that what you think I would be?" I turned to look at him properly, taking in his tense profile, the way his hands gripped the wheel. "A distraction?"

"Isn't that what relationships are? Messy, complicated, unpredictable?" He pulled into the store parking lot but made no move to get out. "I have goals, responsibilities. I can't afford to—"

"To what? Feel something? Live a little?" I ran a hand

through my hair in frustration. "God, Orson, you're allowed to want things for yourself."

"You don't understand."

"Don't I?" I shifted in my seat to face him fully. "You think I don't know about responsibility? About the weight of expectations? I'm literally a prince, in case you've forgotten."

Orson's hands tightened on the steering wheel. "That's different."

"How? Because my obligations come from a crown instead of guilt?" The words came out harsher than I intended, but I couldn't stop now. "You're not the only one who knows what it's like to feel the weight of someone else's expectations."

"My father died saving me." His voice cracked on the last word. "I can't—"

"Can't what? Be happy? Live your life?" I softened my tone. "Do you really think that's what he would've wanted?"

"You don't know what he would've wanted." But there was uncertainty in his voice now. "You didn't know him."

"No, but I know you." I reached for his hand before I could stop myself. He tensed but didn't pull away. "And I know that pushing away everything that might make you happy isn't honoring his sacrifice. It's punishing yourself for surviving."

His breath hitched. "Floris…"

"Tell me you didn't feel something in that bathroom." I squeezed his hand gently. "Tell me you haven't felt this thing between us growing for months. Tell me I'm imagining it all, and I'll back off. We can pretend it never happened."

For a long moment, he was silent. Then, so quietly I almost missed it, "I can't tell you that."

My heart leapt. "Then what are you afraid of?"

"Everything." He finally turned to look at me, his brown eyes vulnerable behind his glasses. "What if it doesn't work out? What if I mess it up? What if—"

"What if it does work?" I interrupted gently. "What if it's amazing? What if allowing yourself to feel something, to want something for yourself, actually makes you stronger?"

"I don't know how." His voice was barely a whisper. "I don't know how to want things for myself anymore."

"Then let me help you figure it out." I brought our joined hands to my lips, pressing a soft kiss to his knuckles. "We can take it slow. No pressure, no expectations. Just... us."

Orson's breath caught at the gesture, and I saw something shift in his expression, like a wall crumbling, just a little. "It's not that simple."

"Why not?"

"Because..." He pulled his hand away, but gently. "You're a prince, Floris. Eventually, you'll have to go back to that life. To responsibilities and public scrutiny and... I can't be part of that world. I'm not..."

"Not what?"

"Not good enough." The words came out in a rush. "Not polished enough, not sophisticated enough, not—"

"Stop." I cut him off, my chest aching at the self-doubt in his voice. "First of all, you're brilliant and kind and absolutely good enough for anyone. Second, do you really think I care about any of that? I like you because you're you. Because you call me out on my bullshit and help me with calculus and make me want to be better, not for the crown or the press, but for myself."

He looked at me then, really looked at me, and I saw a glimmer of hope beneath the fear in his eyes. "I don't want to lose you," he admitted quietly. "Our friendship... it means too much to risk."

"Who says we have to lose anything?" I shifted closer, heart hammering. "Maybe we could gain something instead. Something amazing."

A small smile tugged at his lips. "You sound very sure about that."

"I am." I reached for his hand again, relief flooding through me when he let me take it. "Because I know how I feel when I'm with you. How everything is brighter, better. How you make me want to be more than a prince, more than what everyone expects me to be."

His thumb traced circles on my palm, sending shivers up my arm. "I... I feel that too," he whispered. "But it scares me."

"Good things often do." I squeezed his hand. "But maybe they're worth being scared for."

Orson looked at our joined hands, his expression thoughtful. "What if we take it slow? Figure this out one step at a time?"

My heart soared. "We can go as slow as you need. I'm not going anywhere."

He met my eyes then, and the vulnerability there made my breath catch. "Promise?"

"Promise." I brought our joined hands to my lips again, pressing another soft kiss to his knuckles. "Though we should probably get that cranberry sauce before your mom sends out a search party."

That startled a laugh out of him, breaking the tension. "God, I almost forgot. She's probably wondering what's taking so long."

"We could tell her we got lost in each other's eyes," I suggested with an exaggerated waggle of my eyebrows.

"You're ridiculous." But he was smiling now, that rare, genuine smile that transformed his whole face. "Come on, let's go brave the Thanksgiving crowds."

Inside the store was chaos, last-minute shoppers frantically grabbing forgotten items. We managed to find the cranberry sauce after some searching, though Orson had to reach over an elderly lady who was debating between two different brands.

"I can't believe Americans eat this," I said, studying the can. "It looks like jelly."

"That's because it *is* jelly." Orson's shoulder brushed mine as we waited in the checkout line. "Wait until you see it come out of the can. It keeps the shape and everything."

"That's horrifying." But I was grinning, loving how the awkwardness between us had melted into something softer, full of possibility.

When we got back to the car, Orson hesitated before starting the engine. "Floris?"

"Hmm?"

"Thank you." He turned to look at me, his eyes serious behind his glasses. "For being patient with me. For understanding."

"Always." I reached over to brush a curl from his forehead, my heart skipping when he leaned into the touch. "Though I should warn you, my patience has limits. Especially when you look this adorable."

His cheeks flushed pink. "It'll build character, just like the stairs, the showers, and the lack of AC in our dorm."

I was still grinning by the time we got back.

14

ORSON

In one of my project management classes, my professor had talked about a well-known phenomenon called the curse of knowledge. It basically means that once you know something or are able to do something, it's hard to remember what it's like not to have that knowledge or that skill. That's why help desk people are trained in asking the most basic questions, like, *Is the computer plugged in?* or, *Have you tried turning it on and off?*

For the first twenty-four years of my life, I hadn't known Floris, hadn't stared at him when he smiled, hadn't felt his lips against mine. For twenty-four years, I'd lived in ignorant bliss... and now, barely twenty-four hours after that kiss in the bathroom, I couldn't remember what that had been like. How did it feel not to want him? I had no clue.

The curse of knowledge indeed.

We were on our way to the bayou for a swamp tour—his idea, of course. He'd been fascinated by the concept ever since I'd mentioned it casually at breakfast, and his enthusiasm had been impossible to resist. Then again, most things about Floris were impossible to resist.

"So we might actually see alligators?" He bounced slightly in the passenger seat, reminding me of an excited puppy. "Like, real ones? In the wild?"

"If we're lucky." I couldn't help smiling at his enthusiasm. "Though they're less active this time of year. The water's getting cooler."

"Still. Actual alligators in their natural habitat!" He turned to me, green eyes bright with excitement. "That's so cool. The wildest thing we have back home are some really angry geese."

"Geese can be pretty terrifying."

"True. There's this one at the palace that I swear has a personal vendetta against me. Chased me across the garden once when I was twelve." He grinned at the memory. "The tabloids would've loved that headline: 'Prince Flees from Angry Waterfowl.'"

I laughed, the sound surprising even me. It was getting easier to laugh around him, to let my guard down. Maybe that should've scared me more than it did.

The drive to the bayou was peaceful, the morning sun painting everything in soft gold. Floris kept up a steady stream of commentary about everything from Dutch wildlife to the time he accidentally caused an incident my mispronouncing the German word for humid.

"You did not," I said.

"I absolutely did. The difference was an umlaut; that's what the Germans call those two dots on a letter, in this case a u. *Schwül* with an umlaut means humid or sultry. *Schwul* without one means gay. So I basically told the ambassador the weather was gay. He took offense."

"Only you could accidentally offend an ambassador with weather talk." I shook my head, unable to suppress my smile. "Though I'm surprised he was offended by that."

"Oh, he wasn't offended by the gay part. He was offended I'd mangled his beautiful language." Floris stretched in his seat, and I definitely didn't notice how his shirt rode up slightly. "Germans take their grammar very seriously."

The bayou appeared ahead, misty in the morning light. Spanish moss draped the cypress trees like ghostly curtains, and the air grew heavier with that distinctive swamp smell—earthy and ancient.

"Wow," Floris breathed as we pulled into the small parking area. "It's like something out of a movie."

"Wait until we're actually out on the water." I led him toward the dock where our tour boat waited. "The bayou has its own kind of magic."

"Speaking of magic…" He caught my hand, tugging me to a stop. When I turned to look at him, his expression was soft but serious. "Are we okay? After yesterday?"

My heart stuttered. The memory of that kiss flooded back— his lips on mine, his hands in my hair, the way everything had felt simultaneously terrifying and absolutely right. "Yeah," I managed. "We're okay."

His thumb traced circles on my palm, sending shivers up my arm. "Good. Because I meant what I said about taking it slow, about figuring this out together."

I squeezed his hand, gathering courage from his steady presence. "I know. Thank you for… for understanding. For being patient."

His smile was warm enough to chase away the morning chill. "Though you're making it very difficult when you look at me like that."

"Like what?"

"Like you want to kiss me again."

Heat rushed to my face. "I—"

"All aboard!" The tour guide's voice saved me from having to respond. "Tour's starting in five minutes!"

Floris grinned, clearly enjoying my flustered state. "Shall we?"

The small boat was already half full with other tourists, cameras ready. We found seats near the back, and if we sat closer than strictly necessary, well, the bench was narrow. Floris's thigh pressed against mine, warm even through our jeans, and I tried very hard to focus on what the guide was saying about the bayou's ecosystem.

"The cypress trees you see around us can live for hundreds of years," the guide explained as we pulled away from the dock. "Some of these were here long before New Orleans was founded."

Floris leaned closer, ostensibly to hear better, but his breath tickled my ear as he whispered, "Bet none of them are as old as some of the buildings back home. We've got houses that predate your entire country."

"Show off," I muttered, but I couldn't help smiling.

The boat glided deeper into the bayou, the morning mist creating an otherworldly atmosphere. Water lapped gently against the hull, and birds called from hidden perches in the trees. This place had always felt timeless to me, like stepping into another world where modern concerns couldn't follow.

"There!" The guide pointed to a partially submerged log. "See that bump? That's one of our resident alligators."

Floris practically vibrated with excitement beside me, fumbling for his phone to take pictures. "Oh my god, it's real. An actual alligator!"

"You're like a kid on Christmas morning," I teased, but his enthusiasm was infectious.

"Can you blame me? The most exciting wildlife we get at

home is that murderous goose I told you about." He snapped another picture, then turned to me with such pure joy on his face that my heart did a complicated flip.

The morning sun caught his eyes, turning them the color of spring leaves, and that curse of knowledge hit me again. How was I supposed to pretend I didn't want to kiss him when he looked at me like that?

"What?" he asked, noticing my stare.

"Nothing." I looked away quickly. "You're cute when you're excited."

His smile softened into something more intimate. "Only when I'm excited?"

Heat crept up my neck. "You know you're not."

"Do I?" His voice was teasing, but there was something vulnerable underneath. "Maybe I need reminding sometimes."

Before I could respond, the boat turned sharply, and Floris grabbed my arm to steady himself. The contact sent electricity through my skin, and I found myself hyper-aware of every point where our bodies touched.

"Look there!" The guide's voice broke through my Floris-induced haze. "Another gator, bigger than the last one."

This time, I got my camera out, partly to have something to do with my hands that didn't involve touching Floris. The alligator was impressive, easily twelve feet long, sunning itself on a half-submerged log.

"The males can grow up to fifteen feet," I explained quietly, falling back on facts to ground myself. "They're actually pretty docile unless they're protecting their territory or—"

"Nesting grounds," Floris finished with me, grinning. "I may have done some research last night."

Of course he had. "You never do anything halfway, do you?"

"Nope." His eyes met mine, and suddenly, we weren't talking about alligators anymore. "When I want something, I tend to go all in."

My breath caught. "Even if it's complicated?"

"Especially then." His hand found mine between us. "The best things usually are."

The tour continued, but I was only half-listening to the guide's explanations about the ecosystem and local folklore. Most of my attention was focused on Floris's thumb tracing patterns on my palm, each touch sending sparks up my arm.

"You know what's funny?" he said softly as the boat turned back toward the dock. "I've seen some of the most beautiful places in the world. Palaces, famous landmarks, natural wonders. But somehow, sitting here with you in a swamp boat looking at alligators feels more real than any of that."

I turned to look at him, struck by the honesty in his voice. "Yeah?"

"Yeah." His eyes met mine, soft and sincere. "Because I'm not here as a prince fulfilling some diplomatic obligation. I'm me."

Something warm spread inside me. "I like you being you."

His smile was bright enough to rival the morning sun. "Good, because that's who I want to be. Especially with you."

The boat docked, breaking the moment, but Floris kept hold of my hand as we disembarked. His palm was warm against mine, and I marveled at how natural it felt, how right.

"Want to walk around a bit?" I suggested, nodding toward a nearby nature trail. "There's a boardwalk that goes through the cypress grove."

"Lead the way."

The wooden boardwalk creaked under our feet as we walked, surrounded by ancient trees draped in Spanish moss.

Water rippled below, dark and mysterious, occasionally disturbed by something moving beneath the surface.

"It's beautiful here," Floris said quietly. "But also kind of eerie. Like the trees are watching us."

"They probably are." I squeezed his hand. "Local folklore says the bayou has a memory, that it remembers everything that's happened here."

He turned to look at me, curiosity bright in his eyes. "Is that why you love it? Because it remembers?"

The question caught me off guard with its insight. "Maybe. I used to come here a lot as a teen. Something about this place made me feel connected to him. Like the bayou remembered him too."

Floris stepped closer, his free hand coming up to brush a curl from my forehead. "Thank you for sharing it with me."

"Thank you for wanting to see it." I leaned into his touch slightly. "Most people don't understand why I love it here."

"I do." His voice was soft. "It's part of who you are, like the canals and dikes are part of who I am. These places shape us, make us who we are."

I looked at him then and felt that now-familiar ache. How had this prince, with his designer clothes and royal pedigree, come to understand me so well? How had he slipped past all my carefully constructed defenses?

"What?" he asked, noticing my intense stare.

I struggled to find the right words. "Sometimes, I can't believe you're real. That you're here, in my swamp, holding my hand and actually getting why this place matters."

His smile was soft, genuine in a way his public ones rarely were. "Where else would I want to be?"

And maybe it was the magic of the bayou, or the way the morning light caught his eyes, or that I was tired of fighting what

I felt, but I kissed him. Right there on the boardwalk, surrounded by ancient cypress trees and Spanish moss, I pulled him close and pressed my lips to his.

He made a surprised sound that quickly melted into something softer as he kissed me back. His free hand came up to cup my face, and everything else fell away—my fears, my doubts, all of it gone in the warmth of his touch.

When we finally pulled apart, his eyes were bright with joy and something deeper that made my heart race. "So much for taking it slow," he teased, but his voice was breathless.

"Shut up," I muttered, heat creeping up my neck. "You were looking at me with those eyes, and I..."

"These eyes?" He batted his eyelashes exaggeratedly, and I couldn't help laughing.

"You're impossible."

"You like it." His thumb traced my cheekbone, sending shivers down my spine. "You like me."

"God help me, I do." The admission felt like letting go of a weight I hadn't known I was carrying. "I really do."

Floris's smile was radiant. "Good, because I really like you too. In case that wasn't obvious from all the terrible flirting and lingering looks."

"Was that what those were? I thought you were having vision problems."

He laughed, the sound echoing across the water. "See? This is why I like you. You can match my snark step for step."

A nearby splash made us both jump, probably an alligator sliding into the water. The sound brought me back to reality. We were still standing on a public boardwalk, though thankfully alone for the moment.

"We should head back," I said reluctantly. "Mom will be wondering where we are."

"Right." But Floris didn't move, his hand still warm against my cheek. "One more thing."

"What?"

He kissed me again, soft and quick. "That. For the road."

My heart did that complicated flutter thing again. "You're going to make it very hard to concentrate on driving."

"Good." His grin was mischievous. "Though I promise to behave. Mostly."

The drive back was different from the drive out—charged with possibility but comfortable too, like we'd crossed some invisible threshold into new territory that somehow felt familiar. Floris kept hold of my hand whenever I didn't need it for driving, his thumb tracing patterns on my palm that made it hard to focus on the road.

"So," he said as we neared home, "what are we going to tell your mom?"

I tensed slightly. "About...?"

"This." He squeezed my hand. "Us. Whatever we're becoming."

The question made my chest tight with familiar anxiety, but Floris just waited, patient and steady beside me. "Can we... Can we keep it between us for now?" I asked finally. "Not because I'm ashamed or anything, but..."

"Because you need time to process?" His voice was gentle, understanding. "We can do that. Like I said, we'll go as slow as you need."

Relief flooded through me. "Thank you."

"Though I should warn you," he added with a grin, "I'm terrible at hiding how I feel about you. Your mom's probably already figured it out."

"What do you mean?"

"Orson." His tone was fondly exasperated. "I've been staring at you like you hung the moon since I got here. I'm pretty sure the alligators noticed, and they're not exactly known for their emotional intelligence."

Heat crept up my neck. "You have not."

"I absolutely have. Remember at breakfast when I passed you the coffee and nearly knocked over the orange juice because I was too busy watching you push your hair out of your eyes?"

"That was..." I trailed off, remembering. "Oh."

"Yeah, oh." His thumb traced circles on my palm. "I'm surprised the whole state of Louisiana hasn't noticed how gone I am on you."

My heart did that flutter thing again. "Gone on me?"

"Completely." His voice was soft but certain. "Have been for a while now."

We pulled into the driveway, and I put the car in park but made no move to get out. "How long is a while?"

He was quiet for an uncharacteristically long time. Then he finally said, "Probably since the day we explored Worcester together, when you got so excited about that old concert hall. Your whole face lit up talking about the architecture, and I remember thinking I'd never seen anything more beautiful."

My breath caught. "That long?"

"Yeah." His thumb traced another pattern on my palm. "Though I think I fell a little bit more every time you helped me with calculus, or reminded me to get my laundry, or just... existed in my space. You kind of snuck up on me, Orson Ritchey."

I turned to look at him properly, taking in his earnest expression, the way the afternoon sun caught his eyes. "You snuck up on me too," I admitted quietly. "I had all these walls, all these reasons why I couldn't let anyone get too close. And then you walked right through them with your terrible jokes and your genuine interest in water management and your way of making everything brighter."

His smile was soft, intimate. "So what you're saying is, I wore you down with my charm?"

"More like your persistence." But I was smiling too. "And maybe a little bit your charm."

15

FLORIS

That night, as I lay in Orson's bed, still surrounded by his smell, I couldn't wipe the smile off my face. What a perfect, perfect day. No matter what happened between Orson and me, this would always be a day engraved in my memory, a day filled with pure joy.

It was funny because I had never been a let's-take-things-slow guy. I was more of a let's-see-how-fast-we-can-accelerate person. I had hooked up plenty of times. Hand jobs, blow jobs, a quick fuck in a bathroom—it was all fine with me. Jesus, I had been way too young for my first time anal and the fact that the other guy had been in his twenties was massively problematic now, but back then, I hadn't seen the problem. And to his credit, he'd taken his time with me and it had been a good experience.

But with Orson, everything was different. He made me want to savor every moment, every small step forward. The way his eyes lit up when he talked about architecture, how his rare laughs felt like victories, the subtle ways he showed he cared, like remembering how I took my coffee or grabbing my laundry before it became communal property.

This thing between us felt precious, worth protecting. Worth taking slow. Because Orson wasn't another hookup or fleeting romance. He was someone who saw past my title, past my carefully constructed masks, to the person underneath. Someone who challenged me to be better while accepting me exactly as I was.

I smiled into the darkness, remembering how he'd looked in the morning light on that boardwalk, wild curls catching the sun. How right it had felt to hold his hand, to kiss him surrounded by ancient cypress trees and Spanish moss. For the first time in my life, I was falling for someone who made me want to be patient, to do things right.

A soft knock at the door pulled me from my thoughts.

"Come in?"

The door creaked open, revealing Orson in those tight boxer briefs he wore and a ratty T-shirt that made him look impossibly soft. My heart did that now-familiar flip.

"Hey," he said quietly, hovering in the doorway. "I wanted to check on you. Make sure you're comfortable."

I'd never heard a more pathetic excuse, but I'd play along. "I am." I sat up, patting the bed beside me. "Though I wouldn't mind some company."

He hesitated for a moment before closing the door and crossing to sit on the edge of the bed. Even in the dim light, the slight flush on his cheeks was obvious. "About today..."

"Having second thoughts?" I tried to keep my voice light, though my heart clenched at the possibility.

"No!" His response was immediate, making me smile. "Actually, kind of the opposite."

He took a deep breath, as if gathering his courage. Then in one swift motion, he swung his legs up onto the bed and crawled towards me, determination in his eyes. My breath caught as he settled himself astride my thighs, hands braced on my chest.

"I've been thinking," he said, his voice low and rough in a way that sent shivers through me. "And I've decided that taking things slow sucks."

In one heart-stopping movement, Orson leaned down and captured my lips in a kiss so intense, it blocked out everything else. My mind went blank as he kissed me deeply, like he was trying to make sure I felt every ounce of his need.

I couldn't hold back the groan that rumbled in my chest, couldn't stop my hands from flying to his hips, clutching him hard as I pulled him up against me. He was close, but not close enough. Not yet. I wanted him pressed against me, as tight as he could get. I wanted to feel him everywhere.

I tugged gently and he followed my lead, shifting until he was stretched out on top of me, our bodies aligned. We fit together so perfectly, like we were made for this. Made for each other.

He made a soft, needy sound that vibrated through me like electric current, sending heat flooding through every corner of my body. It was impossible to think when he kissed me like that, when he responded with such urgency that it seemed as if he couldn't bear to stop even for a moment. That he didn't even want to try.

I shifted my weight to one arm so I could free his other hand, cupping his jaw and tilting my head to kiss him deeper, my fingers digging into my hair. His leg slid between mine, sending a jolt of pleasure through me as his thigh brushed against my groin.

I let my hands roam over his back, fingertips skimming the sliver of skin between his shirt and waistband. He shivered and nipped at my bottom lip in retaliation, drawing a low groan from me.

God, he was intoxicating. Every slide of his lips and brush of his tongue left me wanting more, more, more. This was a side of Orson I'd only gotten glimpses of before: bold, decisive, uninhibited. And god, was it a turn-on.

My world narrowed to the feeling of his mouth moving against mine, the slide of his skin against my fingers as I reached beneath his T-shirt, the way he tasted, sweet and so uniquely him. He was everywhere at once, overwhelming in the best possible way.

His hands slid under my shirt, palms hot against my skin as he mapped the planes of my chest, my stomach. I arched into his touch, craving more contact, more friction. More him.

Emboldened by his touch, I slipped my own hands beneath the hem of his T-shirt, reveling in the smooth warmth of his back. He made a soft, desperate sound and rolled his hips against mine, sending sparks of pleasure shooting through me.

As the kiss deepened, Orson pressed his body more firmly against mine, grinding down in a way that made my head spin with desire. We were both hard as iron, our cocks rubbing against each other through the thin fabric that separated us.

In one swift motion, I flipped us over so I was on top, settling between his spread thighs. He looked up at me with dark, lust-blown eyes, lips kiss-swollen and parted. Irresistible. I ducked my head to trail open-mouthed kisses down the column of his throat, relishing the way his breath hitched and fingers tightened in my hair.

"Floris," he breathed, and I felt his hands tugging at the hem of my shirt. "Off. Want to feel you."

I sat back long enough to yank the shirt over my head and toss it aside before diving back in, capturing his lips in another searing kiss. His hands roamed my newly bared skin, leaving trails of fire in their wake. Somehow, he'd gotten rid of his shirt as well, and the sensation of his naked skin against mine made me impossibly hard.

He rocked against me, breath coming in hot, short bursts between kisses. The bed creaked beneath us, but I was past caring if anyone heard, if anyone knew what we were doing. All that mattered was Orson's weight on top of me, the growing confidence in the way he touched me. The way he responded to me, his every gasp and hitch of breath fueling the heat spreading through my body.

When his hands slid under my boxers, calloused fingers skimming over my sensitive skin, reality slammed into me, and I broke the kiss with a gasp. "Orson, wait."

He froze above me, eyes searching mine in the darkness. "What's wrong? Do you not want...?"

"No, no, I want. Believe me." I had to swallow before I could continue. "But we need to talk first, before we go any further."

He frowned, brow furrowing adorably. "Talk? About what?"

I took a deep breath, struggling to gather my scattered thoughts. Orson's warm weight on top of me was incredibly distracting. "About expectations. Experience. What you want, what you're comfortable with."

"Oh." He bit his lip, looking suddenly shy. "I guess that makes sense."

"So..." I began, feeling uncharacteristically nervous. "Have you ever been with a guy before?"

Orson's eyes skittered away from mine for a moment before meeting them again. "Yeah. A couple of times." His cheeks were flushed, from arousal or embarrassment, I couldn't tell. "Nothing too serious though. Mostly hand jobs and I've had a few blow jobs."

I nodded, trailing my fingers lightly up and down his spine in what I hoped was a soothing gesture. At least we weren't starting from zero. "Okay. And what about other stuff? Penetration?"

The flush on his cheeks deepened. "Once. I was on the, uh, receiving end. It was okay, but kind of awkward. We didn't really know what we were doing."

Relief coursed through me at his answer, followed quickly by a pang of jealousy at the thought of him with someone else. I pushed it aside. The past was the past. All that mattered was the present. "That's normal," I assured him. "It takes practice. Communication."

"What about you?" he asked, voice tentative. "I mean, I know you're more experienced than I am."

That was an understatement. I hesitated, then decided to lay my cards on the table. "Yeah, I have a fair amount of experience. With giving and receiving. And I get tested regularly. I'm also on PrEP."

His brow furrowed. "PrEP?"

"Pre-exposure prophylaxis. It's a daily pill that reduces the risk of HIV infection." I shrugged. "I figured, given my lifestyle, it was the responsible thing to do."

Orson nodded slowly, processing this new information. "That makes sense. I'm glad you're taking care of yourself." He paused, biting his lip. "Can I ask, like, how many partners...? Or is that not okay to ask?"

I sighed, running a hand through my hair. This was the part I had dreaded. "A fair number, but always safely. And never anything serious. Until now."

His eyes widened at that, a tentative hope blooming in their depths. "Until now?"

"This is..." I searched for words. I couldn't go too fast, reveal too much, but god, I wanted to. "This is different. I want more than sex, than a hookup."

A slow, sweet smile spread across his face, making my heart turn over. "Yeah?"

"Yes. We'll take it as slow as you want, okay? No pressure. So, in terms of what you want tonight... I'm happy to follow your lead. We can do as much or as little as you're comfortable with."

He cocked his head, as if considering my words. Well, of course he would. This was Orson, after all, a man who never did anything without thinking it through first. "I think I want..." His cheeks turned crimson and Jesus, I wanted to wrap him in bubble wrap and keep this precious little cinnamon roll safe. "I want to fool around a bit? M-make each other come?"

I was so on board with that. "Hands? Mouth?"

"I'm not good at... I'm not sure I'd be good at, you know, giving... oral, since I have no experience, so I might need you to guide me a bit. Show me what to do."

My heart swelled at his words, at the trust he was placing in me. "Of course..."

I cupped his face in my hands, kissing him slowly, thoroughly, trying to pour all the tenderness I felt into the press of my lips. He melted against me, hands coming up to rest on my biceps as he let me take the lead.

I took my time, savoring the slide of our tongues, the way his breath hitched when I nipped at his full bottom lip. My hands roamed his back, fingers dancing over each bump of his spine before dipping beneath the waistband of his shorts to palm the smooth globes of his ass.

He gasped into my mouth, hips jerking involuntarily, and I smiled against his lips. "Like that, do you?" I murmured, giving his cheeks a firm squeeze.

"Y-yes," he breathed, eyes fluttering open to meet mine. They were dark with arousal, only a thin ring of golden brown visible around blown pupils. "Floris, please..."

I loved hearing him say my name like that, all breathy and needy. I wanted to hear it again and again. Keeping our eyes locked, I slowly slid one hand around to the front of his shorts, cupping the hard bulge of his erection through the thin cotton. He let out a strangled moan, hips bucking into my touch, seeking more friction. I obliged, rubbing my palm against him in slow, firm circles that had him panting and trembling above me.

"Floris," he gasped again, and it was the sweetest sound. "I need... I want..."

"What do you need, *lieverd*?" I pressed a kiss to the hinge of his jaw. "Tell me."

"I want to feel you. All of you." His hands tugged impatiently at my boxers. "Can we take these off?"

In answer, I hooked my fingers in the waistband of his shorts and tugged them down over the curve of his ass. He lifted his hips to help, kicking them off and to the side. I quickly shucked my own boxers, leaving us both bare.

For a moment, we stared at each other, drinking in the sight. Orson was beautiful, all lean muscle and smooth, golden skin, his cock flushed and curving up towards his belly. I wanted to touch him everywhere at once, map every inch of him with my hands, my mouth, my lips and tongue.

Then I wrapped my hands around his gorgeous cock. He let out a strangled moan, hips bucking into my touch.

"Fuck, Orson..." I gave him a gentle squeeze. "You're so hard for me already."

"Can you blame me?" His voice was ragged, pupils blown wide with desire. "I've been thinking about this all day. How much I want you."

The confession made my own cock throb. I captured his lips

in another searing kiss as I squeezed him again, then started moving my hand up and down. He was perfect, silky smooth and throbbing with need, the tip already slick with precum. I swiped my thumb over the slit, gathering the moisture and spreading it down his shaft. He whimpered, hips twitching as he tried to thrust into my fist.

"Shh, I've got you," I murmured, pressing a kiss to the underside of his jaw. "Relax, let me take care of you."

"Oh god," he panted against my lips, eyes squeezing shut. "Floris, that feels... Fuck..."

I knew how he felt. The slide of his silky skin against my palm, the way he throbbed and twitched in my grip was dizzying. Intoxicating. I wanted to take him apart piece by piece, to make him fall to shreds in my arms.

I set a steady rhythm, twisting my wrist on the upstroke in the way I knew drove men wild. Orson was no exception. He moaned brokenly, head falling back against the pillow as his hips moved in time with my strokes.

The sight of him, the sounds he was making, the salty-sweet taste of his skin—it was the hottest thing I'd ever experienced. My own cock was painfully hard, leaking against his thigh, but I couldn't focus on my own pleasure. Not when I had Orson naked and wanting in my arms.

"That's it, *lieverd*," I encouraged. "Let go, let yourself feel it."

His only response was another guttural moan, his fingers digging into my shoulders. I could feel his thighs tensing, his balls drawing up tight against his body. He was getting close already.

Wanting to draw it out, I released his cock, ignoring his whimper of protest. I pressed open-mouthed kisses down his chest, pausing to flick my tongue over each nipple before continuing my journey south.

Orson was panting now, hands fisted in the sheets as he watched me through hooded eyes. I maintained eye contact as I settled between his spread thighs, face level with his straining erection.

"I'm going to use my mouth on you now, okay?" I said, waiting for his nod before proceeding.

Orson nodded eagerly, eyes wide and dark with anticipation. "Yes, please..."

I flashed him a wicked grin before lowering my head, breathing hotly over his straining flesh. He shuddered, hips twitching restlessly. I knew he wanted me to take him into my mouth, to give him that wet heat, but I wanted to tease him a bit first.

Slowly, oh so slowly, I dragged my tongue up the underside of his shaft, tracing the thick vein there from base to tip. He let out a strangled moan, head thumping back against the pillow. I lapped at the sensitive spot just below the head before swirling my tongue around the flared crown, gathering the salty-sweet beads of precum that had gathered there.

"Floris," he gasped, sounding absolutely wrecked already. "Please..."

Well, since he asked so nicely. I wrapped my lips around the tip and suckled gently, relishing his choked cry of pleasure. Then, maintaining eye contact, I slowly sank down, taking him inch by glorious inch into my mouth.

His cock hit the back of my throat and I swallowed around him, making him curse and buck up into the wet heat of my mouth.

I set a steady rhythm, bobbing my head as I worked him with lips and tongue. One hand came up to cup his balls, rolling them gently in my palm, as the other gripped the base of his shaft, stroking what I couldn't fit in my mouth.

Orson was lost to sensation, a continuous stream of moans and gasps falling from his lips interspersed with my name. I'd never heard anything so hot.

"Oh fuck, Floris..." he moaned brokenly. "Your mouth, it's... God..."

I hummed around him in acknowledgement and he cried out, back arching off the bed. The stretch of his cock in my mouth was exquisite, his girth just on the right side of challenging. I bobbed my head slowly, taking him deeper each time until my nose was buried in the wiry curls at the base.

He might be in heaven, but so was I, pleasuring him like this... and I never wanted it to end.

16

ORSON

Was it possible to short circuit as a human being? If so, I had to be close. So many sensations were barreling through my body that I was half out of it, almost desperate with the need to come. Floris was sucking me off with gusto, showing his expertise, and I couldn't be anything but grateful to be the beneficiary of his experience.

He did things with his mouth and tongue that I hadn't thought possible, not to mention the fact that he seemed to have no gag reflex at all. My balls were practically resting against his chin, but he was actively swallowing around my cock, humming with contentment every now and then. Every time he did, I went wild.

My hands gripped the sheets as I writhed beneath Floris's expert ministrations. I was barely coherent at this point, reduced to a shaking, sweating mess of need and sensation. Some distant part of my brain knew I should be reciprocating in some way, touching Floris, pleasuring him in return. But I couldn't focus on anything except the wet heat of his mouth, the flicks and swirls of his wicked tongue, the obscene slurping noises that filled the room.

I fisted my hands in his hair, not directing his movements but holding on for dear life as he took me apart. My hips were moving of their own accord with little thrusts that I couldn't control. Floris took it all in stride, letting me fuck his face as I chased my orgasm.

"Floris, I'm gonna..." I gasped out in warning, my voice wrecked. "I can't hold back, I'm going to come."

He hummed around my cock, the vibrations shooting straight through me, and that was it. I came with a shout, my vision whiting out as I spilled down his throat. Floris swallowed it all down eagerly, not pulling off until I whimpered from the oversensitivity.

As I lay there panting and boneless, Floris crawled up my body to press gentle kisses across my face—my forehead, my cheeks, the tip of my nose. I felt utterly spent, like every drop of tension had been wrung out of my body. Floris gathered me close, stroking my sweat-damp hair back from my face as I caught my breath. I went willingly, tucking my face into his neck and breathing in his scent.

We lay like that for a while, basking in the afterglow. "You're amazing," I mumbled, nuzzling into his neck. "That was incredible."

I blinked up at him, still dazed, as he smiled down at me. "You are incredible," he murmured, his voice rough. "The way you let go, the sounds you make... I could watch you fall apart like that all day."

I flushed at the praise, suddenly self-conscious. I wasn't used to being so vulnerable, so uninhibited with another person. "Thank you?"

Slowly, awareness began to return to my sex-fogged brain. I

realized with a start that while I had experienced mind-blowing ecstasy, Floris was still hard against my hip, his own needs unmet.

"Oh god, I'm sorry," I said, pulling back to look at him. "You didn't... I mean, do you want me to...?"

I made a vague gesture towards his groin, feeling a blush heat my cheeks. I wanted to return the favor, but I wasn't sure I had the finesse to give a blow job like he had. The thought of choking, of doing it wrong, filled me with trepidation. But I wanted to make Floris feel as good as he had made me feel. I needed to at least try.

"You don't have to..." Floris started to say, always so considerate. But I cut him off with a firm kiss.

"I want to," I insisted, my voice rough but sure. "I want to make you feel good too. I just... I don't have a lot of experience with oral, so I might not be very good at it."

Floris cupped my cheek, his thumb stroking over my cheekbone. "You could use your hand, if you're more comfortable with that."

I considered this for a moment before nodding. For my first time with him, I was definitely better off with something I actually had done before. My experience was anything but vast, but at least the guys I'd done it with had been satisfied, so that counted for something, right?

Gathering my courage, I rolled us over so that Floris was beneath me. I took a moment to take in the sight of him sprawled out before me, his hair messy from our activities, his chest heaving with each breath. He was so gorgeous, all defined muscles without being bulky. I felt a thrill looking at him, all raw beauty and unguarded vulnerability.

He gazed up at me with a mix of desire and amusement that made my heart skip a beat. A grin tugged at the corners of his mouth as he reached up to tuck a stray curl behind my ear. But I wasn't going to be distracted right now.

Everything about him was captivating, from the flushed head of his cock jutting proudly from its nest of blond curls to the tiny mole on his left hip bone. It was enough to make my head spin, almost enough to make me lose my nerve. But I wanted this, wanted him.

"You're not cut," I said.

He frowned. "Cut?"

"Circumcised."

"Ah. No. It's not common in the Netherlands like here."

Huh, interesting. I hadn't expected something that seemed so standard here to be the exception somewhere else.

Slowly, reverently, I began to explore his body with my hands and mouth, mapping out the planes of his chest, the ridges of his abs, the jut of his hip bones. I wanted to memorize every inch of him, to worship him with my touch the way he had done for me with his mouth. I traced nonsensical patterns on his skin with my fingertips, delighting in the way he shivered and sighed beneath my touch.

"What's the meaning of your tattoos?" I asked, tracing the one on his right upper arm with my fingers. It was a coat of arms with a lion and... My eyes narrowed. "Is that French?"

"It's the Dutch coat of arms and our family motto, *je maintiendrai*. It is French and it means I will maintain." He tapped on his left shoulder. "And this is the Dutch flag with the orange banner. It says Oranje Boven, which means..." He thought for a moment. "It literally means orange above, but it has the spirit of 'long live the king.' Or queen." He shrugged. "Just proud to be who I am, you know?"

He should be. I kissed the tattoo on his right arm, then continued my exploration. Floris let out a low moan as I pressed kisses all over his shoulders. Emboldened, I lavished attention on his chest, licking and sucking and gently biting until he was squirming beneath me, hands fisted in my hair. Each little gasp and moan was like fuel.

Hearing the effect I had on him gave me a rush of power, a daring kind of determination. I could do this. I wanted to do this. My mouth moved with purpose, closing over a nipple and sucking it between my teeth. Floris let out a strangled groan, his body tensing and then shuddering with each sensation.

I rolled the nipple with my tongue, then bit down enough to make Floris toss his head back and gasp out loud. I was determined to wring as many of those sounds out of Floris as I could, to make him feel the same mindless pleasure that I had felt when Floris had been sucking me off.

I moved to the other nipple and gave it the same thorough treatment, licking and nipping and kissing until Floris was bucking beneath me, his entire body taut with need. I had never seen Floris like this, so unrestrained, so overwhelmed, and I couldn't get enough of it.

Downward my journey went, dipping my tongue into his navel, nuzzling the trail of hair below it. Floris's breaths were coming faster now, little whimpers escaping him as I drew closer to where he so clearly wanted me.

My hands skimmed lower, brushing over his thighs, teasing him as I avoided touching his dick. Floris let out a low groan, his hips canting upwards, seeking friction.

"Orson, please," he gasped, desperation leaking into his voice.

I took pity on him then, wrapping my hand around his straining erection. We both moaned at the contact. I took a moment to explore, to catalog the weight of it in my palm, the heat, the silken texture of the skin. He was so hard that the foreskin had peeled back and his tip was wholly visible. Slowly, I began to stroke him, spreading the bead of moisture at the tip with my thumb.

Emboldened, I set a steady rhythm, working him with firm strokes. It was different than getting myself off; the angle was strange and my wrist started to ache after a few minutes. But it was worth it to watch Floris slowly come undone beneath my touch, worth it to hear the breathless little moans and whimpers he let out, to feel him throb and pulse in my grip. His eyes were screwed shut, his kiss-swollen lips parted as he panted for breath. A light sheen of sweat glistened on his skin. He looked utterly debauched, and it was the most erotic sight I'd ever seen. He was breathtaking like this, lost in pleasure that I was giving him. Pride swelled inside me at the knowledge that I could affect him this way, that I could make him feel this good.

I varied my strokes, alternating between long pulls from base to tip and shorter, faster jerks over the head. Floris's hips began to move, thrusting up into my fist as he chased his release.

"Orson," he panted, his voice strained. "I'm close, I'm gonna…"

I doubled my efforts, my hand flying over his cock as I twisted my wrist on every upstroke, the same way I liked it on myself. Floris seemed to approve, if the way his moans increased in pitch and volume were any indication. A few more firm strokes and he was coming with a low cry, spilling over my fist and onto his own stomach. I worked him through it, slowing my strokes but not stopping until he whimpered from the sensitivity.

I finally released him, my hand sticky with his release. Floris lay there panting, his chest heaving as he came down from his high. I stared at him in wonder, marveling at the fact that I had done that, that I had made him come undone so completely.

With a shaky hand, I reached for the tissues on the night-stand and gently cleaned him up. Floris hummed in content-ment, his eyes fluttering open to gaze at me with undisguised affection. My heart stuttered at the tenderness in his expression.

I tossed the soiled tissues in the general direction of the trash can and collapsed next to him on the bed, suddenly exhausted. Floris immediately gathered me into his arms, tucking my head beneath his chin as he stroked his fingers through my hair. I went willingly, relishing the skin-on-skin contact, the steady thump of his heartbeat under my cheek.

We lay there like that for a while, holding each other close as our breathing evened out and our heart rates returned to normal. I felt boneless and blissed out, like I could happily stay right here in this moment forever.

"That was amazing," Floris murmured, pressing a kiss to the top of my head. "You're amazing."

I huffed out a laugh, tilting my head back to look at him. "I'm not sure fumbling my way through a hand job qualifies as amaz-ing, but I'm glad you enjoyed it."

Floris chuckled, the sound rumbling through his chest under my ear. "Trust me, that was not fumbling. You're a natural."

I flushed at the praise, ducking my head to hide my pleased smile against his skin. "You're funny."

Floris's smile was soft as he gazed down at me, his eyes shining with affection. "As long as we get to do this again, I'll gladly have that argument whenever you want."

A pleasant warmth bloomed inside me at his words. The idea that this wasn't a one-time thing, that Floris wanted to continue exploring this new facet of our relationship, filled me with a giddy sort of joy. But for now, I was content to bask in the afterglow, to revel in the feeling of Floris's arms around me, his skin against mine.

We lapsed into comfortable silence, Floris's fingers tracing idle patterns on my back as I listened to the steady thrum of his heartbeat.

"When we get back, I don't want to be too much of a distraction," Floris finally said. "Promise me you'll tell me to back off if you need to."

I smiled. "You mean you want me to employ some of that Dutch directness?"

"Yes. I don't want you to get frustrated with me... or even angry because you feel I'm keeping you from your studies."

He truly understood. Nothing he could've said could've made that clearer. He knew what my studies meant to me. "I will... but please don't stop asking me to do things, okay? I need you to pull me out of my own head, away from my books."

He kissed the top of my head. "Promise."

I'd never registered that us being so different also meant we could give each other what we needed. He was the push I needed to try new things, and I was the one he could be himself with, let down his mask. Maybe we were a better fit than I'd ever realized.

My eyelids began to droop as the long day caught up with me. Our trip to the bayou, coupled with the physical exertion of our lovemaking, had drained me completely. I felt wrung out in the best possible way.

Sated and sleepy, I nuzzled deeper into Floris's embrace, soaking in his warmth and scent. He smelled like sex and sweat and something uniquely him, a combination that I found intoxicating. I breathed him in, letting his presence soothe me, ground me.

"Go to sleep, *lieverd*," Floris murmured, his lips brushing my forehead. "I've got you."

And I believed him. Here, wrapped up in Floris, I felt safe in a way I hadn't in a long, long time. Maybe ever. With him, I could let my guard down, could allow myself to be vulnerable. It was a heady feeling.

My limbs grew heavy as sleep tugged at me insistently. I fought it for a moment, wanting to stay awake and savor this closeness, this perfect moment. But my exhaustion won out in the end.

The last thing I remembered before slipping into slumber was the gentle press of Floris's lips against my temple and the whispered words, "Sweet dreams, *lieverd*."

17

FLORIS

I wasn't the kind of guy to spend the night or to let my hookups stay over. Granted, part of that was also because I could hardly bring them back to the palace or anywhere where the press could easily spot them, but that was not the only reason. Staying over meant facing the morning after, meant possible complications and people wanting more than sex, which had been a definitive *hell, no.*

Until now.

Waking up with Orson plastered against me like a little octopus should've made me panic, but it didn't. Instead, as soon as I realized where I was and more importantly, who was softly snoring in my arms, a deep peace filled me.

I stared down at Orson's sleeping face, tracing the curves of his cheeks, the line of his jaw, with my gaze. His dark lashes fanned against his skin, his lips slightly parted as he breathed. He looked so innocent, so unguarded. So beautiful.

A lump formed in my throat. What the hell was I doing? This wasn't me. I didn't do feelings, and I certainly didn't do relationships. I'd learned long ago that those things only led to pain and disappointment. It was safer to keep things casual, superficial. To not let anyone get too close.

But with Orson... God, it was different. From the moment we met, there had been this undeniable pull toward him. Like gravity. I couldn't resist it even if I wanted to. And if I was being honest with myself, I didn't want to resist anymore.

Carefully, so as not to wake him, I brushed a stray curl off his forehead. He sighed in his sleep and nuzzled closer, his arm tightening around my waist. My heart squeezed almost painfully in my chest.

I was in deep trouble here.

But then Orson stirred, his eyes blinking open sleepily. When his gaze met mine, a blush crept into his cheeks, as if he too was realizing the position we were in.

"Morning," I murmured, my voice still rough from sleep.

"Morning," Orson replied, his eyes wide and a little shocked. "I... I didn't mean to fall asleep on you like that. I'm sorry."

I chuckled, tightening my arms around him. "Don't be. I liked it."

Orson's blush deepened, but a small smile tugged at the corners of his mouth. "Me too."

We lay there for a few more minutes, enjoying each other's presence, until the smell of coffee and bacon wafted up from downstairs. Orson groaned, burying his face in my chest. "That'll be my mom. There's no way she'll have missed me not sleeping on the couch."

I ran my hand up and down Orson's back. "We should probably head down there, huh? Face the music."

Orson lifted his head, biting his lip nervously. "I don't know what to say to her. This is all so new."

I repressed a smile at Orson's embarrassment, finding it absolutely adorable. "We'll figure it out together," I assured him, pressing a kiss to his forehead before untangling our limbs and climbing out of bed.

After a quick stop in the bathroom to make ourselves presentable, Orson and I got dressed and headed downstairs together, Orson fidgeting nervously the whole way.

Diana was at the stove, frying up eggs and bacon, humming softly to herself. She turned as we entered, a knowing smile on her face.

"Good morning, boys," she said cheerfully, as if this was any other day and her son hadn't just spent the night wrapped in another man's arms. "Breakfast is almost ready. I hope you're hungry."

"Starving," I replied easily, taking a seat at the table while Orson stood there awkwardly, looking like he wanted the floor to swallow him whole.

"Orson, honey, why don't you set the table?"

"Sure, Mom." Orson's voice was a little shaky as he moved to grab silverware. I could practically feel the nerves radiating off him.

Diana's gaze landed on me, her eyes twinkling with amusement. "Sleep well, Floris?"

I grinned at Diana, not missing the mischievous glint in her eye. "Yes, ma'am, like a baby."

Orson made a strangled noise as he placed forks and knives around the table. His cheeks were flaming red now. I had to bite the inside of my cheek to keep from laughing.

Diana just hummed contentedly as she slid the eggs and bacon onto a serving platter. "I'm so glad. You know, Orson's mattress isn't the most comfortable. I keep meaning to replace it." She winked at me conspiratorially.

"Mom!" Orson sputtered, nearly dropping the stack of plates he was holding. He set them down with a clatter.

"What? I'm just saying." Diana placed the platter on the table and took a seat, acting completely oblivious to her son's mortification. "Well, dig in before it gets cold."

Orson finally sat down next to me, his knee bouncing anxiously under the table. I placed my hand on his thigh, giving it a reassuring squeeze.

"At least it's more comfortable than the couch," Diana said, and I had to give her props for the flawless delivery of that line. Of course, she then went for the kill. "Though I suspect Orson didn't spend much time on it last night."

Orson dropped a fork, his face flaming red. "Mom!"

"What? Am I wrong?" Diana arched an eyebrow at her son.

Orson opened and closed his mouth a few times before sighing. "No. You're not wrong. Floris and I, we're... together. Sort of. It's new."

Diana's teasing expression softened into one of genuine happiness. She rounded the table and pulled Orson into a tight hug. "Oh, honey. I'm so happy for you."

Over his mom's shoulder, Orson met my gaze, his eyes wide with surprise and relief. I smiled encouragingly at him.

When Diana released him, there were tears shimmering in her eyes. "Your father would be so proud of you, Orson. So proud. All we ever wanted was for you to find someone who makes you as happy as he and I were together."

Orson's own eyes welled up at the mention of his dad. "You really think so?"

"I know so," Diana said firmly, cupping Orson's face in her hands. "He loved you so much, Orson. And he would've loved seeing you like this, opening your heart to someone special."

A few tears escaped down Orson's cheeks. I had to swallow past the lump in my own throat. Seeing him so emotional, so vulnerable, made me want to wrap him up in my arms and never let go.

Orson swallowed hard. "Thanks, Mom. That means a lot."

He glanced over at me again, a tentative smile on his face. I reached out and took his hand, interlacing our fingers.

Diana wiped at her eyes and laughed. "Listen to me getting all sentimental. I'm so thrilled you two found each other." She patted Orson's cheek affectionately before returning to her seat.

Just then, Tia came bounding down the stairs, her hair in a messy ponytail. "Morning, everybody!" she chirped, plopping down next to her mom and helping herself to a heaping pile of eggs and bacon.

"Morning, sweetie," Diana replied, pouring Tia a glass of orange juice. "Sleep well?"

"Yep! Though not as well as Orson, I bet," Tia said with a cheeky grin, waggling her eyebrows suggestively.

"Tia!" Orson groaned, covering his face with his hands.

I couldn't help it; I burst out laughing. This family was something else.

"So you're a prince, right?" Tia mercifully turned her attention to me.

The kitchen grew quiet. "How did you know?" I asked.

She shrugged. "I overheard Mom saying something to you and googled you. It's not like it was hard to find."

That made sense. "That's right. I'm part of the royal family of the Netherlands. My uncle is the king, King Friso."

"That is so cool! Do you live in a castle? Do you have servants? Ooh, do you have a crown?" Tia rapid-fired questions at me, her eyes sparkling with excitement.

"I grew up in a palace, though it kinda looks like a castle too," I replied, amused by her enthusiasm. "And yes, there are staff. We don't like to call them servants. There's a crown, but it only comes out for special occasions. But I try to live a pretty normal life, as much as I can anyway."

"Wow!" Tia was clearly star-struck. "I can't believe my brother is dating a prince. That's like something out of a Disney movie!"

Orson made a choking noise, his face somehow turning even redder. I squeezed his hand under the table, not bothered in the least by her questions. "I'm afraid reality isn't quite as charming as the movies, but we do try."

"Does that mean you're gonna make Orson a prince too? Since you're together and all." Tia grinned mischievously at her brother, who looked like he wanted to slide under the table.

"Tia, shut up," Orson mumbled, his face still beet red.

"But isn't that how it works? That if you marry a prince, you become a prince too? Or in my case, a princess? Hey, do you have any brothers, maybe?"

I chuckled at Tia's antics, finding her blunt curiosity refreshing. "Orson would make a very handsome prince," I said with a wink, making Orson groan again.

"You're not helping," he muttered under his breath, but a small smile tugged at his lips.

"As for brothers, I'm afraid you're out of luck," I told Tia apologetically. "I have one older brother, but he's already engaged. But if I come across any eligible princes, I'll be sure to send them your way."

"Deal!" Tia grinned at me, clearly delighted by the idea.

Diana shook her head fondly. "Tia, let the poor man eat his breakfast now. You can interrogate him later."

"Fine, fine." Tia sighed dramatically before shoveling a forkful of eggs into her mouth.

Orson shot me an apologetic look across the table but I smiled reassuringly back at him. His family was a trip, but in the best way possible. Tia was super sweet, but I could see what Orson had mentioned about her being young for her age. She acted more like a teenager than a twenty-year-old.

The rest of breakfast passed in a blur of easy conversation and laughter. Diana asked me questions about my family and what it was like growing up royal, but in a casual, curious way that didn't feel prying. I found myself sharing stories I hadn't told many people, about sneaking out of the house with my brother as a kid, some of my more infamous moments with the press as a child, and the pressure I sometimes felt to live up to expectations.

"How different is Dutch culture compared to American?" Diana asked me.

"Very different in some ways," I said, taking a sip of coffee. "The Dutch are famously direct. We say exactly what we think, which can come across as rude to Americans. Like, if someone asks how you like their new haircut and it's terrible, we'll tell them it's terrible."

"That sounds awkward," Tia said, wrinkling her nose.

I laughed. "It can be! But we see it as being honest and helpful. Why let your friend walk around with bad hair if you can prevent it?"

"What else is different?" Diana asked, genuinely interested.

"Well, we have this concept called *gezellig*, which has no translation in English. It's kind of like cozy, but more than that. It's a feeling, a mood. Enjoying a warm, welcoming atmosphere. Like this," I gestured around the kitchen table. "Having breakfast together, talking, laughing, that's *gezellig*."

"Fascinating," Diana said.

"But I think what stands out most is our ability to compromise and find a middle ground that works for everyone. We call it the *polder model*, named after our *polders*, which is the Dutch word for reclaimed land. We basically acknowledge that no one will ever get exactly what they want, so we agree to disagree and find common ground in the middle. We have to, since our parliament has fifteen political parties represented."

"Fifteen?" Orson's eyes grew wide. "For real?"

I waved my hand dismissively. "Two-party systems are for wimps."

"But how does anything get done with fifteen parties?" Orson asked, his analytical mind clearly trying to work out the logistics.

"That's where the polder model comes in. We have to work together, find compromises. No party ever has a majority, so coalition-building is essential. It's messy and slow sometimes, but it works."

"Like how you and Orson worked out your differences?" Diana suggested with a knowing smile.

I grinned, catching Orson's hand under the table. "Exactly. Though I'd say in our case, the compromise heavily favored me getting my way and dragging him out of the library occasionally."

"Hey!" Orson protested, but he was smiling too. "I go willingly. Sometimes."

"After extensive negotiation and careful consideration of all variables," I teased. "Very Dutch of you, actually."

Tia rolled her eyes. "You guys are disgustingly cute. I can totally see you get married and have, like, kids."

"Tia, let them be," Diana warned.

I appreciated her correcting Tia, even as I found myself pondering those very intentions myself.

What were Orson and I doing? Where was this headed? The rational part of my brain screamed that it was too soon to be thinking about anything long-term. We'd only just gotten together, for god's sake. But another part, a part that seemed to be growing louder by the minute, whispered that this was different. That Orson was different. Special.

I glanced over at him as he laughed at something his sister said, his eyes crinkling at the corners, his full lips stretched into a wide smile. My heart turned over in my chest. Yeah, definitely special.

18

ORSON

I stared at the blinking cursor on my laptop screen, the blank document reflecting in my glasses like an accusation. The paper was due in three days, but my mind kept drifting back to the weekend. Spending that time with Floris had made it the best Thanksgiving ever. Maybe the best weekend ever, period. The way he'd listened to me as I told him about my dad, the pure joy on his face when we saw the gators, and how sweet and kind he'd been with my mom and Tia... Each memory was a welcome distraction and a source of anxiety all at once.

Two days back at Vernon Technical College, and I'd managed to write exactly three sentences of my paper for environmental engineering. Three sentences in forty-eight hours. At this rate, I'd have a complete first draft somewhere around my fiftieth birthday. And it wasn't like the topic I'd picked—the environmental impact of the Hoover dam—didn't interest me. It did. It was just that... Well, it was Floris.

Had I really brought Floris van Oranje Nassau—a literal prince—home to meet my mother and sister? Had Floris really charmed Tia into showing him her science fair project? Had he really sat at our worn kitchen table, asking my mom thoughtful questions about her biology classes while she was making soup from the leftover turkey?

It seemed impossible, like a particularly vivid hallucination. More impossible still was the fact that Floris had enjoyed himself. Sure, he might've had training into always being polite, even when he was bored out of his mind, but no one was that good an actor.

I pulled up the photos on my phone. Evidence that it had really happened. There was Floris, his whole face lit up like a Christmas tree, pointing at a gator. There he was on the street-car, green eyes wide as he took in the city, framed by the window like a Renaissance painting. And I had even taken a selfie with the two of us, something I had never done in my entire life. His smile was so broad, I couldn't help but respond to it, even now.

It had happened. It was real. But for how much longer?

That was the question that burned on my mind, a constant, uncomfortable heat that I recognized as fear. People like Floris didn't end up with people like me. It wasn't how the world worked. Someday—maybe tomorrow, maybe next week, maybe next month if I was lucky—Floris would realize he could do better than a compulsive, anxious math nerd with a tragic backstory.

That wasn't even a dis at myself but more of an acknowledge-ment of who I was. I didn't hate myself or anything, nor did I consider myself a basket case or lost cause. But Floris was a prince. He was literal royalty, and on top of that, he was insanely good-looking, smart, charming, and did I mention hot? We weren't playing in the same league, even if we were batting for the same team, to stay in that metaphor. He was major league while I was not even good enough to make it onto a high school team.

No, at some point, this thing between us would end. Floris would grow tired of me or simply meet someone else, someone more suitable for him. But until then, I would take what I could get. I would memorize every touch, catalog every smile, document every moment like the methodical, detail-oriented person I was. And when it ended—not if, *when*—I would at least have that.

That was why, when we were on the plane back, I'd asked Floris to keep our relationship private at school. "I'm not ready for everyone to know," I'd said, the lie bitter on my tongue.

The truth was more pathetic: I couldn't bear the thought of becoming known as Floris's ex. Of being pitied when the inevitable happened and his identity leaked. Of the whispers that would follow me through the halls of VTC, wondering what I'd done wrong, how I'd managed to lose a literal prince.

Floris had agreed easily, with a casual shrug and a smile. "Whatever you want, I understand."

And he probably did. After all, he'd been stalked by paparazzi his entire life. Privacy was a luxury to him.

The door to our room swung open, shocking me out of my spiral of self-doubt. Floris stood in the doorway, a laundry basket balanced on his hip. His damp hair curled against his neck, and he wore nothing but a pair of gray sweatpants slung low on his hips. Droplets of water clung to his shoulders, catching the light from the desk lamp.

"I remembered," he announced triumphantly, hoisting the laundry basket a bit higher. "I put my laundry in this afternoon and actually remembered to take it out of the dryer."

I couldn't help the smile that tugged at my lips. "Gold star for you," I said, spinning my desk chair to face Floris fully. "Did you also remember to keep your red socks away from your white shirts? I mean, you own a vast collection of pink shirts by now. No need to add to it."

"I did, actually. But pink suits me, don't you think?" Floris grinned, setting the basket down and striking a pose, flexing one arm in a parody of a bodybuilder. "With my complexion?"

I rolled my eyes, but the knot in my chest loosened slightly. This was the thing about Floris, he made everything easier somehow. Made the world seem less threatening, more manageable. Made me forget sometimes the heavy load I carried.

"That one oversized shirt you have looks ridiculous on you now that it's pink," I said, but there was no heat in it. "Like a flamingo."

"A very handsome flamingo." Floris crossed the room to stand behind my chair. His hands came to rest on my shoulders, thumbs pressing gently into the tense muscles at the base of my neck. "How's the paper coming?"

I gestured helplessly at the blank document. "Could be better."

"Are you stuck?"

"I keep getting distracted." I tilted my head back to look up at Floris. From this angle, with the ceiling light behind him, Floris looked almost otherworldly: his sharp jawline, the constellation of freckles across his nose, those impossibly green eyes framed by thick lashes.

"Distracted by what?" His thumbs continued their gentle massage, now making small circles at the nape of my neck.

"You know what." Even after the weekend we'd spent together, even after the kisses and touches we'd shared, I still found it hard to say these things out loud.

"Hmm, I'm not sure I do," Floris teased, leaning down so his lips were inches from my ear. "Perhaps you should enlighten me."

A shiver ran down my spine. "I should be working. This paper is 20 percent of my grade."

"And it will still be 20 percent of your grade after you take a short break," Floris reasoned, his breath warm against my skin. "You've been staring at the screen for hours. Your brain needs to reset."

The responsible, disciplined part of me—the part that had gotten me a full scholarship to VTC, the part that triple-checked every calculation, the part that never missed a deadline—was screaming at me to turn back to the laptop. But then Floris's lips brushed against the sensitive spot just below my ear, and the responsible part of me was drowned out by a chorus of other, less disciplined urges.

"Twenty minutes," I said, my voice embarrassingly breathless. "Then I really need to work."

Floris's answering smile was both victorious and hungry. "Twenty minutes."

He took my hands and pulled me up from the chair. We moved to my bed, the narrow dorm mattress creaking slightly under our combined weight. Floris lay back against the pillows, pulling me down on top of him. For a moment, we just looked at each other, the air between us charged with possibility.

Then Floris's hand came up to cup my cheek, his thumb tracing the line of my cheekbone with a tenderness that made my chest ache. "I missed you today," Floris whispered. "Was thinking about kissing you again all day."

The words sent a different kind of shiver through me—not desire this time, but fear. How long would Floris want me? How long before the novelty wore off? Before Floris realized that I wasn't special, wasn't extraordinary, wasn't enough?

But then Floris was kissing me, and I couldn't think at all.

Floris kissed the way he did everything else: confident, thorough, with a single-minded focus that made me feel like the center of the universe, as if nothing else existed but us. His lips were soft, coaxing my mouth open, his tongue sliding against mine in a way that made heat pool in my stomach. It was overwhelming and exhilarating, a powerful and much-needed reminder that he wanted me, even if I couldn't quite figure out why.

My hands found their way to Floris's chest, palms flat against the warm skin, feeling the steady thump of his heart. Floris hummed appreciatively against my mouth, one hand sliding down to grip my hip, the other tangling in my curls, pulling me impossibly closer until I was completely surrounded by him.

We'd done this before, the kissing, the touching, the exploration of each other's bodies. But each time felt new somehow, a fresh discovery. I marveled at the way Floris responded to my touch, the small catches in his breath, the way his pulse quickened beneath my fingertips.

Floris broke the kiss, his lips trailing down my jaw, my neck, finding the sensitive spot at the hollow of my throat. A soft sound escaped me, something between a gasp and a moan.

With a fluid motion, Floris flipped our positions, pressing me back against the pillows. His hands slid under the hem of my T-shirt, pushing it up to expose my torso. I raised my arms, allowing Floris to pull the shirt over my head.

Floris took a moment to look at me, his gaze traveling over my chest, my shoulders, down to the trail of dark hair disappearing beneath the waistband of my jeans. "You're beautiful," Floris said, with such sincerity that I almost believed him.

I wanted to argue with him, but it seemed senseless anyway. He was as stubborn as I was, so what was the use? Instead, I pulled him down for another kiss, deeper this time, hungrier. Floris made a pleased sound against my mouth, his hands roaming over my chest, thumbs brushing over my nipples in a way that made me arch against him.

Floris broke the kiss again, but only to move lower, his lips tracing a path down my neck, my chest, my stomach. When he reached the waistband of my jeans, he paused, looking up through his lashes. I nodded my consent.

With deft fingers, Floris unbuttoned my jeans, sliding them down my legs along with my boxers. The cool air of the dorm room hit my heated skin, making me shiver—or maybe that was the way Floris was looking at me, like I was something precious, something worth savoring.

Floris maintained eye contact as he lowered his head, his breath warm against my most sensitive skin. And then his mouth was there, hot and wet and perfect as it wrapped around my cock, and for a moment, my mind went completely, blissfully blank. All the worry and stress melted away as he alternated between gentle, teasing licks that danced across my skin and taking me deeper with a practiced rhythm.

Wait.

I didn't want to do this again, with Floris giving me oral and not being able to return the favor. He couldn't always be the one to give and not get back in equal measure. No, I needed to learn this. I wanted to learn this. I wanted to make Floris feel what I had felt, wanted to see him come undone the way he'd sent me sky high back in New Orleans.

I gently pulled him off my cock.

Floris looked worried. "Everything okay? Did I do—"

"Show me how to do that. I want to try."

A flash of surprise crossed Floris's face, quickly replaced by desire. "You don't have to."

"I want to learn. Will you teach me?"

Floris swallowed hard. "Okay, but you can stop any time you want. If you don't like it, or if your jaw gets tired, or—"

I silenced him with a kiss. "I want this. I want you."

We shifted positions, Floris lying back against the pillows, me kneeling between his legs. Floris helped me remove his sweatpants, lifting his hips to allow me to slide them down. He wasn't wearing anything underneath.

For a moment, I looked, taking in the sight of Floris: his broad shoulders, the colorful tattoos on his upper arms, the dusting of freckles across his chest, the trail of blond hair leading down to where he was hard and ready.

"You're staring," Floris said, a rare note of self-consciousness in his voice.

"You told me I was beautiful. I'm returning the favor."

Floris's cheeks flushed, the color spreading down his neck to his chest. "Don't you want to touch?"

I did want. I reached out, wrapping my fingers around Floris, feeling the weight of him in my hand. Floris's breath hitched, his eyes fluttering closed for a moment.

Encouraged, I continued, watching Floris's face for reactions, cataloging what made his breath catch, what made his hips rise to meet my hand. When I felt confident, I lowered my head, mimicking what Floris had done to me.

It was different than I'd expected: the taste, the feel. But not bad different. Just... new. Unfamiliar. I licked around his cock head, then suckled gently. This, I could do. I could make him feel what he'd made me feel.

"That's perfect," Floris murmured, his hand coming to rest lightly on my head, not pushing. "Your tongue on my slit feels really good."

The praise sent a thrill through me, making me more eager, more bold. I teased his slit a little more with the tip of my tongue, his salty precum flooding my mouth. I didn't mind it. It wasn't yummy, but it wasn't gross either.

His cock was steel velvet in my hand, and I lapped up long strokes along his length, holding him at the base. I'd read once that pubic hair had the biological function of trapping scent, and I could understand that now. Even though he had just showered, I could smell him there, a heady, musky odor that was strangely arousing.

"If you use your hand and your mouth together," Floris suggested, his voice strained, "it's easier to control the depth."

I followed the advice, finding that Floris was right. It was easier this way, more comfortable. I was careful at first, cautious, afraid I'd do something wrong. But Floris's reactions—every breathless gasp, every low moan—spurred me on, gave me the confidence to keep going and find a rhythm. I wanted more of that. Wanted to see him completely unravel.

A trembling breath escaped Floris, and I glanced up, catching sight of his face. His eyes were closed, his head thrown back, mouth slightly open. He looked wild and undone and so beautiful, it made my heart lurch. I released him from my mouth, licked long and slow up his shaft, then took him in again.

I redoubled my efforts, alternating between taking him deeper —though nowhere near as deep as he'd taken me—and teasing him with soft, shallow sucks at the tip. Floris's fingers tightened in my hair, still not pushing, just holding on as if he needed something to anchor himself. The thought made me shiver, made me more eager to continue, to bring him to the edge and push him over.

"Orson," Floris warned, his voice tight. "I'm close. You can... You don't have to..."

But I didn't stop. I wanted this, wanted to give this to Floris, wanted to see him come apart the way Floris had seen me. I increased my pace slightly, my hand working in tandem with my mouth.

Floris gave a broken cry, his body tensing, and then he was coming, his hand tightening in my hair. I swallowed, surprised by the taste but not unpleasantly so.

When it was over, I moved up to lie beside Floris, oddly proud of myself. Floris looked at me with heavy-lidded eyes, a lazy smile spreading across his face.

"You're a quick learner." He reached out, brushing a curl back from my forehead. "That was incredible."

I couldn't help the smile that tugged at my lips. "I had a good teacher."

Floris laughed, pulling me closer. "We should get up," he said, though he didn't move. "You have a paper to write."

The paper. I had almost forgotten. I glanced at the digital clock on my nightstand. We'd been at this for nearly an hour, not the twenty minutes I'd promised myself. I should get up, should get back to work.

But Floris was warm against me, his heartbeat steady under my palm. And I was suddenly, overwhelmingly tired, the kind of bone-deep fatigue that comes after intense physical and emotional exertion. "Five minutes," I murmured against Floris's chest. "Gonna rest my eyes for five minutes."

Floris's arms tightened around me, a protective circle. "Five minutes." He pressed a kiss to the top of my head.

I knew, somewhere in the back of my mind, that five minutes would turn into the whole night. That I'd wake up in the morning with Floris still beside me, and my paper still unwritten. That I'd have to scramble to catch up, to meet my self-imposed deadlines.

But as sleep claimed me, held safe in the circle of Floris's arms, I couldn't bring myself to care.

19

FLORIS

I sprawled across my too-small dorm bed, staring at the ceiling with what must have been the stupidest grin on my face. My chest felt like it was filled with helium, my heart so light, I worried it might float right out of my body. This feeling—this ridiculous, wonderful weightlessness—had to be what true happiness felt like. And it all circled back to one curly-haired, nervous, brilliant person: Orson Ritchey.

It had been three-and-a-half months since I'd met Orson, two weeks since our first kiss, and approximately twelve hours since I'd realized I was falling in love with him.

In love. The phrase felt foreign in my mind, like trying on clothes in a style I'd never dared to wear before. I'd had hookups with anything ranging from bad encounters to spectacular sex, but nothing that had ever made me feel like this. Nothing that had made me want to build something real, something lasting.

Last night, we'd stayed up talking until three in the morning, Orson's head resting on my chest, his wild curls tickling my chin. He'd been explaining the technical details of how the Egyptians had structured the pyramids, his long fingers drawing invisible diagrams in the air. I'd barely followed his explanation, but I'd been enraptured by the animation in his voice, the intelligence in his gorgeous, brown eyes, the way his whole body seemed to vibrate with the joy of explaining something he loved.

And then he'd stopped mid-sentence, looked up at me, and said, "You're not listening to a word I'm saying, are you?"

"I'm listening to every word. I just don't understand half of them."

He'd laughed then, that unexpected laugh that transformed his sharp, serious face into something mischievous and young. "You don't have to pretend to be interested in my obsessions."

"I'm not pretending to be interested in you," I'd said, and the words had slipped out before I could analyze them, measure them, weigh their impact the way I'd been taught to do with every utterance since childhood.

The memory made my stomach flip pleasantly. I needed to talk to someone about this feeling, someone who would understand the complications that came with being me. Someone I could trust not to breathe a word until I was ready to talk to anyone else about it. I reached for my phone and pulled up my brother's contact.

Laurens and I had always been close, partially because we were barely two years apart in age and mostly because we'd always had to have each other's backs. Growing up in the public eye did things to you as a kid, and we'd always been able to count on each other.

Laurens picked up on the third ring. "Well, well. If it isn't my little brother, the American college student. To what do I owe this honor?"

"Can't I just call to say hello?" I asked, sitting up and leaning against the wall, knees pulled to my chest. "Maybe I missed your charming personality and judgmental sighs."

"You could, but you never do." His voice was warm with affection despite the teasing. "And my sighs aren't judgmental, they're aristocratic. We practiced them extensively in prince school, remember?"

I snorted. "Ah yes, right between 'Eating Soup Without Slurping' and 'How to Smile for Official Portraits.' Those were the days."

"Everything okay over there? Classes going well? No international incidents this time?"

I let out an indignant huff. "You're making it sound like I cause incidents all the time."

"Well, I wouldn't quite go that far, but there have been some... misunderstandings."

"Misunderstandings that were not my fault," I protested, though I couldn't help grinning. "And no, no incidents. Actually, everything's kind of perfect."

There was a pause on the other end. "Okay, now I'm intrigued. You sound different."

"Different how?"

"Happy," he said simply. "Not the 'I'm pretending everything is fine for the press' happy, but actually happy."

I took a deep breath. "I met someone."

"Ah." Just that one syllable, but it carried volumes of understanding. "Tell me about him."

My sexuality had never been an issue for my family, including Laurens. He hadn't been surprised when I'd told him and ever since, he'd shown his wholehearted acceptance in every single way.

The knot of tension between my shoulders loosened. "His name is Orson, and he's brilliant. Literally brilliant, probably the smartest person I've ever met. He's studying civil engineering and he's super passionate about restoring old buildings. He's from New Orleans originally, and his mom and sister are amazing, and—" I cut myself off, embarrassed by my own enthusiasm.

"He sounds wonderful," Laurens said softly.

"He is. He's super cute, and he has the most amazing eyes... and when he laughs, really laughs, it's like... like..."

"Like watching the sun come out?"

"Yeah." I ran a hand through my hair, smiling at how well my brother understood. "Exactly like that."

"How did you meet?"

"He's my roommate."

Laurens chuckled. "Only you, bro. Only you. Well, at least that makes it easy to stay discreet."

"He wants to keep it under wraps for now. He's very new at this. Not in the closet, but inexperienced with relationships."

"Relationships," Laurens said slowly. "So this is not casual, then. It's serious."

"It feels serious," I admitted. "More serious than anything I've felt before. I think... I think I'm in love with him, Laurens."

The words hung in the air between us, across the ocean that separated Massachusetts from the Netherlands. My brother was silent for a moment, and I could picture him in his office, elbows leaning on the desk as he looked pensive.

"Well, that's certainly new," he finally said. "Does he know who you are?"

"Yes. He knows everything. Including the video."

"Good, good. I'm glad. And he's okay with it?"

"He seems to be."

"That's a big hurdle taken, then. So, what's the problem? Why the call?"

I shifted on the bed, the mattress creaking under me. "I want to tell Mom and Dad. About him. About us. But I don't know how they'll react. He's not exactly what they might've expected."

"Because he's American?"

"Because he's a regular guy. No title, no family connections. A middle-class kid from New Orleans."

Laurens laughed outright at that. "Floris, you do realize that Grandmother married a complete commoner who became everyone's favorite prince consort, right? And that our cousin married the daughter of the gardener? You're overthinking this."

I hadn't realized how much I needed to hear those words until they were spoken. "You think they'll be okay with it?"

"They'll be thrilled you've found someone who makes you happy," Laurens said firmly. "Especially after that mess with that video. They've been worried about you, you know."

The mention of "that mess" sent a familiar twinge through me. The injustice still stung.

"I know they worry. That's part of why I want to tell them properly, before they hear rumors."

"Good plan. But speaking of rumors..." He paused, and my stomach tightened. "Floris, Margriet has been getting questions."

Margriet was the royal family's chief spokesperson, a formidable woman who managed our public image with iron efficiency.

"What kind of questions?"

"The usual. Where you are, what you're doing, why you haven't been seen at any functions lately. There's some speculation that you're in rehab or having some kind of breakdown."

I closed my eyes. "Fantastic."

"It's nothing we can't handle, but I wanted to warn you that they might start looking for you. You know how persistent they can be."

My stomach soured as the weightless feeling of earlier dissipated. I knew exactly how persistent they could be. As a child, it had been carefully planned moments for the press, with the agreement that they'd leave us kids alone otherwise. For the most part, they had, but whenever we appeared for official events, they were allowed to take pictures too. There were some lovely ones of me picking my nose at age three.

But once we turned eighteen, that agreement ended and the press had free reign. It was part of being fifth in line to the Dutch throne: not important enough to warrant full security detail at all times, but interesting enough to sell magazines.

"I don't want that for Orson," I said, and my voice came out raw. "He doesn't deserve to have his life invaded like that."

"No, he doesn't, but if this relationship is as serious as it sounds, it's something you'll both have to face eventually."

The thought made me physically ill. I pictured Orson, with his shy smile and his self-consciousness, being pursued by photographers. I imagined his private life splashed across tabloids, his past dissected, his family harassed. All because he'd had the misfortune to fall for me.

"I don't know if I can do that to him," I whispered.

"Floris." Laurens's voice was gentle but firm. "You can't make that decision for him. You need to talk to him about it, be honest about what being with you might mean. Let him decide if it's worth it."

My free hand clenched into a fist. "And if he decides it's not?"

"Then that's his choice to make. But from what you've told me about him, he sounds like someone who knows his own mind."

I thought about Orson's determination, his focus, the way he meticulously worked through problems until he found a solution. He wasn't impulsive. If anything, he overthought everything, analyzed all possible outcomes before making a move. It was one of the things I loved about him, how different it was from my own tendency to speak first and think later.

"You're right. I need to talk to him."

"And to Mom and Dad. Sooner rather than later. They're planning to come visit you in the spring. It would be better if they weren't blindsided."

My parents had scheduled a "private" visit to the United States, with a few days set aside to see me at school. Private in royal terms meant only a dozen staff members and minimal press coverage.

"I'll call them," I promised. "And I'll talk to Orson."

"Good. And Floris? For what it's worth, I'm happy for you. It's about time something good happened in your life."

His words sent a rush of warmth through me, mingled with a twinge of apprehension. "Thanks, Laurens. I appreciate it."

After we hung up, I sat motionless on my bed, phone clutched in my hand. The happiness I'd felt earlier hadn't vanished entirely, but it was now shot through with anxiety, like cracks in a beautiful vase. I had to warn Orson about what might be coming. I had to give him the chance to walk away before things got complicated.

The thought made my chest ache with a pain that felt physical. My hands weren't exactly numb, but I felt a warmth, an uncomfortable heat that I recognized as fear, fear of losing something precious before it had fully begun.

But before I could analyze that any further, my phone rang again. When I spotted the number, I frowned. Tore? Why would he be calling me?

"Tore? Is everything all right?" I asked, unable to keep the concern out of my voice.

"I've royally mucked things up, Flo," he blurted out. "I need your advice."

I pushed my own worries to the background. "I'm listening. What's going on?"

The call didn't take long and I saw the irony in the fact that I was telling him the exact same thing that Laurens had advised me: to communicate. In my case, with both my parents and Orson, and in Tore's case, with the guy he'd insisted for so long he hated. Had I called it or what when I'd labeled it foreplay?

At least I wasn't the only one with relationship trouble... though that was barely a consolation. I needed to talk to Orson about the press, and I needed to do it soon.

But how would he react? I had a feeling I wasn't gonna like it.

20

ORSON

Snow fell thick across campus, blanketing the world, erasing it. I hurried from the grand lecture hall to our dorm room as quickly as I could, though careful not to slip on the slick surface. Even after over three years here, snow was still foreign to me, the stuff of pretty Christmas cards and Facebook posts, not my actual reality. I hadn't made my mind up as to whether I actually liked the stuff.

I pulled my hat low over my ears, stuffing my hands in my pockets. Around me, groups of students hurried across the white fields, heads down against the biting wind, looking for cover. I was no different, feeling the sting of each flake as I trudged past the library, past a bunch of snow-covered benches, past the dining hall and finally on to the dorms. A chill crept under my layers, and I shivered.

When I turned the corner, I came to a sudden stop, my feet almost sliding right from under me. Floris stood in the center of the lawn in front of Smelter Hall, arms outstretched, open-mouthed and shocked, or thrilled, or maybe a combination of both. Like he'd never seen it, like he'd been waiting forever. A million white crystals covered everything, even him, turning his orange coat into an overgrown marshmallow.

"What are you doing?" I called, trying to sound casual, but my voice caught on the words.

Floris spun around, too fast, nearly slipped on a patch of ice. "Orson! It's snowing!" he said, as if he had invented the white stuff himself and I should be impressed. He pointed toward the sky, where heavy, gray clouds twisted into strange, dark shapes. "Isn't it brilliant?"

"It's snow," I said, because that seemed to cover it, and someone had to point out the obvious. "Don't you have this back home?"

He laughed, a cloud of steam billowing around him. "Not like this! It's so much!" He moved through the falling whiteness, his hair and lashes turning frosty, until he was close enough to touch. "Don't you love it?"

"In moderate amounts... and not when it's this cold. The feel temperature is, like, in the low twenties."

He grinned. "I have no idea what that even means. Using Celsius, remember?"

Oh god. I'd learned the formula back in high school. What was it again? Multiply by... multiply by one-point-eight and then add thirty-two. I did a quick calculation. "Minus five... give or take."

"Minus five? That's not that cold. Come on," he said, and he took my hand. I wasn't prepared, not for the touch of his bare fingers against my gloves or for the way his eyes crinkled at the edges, flecks of snow catching in his smile. He pulled, trying to drag me out into the open. I let him, even though I knew I shouldn't.

"Are you trying to kill me?" I said, when we stopped, our breath mixing like we were making clouds.

"Nah. You're way too pretty for that..." He let go of my hand to flick a snowflake off my cheek, touching me lightly, his fingertips brushing my skin like he'd always been there and always would be.

I couldn't take it. I was helpless. Hopeless. I leaned forward, before he could finish the motion. Before he could pull away. Before I could think and change my mind. I kissed him, right there on the open commons, with snow in our eyes and a hundred people around us. The last thing I saw was the shocked look on his face.

And then he kissed me back. His mouth covered mine, his lips cold against mine, and our tongues met and danced. I closed my eyes, sinking into the kiss with all I had... until my feet slipped right from under me and I lost my balance.

I fell back, flat on the frozen ground, the air knocked from my lungs. Floris landed on top of me, as shocked as I was, as breathless. But he recovered first, propping himself up on his elbows, looking down at me like he'd won the lottery. He laughed, and his laughter rolled through me, making my heart pound against the thin layers of my winter coat.

"What the hell got into you?" he said.

In lieu of the answer I didn't have, I kissed him again. His lips tasted like wind, like snow, like all the daydreams I had about him. He kissed me until I forgot about all the people who might be watching. Until I forgot about everything except the feel of his mouth and the weight of his body and the way his leg pushed between mine, sending little shocks up my spine.

It was insane. It was reckless. It was the most reckless thing I'd ever done, but I couldn't stop. I grabbed his collar and pulled him closer, turning us both, rolling through the wet snow, until it soaked through my jeans and leaked through his coat and melted in our hair.

"I thought you wanted to keep it a secret," he said, between kisses, sounding like it was the best joke he'd ever heard.

"I changed my mind," I said, breathless, even though my mind had gone completely blank, and it was my heart, or maybe some other part, doing the thinking.

Floris laughed, pressing his hips to mine, a little more than teasing. "I like it," he said.

The cold was creeping up on us, and the clouds seemed to lower themselves to the ground. But we didn't stop until we were soaked to the bone, until Floris's lips turned blue and my hair stuck to my forehead in frozen clumps. A group of students ran past us, feet crunching in the snow, faces flushed with wind and laughter. They whistled and cheered and yelled things I couldn't hear above the pounding in my ears.

"Okay," Floris said, standing and reaching down to pull me up. "Before I turn into a Floris-cicle."

"You and the lame jokes," I said, because he had a habit of thinking everything was hilarious, but secretly, or not so secretly, I loved it.

He draped his arm over my shoulders as we headed toward Smelter Hall, our footprints already disappearing behind us.

Inside, everything felt too warm and too loud. The darkwood paneling, the hallways of heavy doors, even the banisters on the iron staircase seemed to vibrate, filled with chatter and commotion. A burst of students poured past us, shaking off coats and backpacks, thawing and dripping all over the linoleum.

Up in our room, we peeled off our wet clothes. Floris tossed his bright-orange jacket over a chair, and I kicked off my boots, my fingers trembling with cold, unable to keep up with the task. My shirt went next, then my jeans, until I stood there in nothing but damp boxer shorts. Floris's eyes were glued to me, but instead of being embarrassed, I shivered with the thrill of it.

He grabbed a towel from the rack and tossed one to me. I caught it, almost fumbled.

"Getting naked is smart," Floris said. "So we don't freeze."

He dropped his own shirt to the floor, his tan skin glowing against the whiteness outside.

"Not freezing is good," I said, unable to take my eyes off the freckled expanse of his chest.

He grinned, wrapping the towel around his waist. "You know what's even smarter?"

"No, but please enlighten me."

He stepped closer, only inches from me now. "Getting warm." He let the towel slip. "In bed. Skin to skin contact will help us warm up fast."

He held my gaze, and my heart leapt. He didn't break eye contact as he backed up toward his bed, sitting down on the edge, the springs groaning in a familiar way.

"We wouldn't want you to die of hypothermia," I said, as if I cared. As if I didn't think I might be the one dying from the need to have him touch me. I tossed my towel on the floor and climbed in next to him, next to the skin I wanted to memorize before we left for break, before it disappeared and became someone else's. "I'd feel so guilty."

"Can't have that." He pulled me down, wrapping himself around me like a blanket, the cute kind with a face and paws and ears, the kind you don't want to take off. His hands moved over my shoulders, along my arms, leaving a trail of sparks. "Is this better?" he asked.

It was too much. It was not enough. "Definitely, but to be sure, don't stop."

He laughed and kissed me, letting his weight settle over me until all I felt was him. "I'm going to miss you so much over Christmas break," he said, pulling back enough to see my face, but not enough to break the pressure that was building between us.

We were both flying out in a few days, and for the first time, I was not looking forward to going home. Christmas break had always been my favorite, but now the time away from Floris doomed over me like a heavy, dark cloud.

"Really?" It came out needier than I'd meant, more than I'd meant, but this whole thing felt unreal, and I needed to hear it again.

"It will be torture."

"Even though you'll meet countless tall, blond, attractive Dutch guys?"

He pushed my hands above my head, pinning them to the pillow. "Maybe. But none of them will be you." His fingers tightened, squeezing my wrists. "None of them will be this hot."

He let go and kissed his way down my neck, across my shoulder, then worked back to my mouth. He kissed me until I forgot about being cold and the snow and Christmas break and everything else.

His hands moved lower, teasing, until I gasped against his mouth. "What do you want?"

I swallowed. "You."

He kissed me again. "I'm gonna need you to be more specific."

"What are my options?"

"You want a multiple-choice question?"

I snickered. "I was thinking more along the lines of a menu, but yeah. What do you recommend, chef Floris?"

He snorted. "Our special of the day is... anal play. Would you be interested?"

He hadn't even finished before I nodded. "Yes, Chef."

"Thank you for trusting me."

His hand slipped past my stomach, over my hips, making me shiver in ways that had nothing to do with being cold. He reached for the lube, which made me so ridiculously happy that I wondered if he could see me smiling in the dim light. Another big step I got to take with him.

Floris took his time, slicking his fingers, rubbing them together, then sliding them down my crack until they rested lightly against my...

I took a deep, shuddering breath.

My anus. My hole. Floris was gonna put his finger inside me and play with me. And I would let him because everything we'd done so far had felt amazing, so this would, too.

"Good?" he asked, and had to blink a few times to process his question.

I couldn't talk. I nodded again, eyes wide.

He rubbed his finger against me, against my hole, and nerve endings I'd never known I had lit up. Like falling dominos, they spread sensations through my body, wider and wider in concentric circles, as if every part was somehow connected to where he was touching me. Maybe it was. Anatomy had never been a particular interest of mine.

He pressed harder, slower, making circles. Then his finger slipped in, and I had no idea it could feel that good. It hurt a little, but inexplicably, it was the kind of hurt that made you want more.

The slick slide of his finger in and out of me was strange but good, alien but oh so welcome. He pumped his finger, working me open, and the sensation made me clench around him. His low chuckle reverberated through me. "Good?" he asked again.

This time, I got my mouth to work. "Good. Really good."

"I love watching you. For someone who is usually so reserved, you show everything during sex."

Wasn't that good to know? I had learned something about myself. "Thank you, I think?"

He chuckled. "Definitely not a bad thing."

Then he added another finger, scissoring me, and my head spun. My body felt like it was catching fire and burning to ashes every single thought, every fear, every single reason I ever had for keeping my distance from Floris.

I pulled his mouth to mine, shaking, never ready for what he gave me but wanting it anyway. He pushed deep, then angled his hand and twisted it, finding a spot that made my entire body tremble and my vision blur.

"H-holy shit, what is that?"

"Meet your prostate, *lieverd*... It doesn't work this way for everyone, but yours is sensitive."

Sensitive. What an understatement. "Clearly," I said dryly, and he chuckled.

"Want me to do it again?"

"For someone as smart as you, you certainly know how to ask stupid questions."

He was still laughing when he found that spot again and rubbed against it, and the smile on my own face turned into a moan that was embarrassingly loud and long. As he continued, he drew sounds from me I'd never made before, sounds I hadn't even thought I could make. I was shaking, shivering, unbearably hot and yet somehow cold at the same time, my skin itching and burning.

Relentlessly, he pushed me higher and higher until I gripped his shoulders and came hard, yelling his name. Pretty sure the whole dorm had been able to hear me, but I was past caring.

"Shit," I said, when I could breathe again, when I remembered I needed to breathe. "That was spectacular."

"I think it's safe to say you liked that menu item."

I snorted. "So far, it's my favorite."

"Well, you've only sampled a few specialties available, so maybe that will change."

"I'll take whatever you're serving." Okay, I needed to stop with the mushy shit before I truly embarrassed myself. "But thank you."

"You're welcome."

Should I return the favor? Couldn't be that hard, right? A thought occurred to me. "Are you a top or a bottom? Or do you like both?"

He flashed me a wide grin. "Is it strange that I'm proud of you for asking that? And I'm vers, though I do prefer to top."

Hmm, which one would I prefer? I was definitely open to trying both, but I had a sneaky suspicion I would prefer bottoming. My one and only experience hadn't been stellar, but Floris would make it good for me. That much I was certain of. "I wouldn't mind letting you top me."

I was very proud of how casually I'd managed to deliver that line. Maybe I was getting the hang of this sex thing. Of course, that was when the realization hit me that once again, Floris had made me come and I had not returned the favor. I really needed to learn to multitask.

"It's really hard to think when you touch me like that," I said.

Floris frowned. "Huh? I'm not following."

"I didn't... You're still..." I gestured at him, half-hard by now. "I should've done something about that. Touched you, I mean."

Understanding lit up his face. "No worries. My first few times, I was completely overwhelmed and couldn't figure out how to multitask. It's okay. It takes some getting used to."

Phew. "Thanks. Glad to hear I'm not the only one. So do you want me to... blow you?"

He kissed the top of my forehead. "I'm good, but thank you. Can we snuggle instead?"

We sure could, and I sank into his embrace, splaying myself half on top of him. We stayed like that, breathing in each other's heat, too wired to sleep, but too exhausted to move.

"I don't want to put pressure on you, but you said you were okay with us going public?" Floris asked after a while. "I mean, you did kiss me in public."

"I did." I knew I could still change my mind. Floris would let me. But was that what I really wanted? Did I always want to have to hide? Even knowing it would end at some point, didn't I want to spend every possible moment with him, consequences be damned? I took a deep breath. "And yes, I am. If you are too."

Floris let out a soft gasp. "Very much so." His arms tightened around me for a moment. "But let me talk to my parents first. I promised my brother I would, but then I chickened out."

Floris who chickened out? That was unexpected. "Of course. Let me know when we can, you know, go public."

"I will. You know the press will—"

"We'll deal with that when we have to."

I very much preferred to stick my head in the sand when it came to that, thank you very much.

"I'll miss you," he whispered after a long pause, almost too soft for me to hear.

I couldn't stop myself. "I'll miss you too."

I lay there for a long time, listening to the quiet of the dorm, to the wind howling at the windows, to Floris breathing. I lay there, letting the warmth fill me up. Letting myself hope. Maybe it could last.

Maybe.

21

FLORIS

Our traditional Christmas brunch at home had always been one of the highlights of the year for me, but this time, I struggled to get into the Christmas spirit. It wasn't for a lack of effort. The kitchen staff had outdone themselves, and the table was decked out with festive decorations like holly and pine garlands, twinkling lights, and red and green table settings. The food was beautifully arranged on platters and dishes, showcasing the various kinds of freshly baked bread, pancakes, smoked salmon, different kinds of deli meats, cheese, fresh fruit, and of course, a *kerststol*, the traditional Christmas bread with almond paste in the center.

It even smelled amazing. The delightful aroma of freshly brewed coffee wafted through the air, mingling with the scents of freshly baked croissants and the unique smell of fresh pine trees. We always got real Christmas trees, dug out with roots intact and replanted two days after Christmas. Better for the environment, my mom insisted, plus so much nicer than fake trees. She had a point.

But I wasn't in a festive mood. I usually loved hanging out

with my parents and my brother and his fiancée, Maaike. They were engaged for six months now and had dated for two years before taking this step. Somehow, they had managed to keep their relationship private for the first few months. I liked her. She was sweet and funny, but she also knew when to put her foot down, which my brother needed from time to time.

So yes, I genuinely liked spending time with my family. We didn't get to do that nearly often enough, so when we had a whole day to ourselves without any public obligations, it was a luxury. But my thoughts kept drifting to Orson.

I missed him. I missed his wild curls in the morning and how he always had bed head no matter how much he tried to tame it. I missed his quiet intensity when he studied, the way his brow would furrow in concentration and how he'd absently push his glasses up his nose. Most of all, I missed those rare moments when he'd let his guard down completely: his unexpected laugh that transformed his whole face, the way his eyes lit up when talking about historical architecture, how he'd unconsciously lean into me when we watched movies together.

Even the little things felt like missing puzzle pieces in my day. The way he'd wordlessly hand me coffee in the morning, somehow always knowing exactly when I needed it. His exasperated sighs when I left my laundry in the dryer too long, though he'd still bring it up to our room. The soft, private smile he saved just for me when he thought no one else was looking. Three weeks apart felt like an eternity, and it had only been a few days. Somehow every hour without him stretched endlessly.

"You're awfully quiet this morning," Mom said, passing me the bread basket. "Everything okay?"

I forced a smile, taking a slice of the Christmas bread without really seeing it. "Just tired, Mama."

"Tired?" Laurens arched an eyebrow from across the table.

"You? On Christmas morning? Who are you and what have you done with my brother?"

Maaike elbowed him gently. "Leave him alone. He's probably missing his friends from college."

If only she knew. I caught Laurens's knowing look and quickly focused on buttering my bread.

"How's Tore doing?" Dad asked. "Have you talked to him?"

I nodded. "We spoke briefly yesterday. He's still trying to come to terms with it all."

His uncle, King Ragnar of Norway, had died unexpectedly after a massive heart attack in public. Uncle Friso and Aunt Annette had flown in for the solemn and somber funeral and I had changed my flight home into one to Norway. I'd barely seen Tore, but I'd been there, and that mattered. Greg and Nils had shown up too, and we'd stayed together.

"He was so young," Mom said. She shot my father a look. "You'd better take good care of yourself, Marc. You're almost the same age."

I could see the protest on my father's lips, but it died just as quickly, probably because he realized how deeply worried she was. "You know I will, *lieve schat*."

The conversation continued, but my thoughts drifted again. Was Orson awake yet? Probably not, considering the time difference. What was Christmas morning like at his house? I imagined him still sleepy-eyed, wild curls even messier than usual, maybe wearing that soft, green sweater that brought out the gold flecks in his eyes...

"Floris?" Dad's voice pulled me back to reality. "Your mother asked you a question."

"Sorry, what?"

"I asked how your finals went," Mom repeated patiently. There was something in her expression, a maternal intuition that made me wonder if she could read more into my distraction than I wanted her to.

"Oh. Good. Really good, actually." Thanks largely to Orson's patient tutoring and ability to explain complex concepts in ways that actually made sense. "The civil engineering program at Vernon Tech is excellent."

"And life in America? How are you liking that?" Maaike asked.

"Different." I forced myself to pay attention. "Did you know they start classes at eight in the morning? I thought their constitution forbade cruel and unusual punishment."

Dad chuckled. "I'm sure you'll survive."

"Barely. And don't get me started on their food portions. Everything comes supersized. The other day, I ordered a 'small' coffee and got what we'd consider a bucket. Though I have to admit, I'm developing a concerning addiction to something called 'mac and cheese.' It's basically pasta drowning in cheese sauce."

Mom wrinkled her nose. "That sounds... unhealthy."

"Oh, it absolutely is. But it's like a warm hug for your stomach. Plus, they have this thing called 'dining dollars' which basically means I can eat my feelings without actually seeing money leave my wallet. Dangerous system, really."

"And the classes?" Dad asked, as always more interested in academics. He was an engineer himself, so I definitely took after him in that aspect.

"Challenging but good. Half my class struggles with converting to the metric system, but that's one challenge I don't have. On the other hand, I still can't figure liquid ounces out. Every time I order a drink and they ask which size, I have to guess."

The conversation flowed easily, my family's genuine interest in my experiences making it simple to share. It felt good to talk about the little cultural differences that still caught me off guard, like how Americans thought nothing of striking up conversations with complete strangers, or how they seemed physically incapable of pronouncing my name correctly. The rolling r was too much, apparently.

"Have you made any friends?" my mom asked.

My heart skipped at the opening she'd inadvertently provided. This was my chance. I'd promised Laurens I'd tell them about Orson, and really, there wouldn't be a better moment. We were all together, relaxed, no pressing engagements or staff hovering nearby.

I took a deep breath. "Actually, there's something I wanted to tell you all." I glanced at Laurens, who gave me an encouraging nod. "I've met someone."

The silence that followed felt heavy with anticipation.

Mom's face lit up immediately. "Oh? Tell us about him."

"His name is Orson," I said, watching carefully for their reactions. "He's my roommate, actually. He's studying civil engineering too, and he's brilliant. Probably the smartest person I've ever met."

"A roommate?" Dad's eyebrows rose slightly. "That's convenient."

I couldn't help but laugh. "Trust me, it wasn't planned. But he's amazing. He's from New Orleans originally, and he's incredibly focused and dedicated to his studies. He wants to work in disaster prevention, specifically flooding. You'd love talking to him, Dad."

"And how serious is this?" Mom asked, her voice gentle but probing.

I met her eyes, knowing honesty was crucial here. "I'm in love with him."

Dad's coffee cup clinked against its saucer. "Aren't you a bit young to be throwing around words like love?"

"Marc," Mom chided softly, but I shook my head.

"No, it's okay." I straightened in my chair, channeling every lesson in poise I'd ever learned. "I know I'm young, and I know my track record with relationships isn't exactly stellar. But this is different. Orson is different."

"Different how?" Dad pressed.

"He sees me," I said simply. "Not the prince, not the tabloid target, but the real me. He challenges me to be better, helps me with my studies, calls me out when I'm being ridiculous. And he's so brilliant and passionate about what he does, even though he tries to hide it."

"Hide it?" Mom's brow furrowed.

I hesitated, not sure how much of Orson's story was mine to tell. "He lost his father during Hurricane Katrina. He was only four. It changed him. He's very focused. Sometimes too focused."

Understanding dawned in Mom's eyes. "Ah. And you help him find balance?"

"I try." I smiled, thinking of all the times I'd dragged Orson away from his books, shown him it was okay to live a little.

"And does he understand what being with you means?" Dad asked carefully. "The public scrutiny, the responsibilities, the expectations?"

The question made my stomach clench. "We're working on that part. He knows who I am, obviously, and for his own reasons, he's fine with keeping things private for now. But I haven't fully explained what might happen when the press finds out."

"You need to tell him," Dad said firmly. "Before it blindsides him. You know how ruthless the tabloids can be."

I did know. The memory of that edited video, of headlines

screaming accusations, made my chest tight. "I'm afraid," I admitted quietly. "Not of telling him, but of what might happen after. He's such a private person, and his family's been through so much already. I don't want to put them through more trauma."

"Oh, sweetheart." Mom reached across the table to squeeze my hand. "You can't protect him from everything. He has the right to make his own choice about whether this—whether you—are worth the complications that come with our life."

"I know." I stared down at my barely touched Christmas bread. "But what if he decides it's not? What if—"

"Then that would be his choice to make," Mom said gently. "But from what you've told us about him, he sounds like someone who knows his own mind."

Laurens snorted into his coffee. "That's exactly what I told him."

I shot him a grateful look, appreciating his support. "You should see him when he's working on a problem. He analyzes every possible angle, considers all variables. He's probably the most thorough person I've ever met."

"Then trust him to apply that same thoroughness to this decision," Dad said, his voice softening. "Give him all the information he needs, then let him choose."

"And if he chooses you," Mom added with a warm smile, "we'd love to meet him."

Warmth spread through my chest. "You'll love him, I promise."

"Speaking of the press," Dad said.

I sighed. "They're asking about me, I know. Laurens told me."

"Not merely asking," Dad said, setting down his coffee cup. "They're starting to dig. Margriet's had inquiries about your absence from certain events, and someone spotted you at Logan Airport last month."

My stomach dropped. "How close are they?"

"Close enough that we need to get ahead of this," Mom said. "We can control the narrative if we announce your studies officially, maybe arrange some carefully managed press coverage—"

"No." The word came out sharper than I intended. "I mean, not yet. Please. Let me talk to Orson first. He deserves to hear everything from me, not from some press release."

Dad studied me for a long moment, and I recognized his analytical face, the one he used when considering all factors before making a decision. The man was nothing if not thoughtful and thorough, rarely making an impulsive call. "You really care about him."

"I do." I met his gaze steadily. "More than I've ever cared about anyone."

Something in his expression softened. "Then you need to tell him soon. The press will find you eventually. They always do. Better he hears it all from you first."

"I know." I ran a hand through my hair. "I don't want to ruin what we have. Things are so good right now, you know?"

"Sometimes," Maaike spoke up unexpectedly, "the hard conversations are what make relationships stronger." She smiled when we all turned to look at her. "What? I've had my share of 'by the way, you might be photographed grocery shopping' talks with Laurens."

My brother's expression softened as he looked at her, and I felt a pang of longing. That's what I wanted with Orson, that easy understanding, that shared knowledge that whatever came, we'd face it together.

"How did you adjust?" I asked her.

Maaike considered for a moment. "Honestly? It was terrifying at first. The idea that someone might be photographing me buying tampons or having a bad hair day?" She shuddered dramatically. "But then I realized something important: the press might be interested in my life with Laurens, but they don't get to define it. We do."

"That's... actually really helpful." I smiled at her, grateful for the perspective. "How did you tell your family?"

"Oh, that was fun." She grinned. "My dad nearly choked on his coffee when Laurens showed up for Sunday dinner. Turns out I probably should've warned them that I was dating a prince. Though in my defense, how exactly do you casually mention that in conversation? 'Pass the salt, and by the way, my boyfriend's fourth in line to the throne'?"

We all laughed, and some of the tension eased from my shoulders. "Orson's family already knows, actually. His mom figured it out from Google."

"Smart woman," Mom said approvingly. "And how did she react?"

"She was amazing, actually. Treated me like any other guest. Made sure I tried her gumbo, teased me about my attempts at American slang." The memory made me smile. "She has this way of making everyone feel welcome, you know?"

"Sounds like someone I'd like to meet," Mom said softly, and my heart lifted at the implicit acceptance in her voice.

"You will," I said, then quickly added, "If things work out. If he wants that."

"If he's half as special as you make him sound, he'd be a fool not to," Dad said, surprising me with his warmth. "Though I have to ask: does he like football?"

"Marc!" Mom rolled her eyes. "That is not a requirement for dating our son."

"It should be," Dad protested with a grin. "We can't have

someone who doesn't appreciate the beautiful game in the family."

I tried to picture Orson with a football, or, as he would call it, a soccer ball, but I couldn't even imagine it. He was *so* not the athletic type, but I didn't care one bit. "I don't think he's even aware the game exists, but that's okay. He has plenty of qualities to make up for that."

As the talk transitioned into updates about the Eredivisie, our premier football league, and how well Ajax, our club, was doing, my thoughts drifted back to Orson. God, I missed him. Did he miss me too?

22

ORSON

Seeing my uncle Bill, my father's younger brother, always triggered me. He looked too much like my dad, sounded too much like him. Spending time with him was a painful reminder of what we all had lost, and somehow, we always talked about my dad when Uncle Bill came to visit. It wasn't that I didn't like him. He'd clearly loved my dad and he was nice enough and so was Aunt Lydia, but I still always ended up feeling sad.

When my mom had told me they were coming to visit us for Christmas—they lived in Oklahoma—I had screamed on the inside. Of course, I'd shown nothing of those emotions to my mom and had merely replied I was looking forward to seeing them, as well as my two cousins, Sasha and Heather. Nothing could be further from the truth. My cousins were airheads, interested in nothing but boys, fashion, and celebrity gossip. Even Tia struggled to connect with them.

Of course, missing Floris didn't help.

I had expected to feel some sadness over not seeing him, but I hadn't counted on this deep sense of... of loss, almost like grief. How could I miss him this much after such a short time together? We were talking mere weeks, not even months, and yet my heart hadn't gotten that memo and ached like we were separated after being together for years.

Uncle Bill and Aunt Lydia had brought their usual holiday chaos with them. My cousins were arguing over the number of calories in a dinner roll while my uncle dominated the conversation with his voice that sounded so much like my dad. The dining room was decked out in Mom's festive decorations, tiny white lights twinkling along the windowsills and her prized angel centerpiece casting soft shadows across the tablecloth.

We sat down for dinner at four. Steam rose from the golden-brown turkey that had taken Mom hours to perfect, surrounded by all the traditional sides: creamy mashed potatoes with rivers of gravy, green bean casserole topped with crispy onions, sweet potatoes crowned with toasted marshmallows, and Mom's famous cornbread dressing that always made the whole house smell like sage and childhood memories. But even with all this comfort and familiarity around me, my thoughts kept drifting back to Floris, wondering what Christmas dinner looked like in a Dutch palace, if he was thinking of me too.

"Pass the potatoes, please," Heather called from across the table, barely looking up from her phone. Her perfectly manicured nails clicked against the screen as she typed.

I handed over the dish, trying not to feel irritated by her constant texting. At least it meant less awkward conversation.

"So, Orson," Uncle Bill said, his voice so similar to Dad's, it made my chest tight. "How's college treating you? Still on track with civil engineering?"

"Yes, sir." I pushed my glasses up, a nervous habit I couldn't seem to break. "Classes are going well."

"Good, good." He nodded approvingly. "And after this?"

"I'm hoping for a job with a big engineering firm."

"Your father would be proud. Following in his footsteps, doing something meaningful with your life."

The words hit like a physical weight, pressing down on my shoulders. I caught Mom's slight frown, the way she opened her mouth as if to say something, then thought better of it.

"Orson's at the top of his class," Mom said instead, her voice carrying that particular mom-tone that meant she was being protective. "His professors are very impressed with his work."

"As they should be." Bill's expression turned serious. "It's what Henry would've wanted, isn't it? Using your education to prevent other tragedies."

I could feel it coming, that familiar pressure building. The weight of expectations, of duty, of trying to live up to a sacrifice I could never repay.

"Orson should study whatever he wants." Mom's tone was sharper now. "We shouldn't put a moral obligation on his shoulders."

Bill's face grew tight. "I'm saying that he has a responsibility. Henry died making sure he lived, and—"

"And Orson's dating a prince!" Tia blurted out, clearly trying to change the subject.

The silence that followed was deafening. I stared at my sister in horror, heat rushing to my face. Of all the ways I'd imagined this coming out—and I had imagined several, usually involving careful explanation and context—this wasn't one of them.

"A what now?" Sasha's head snapped up from her phone, suddenly interested in the conversation. "Like, an actual prince?"

"He's not... We're not..." I stammered, but Tia was already pulling up something on her phone.

"His name is Floris," she announced. "He's from the Netherlands. Look!"

She turned her phone around, showing what appeared to be an official royal family photo. Floris stood tall and elegant in a crisp, blue suit, looking every inch the prince he was. My chest tightened at the sight of him, even in a photo.

"Oh my god!" Heather abandoned her own phone to lean closer. "He's gorgeous! How did you even meet someone like that?"

"He's my roommate," I muttered, wishing I could disappear into my chair. "It's not a big deal."

"Not a big deal?" Sasha's eyes were wide. "You're dating actual royalty! That's like, totally a big deal!"

Uncle Bill set down his fork with deliberate care. "Is this true, Orson?"

Something in his tone made me sit up straighter, defensive. "Yes. We've been seeing each other for a few weeks."

"A few weeks?" Bill's expression darkened. "And you think that's appropriate? Getting involved with someone like that?"

"Bill," Aunt Lydia said softly, but he waved her off.

"No, this needs to be said." He fixed me with a hard stare. "You have responsibilities, Orson. Goals. Your father died making sure you'd have a chance to make something of yourself, to help prevent other families from going through what we did. And now you're getting distracted by some European playboy?"

His words were sharp daggers, but beneath the pain, something else stirred. Anger.

"You don't know him."

"I know his type. They're all rich, spoiled little brats. Is this really what your father would've wanted for you?"

"Bill!" Mom's voice cracked like a whip. "That's enough."

But the words were already out there, hanging in the air like poison. I could feel everyone's eyes on me, waiting for my response.

"You don't get to use my father like that." My voice came out steadier than I expected, despite the trembling in my hands. "You don't get to decide what would make him proud."

"I knew him better than you did," Bill shot back. "You were only four—"

"Exactly." I pushed back from the table, my chair scraping against the floor. "I was four when he died saving me. Not you. Me. I'm the one who's lived with that every day since. I'm the one who's tried to be perfect, to be worthy of his sacrifice."

"Then act like it!" Bill's face was red now. "Focus on what matters instead of getting caught up in some fairy-tale romance that'll never work out anyway. You don't belong in that world, Orson."

"Bill, stop it right now." Mom stood up, her hands flat on the table. "You have no right—"

"I have every right! Henry was my brother, and I won't stand by while his son throws away everything he died for!"

The words hit like a physical blow, but something inside me snapped. All the pressure, all the guilt, all the carefully contained emotions I'd been holding back for years came rushing out.

"You think I don't know what Dad died for?" My voice shook with anger and something deeper, rawer. "You think I don't feel it every single day? But Floris..." I swallowed hard, thinking of gentle hands and understanding eyes, of someone who saw past my walls to the person underneath. "Floris makes me better. He challenges me to think differently, to see beyond equations and safety factors. He makes me want to *live*, not just exist."

"And what happens when he gets bored?" Bill demanded. "When he realizes you're not cut out for his world? What then?"

"Then at least I'll have known what it's like to be happy!"

The words exploded out of me. "To be more than the kid whose father died saving him!"

Silence fell over the table. Even Sasha and Heather had stopped playing with their phones, staring at me with wide eyes. Mom reached for my hand, but I pulled away, needing space.

"Orson," Mom started softly, but I was already pushing back from the table.

"I need some air." I headed for the front door, grabbing my jacket from the hook. Behind me, I could hear Mom telling Uncle Bill exactly what she thought of his behavior, her voice carrying that rare edge of true anger.

The December air hit me like a slap, crisp and fresh. We were experiencing an unusual cold spell, though it didn't come close to Massachusetts weather. I sat on the front steps, wrapping my arms around myself, trying to steady my breathing. The Christmas lights from neighboring houses blurred through unshed tears.

The door opened behind me, and soft footsteps approached.

"I'm sorry," Tia said quietly, sitting beside me. "I shouldn't have blurted it out like that."

I sighed, unable to be angry with her. "You were trying to help."

"I wanted Uncle Bill to get off your back." She bumped my shoulder gently. "I never expected him to react like that."

"Neither did I." I stared at the twinkling lights across the street, thinking of Floris's smile, the way his eyes crinkled at the corners when he laughed. "But maybe he's right. Maybe I don't belong in Floris's world."

"That's bullshit." The curse word sounded forceful. "You belong wherever you want to belong. And from what I saw at Thanksgiving, Floris wants you in his world."

"It's not that simple."

"Why not?" She turned to face me fully. "Look, I may be younger than you and not, like, experienced with relationships, but I'm not blind. I saw how he looks at you, like you're the most fascinating thing he's ever seen. And I saw how you are with him —happier, lighter. More... you."

"More me?" I repeated, confused.

"Yeah. Like... okay, remember when we were kids and you used to get so excited about old buildings? How you'd drag me around the French Quarter, explaining about architectural styles and historical preservation? You stopped doing that at some point, instead focusing on nothing else but studying. Everything became about safety and prevention and being perfect." She paused, choosing her words carefully. "But with Floris, I saw that old spark come back. When he was here, you lit up like you used to. I overheard you talk to him about the classic New Orleans architecture, and he got it. He actually listened and asked questions and seemed genuinely interested in what you were saying."

I remembered that day: Floris's enthusiasm, his intelligent questions, the way he'd encouraged me to share my knowledge. "He makes it easy to get excited about things."

"Exactly!" Tia grabbed my hand. "And that's what Dad would've wanted for you. Not just surviving, but *living*. Being passionate about something. Being happy."

"But Uncle Bill—"

"Uncle Bill isn't Dad." Her voice was firm. "He didn't know Dad's heart like Mom did. And Mom loves Floris. You can see it in her face whenever she talks about you two."

I thought about Mom's warm acceptance, how she'd welcomed Floris into our home without hesitation. "She does seem to like him."

"Because she sees how good he is for you." Tia squeezed my hand. "And because she's not stuck in the past like Uncle Bill.

She wants you to live your life, not spend it trying to make up for something that wasn't your fault."

The words hit home, echoing what Floris had been trying to tell me all along. "I miss him," I admitted quietly. "More than I thought possible."

"Then call him." Tia picked up my phone from where I had put it down next to me and held it out. "Right now."

"It's after 11 p.m. there."

"So? He won't mind if it's you."

The simple truth of her words made my chest tight. I took the phone, staring at it for a long moment before hitting the call button. It rang a few times before Floris's voice came through, warm and familiar. "Orson?"

Just hearing him made something in my chest unclench. "Hi. Yes, it's me."

The background noise on his end quieted, like he was moving somewhere private. "Is everything okay, *lieverd*?"

"I just..." I swallowed hard. "I needed to hear your voice."

There was a pause, then softly: "God, I miss you too."

"Today's been rough," I admitted, aware of Tia still sitting beside me but needing to get the words out. "My Uncle Bill is here, and he looks so much like Dad, and then Tia accidentally told everyone about us, and—"

"Breathe, *lieverd*," Floris interrupted gently. "Start from the beginning."

I took a shaky breath, letting his voice ground me. "My uncle, my dad's brother, he always pushes about following in Dad's footsteps, about living up to his sacrifice. And then Tia mentioned you, trying to change the subject, and he... he said some things."

"What kinds of things?" Floris's voice had taken on that protective edge I'd come to recognize.

"That I don't belong in your world. That I'm getting distracted from what matters, from what Dad died for." My voice cracked slightly. "That you'll get bored eventually and—"

"Stop." The word was firm but gentle. "First of all, you belong wherever you want to belong. Second, you're not getting distracted. You're the most focused, dedicated person I know. And third..." His voice softened. "I could never get bored of you, Orson Ritchey. You fascinate me more every day."

Warmth spread through my chest, and beside me, Tia made a quiet "aww" sound. I'd forgotten she could hear his side of the conversation.

"I'm..." I struggled to find the right words. "Sometimes, I feel like I'm betraying Dad by wanting something for myself. By wanting you."

"Oh, *lieverd*, your father didn't die so you could spend your life feeling guilty for surviving. He died so you could live. Really live, not just exist."

"That's almost exactly what Tia told me."

"Smart girl," Floris said, and I could hear the smile in his voice. "She's right, you know. And from everything you've told me about your dad, everything your mom has said, he would want you to be happy."

"But what if..." I trailed off, the words sticking in my throat.

"What if what?" Floris prompted gently.

"What if I'm not enough?" The fear that had been lurking beneath everything else finally surfaced. "What if Uncle Bill is right and I can't handle your world? I'm just... me. Some ordinary kid from New Orleans who's terrified of messing up."

"Just you?" Floris's voice was soft but intense. "Orson, you're brilliant and kind and so much stronger than you know. You survived something terrible and turned it into motivation to help others. You see beauty in old buildings that most people would walk right past. You notice details others miss, you care about things deeply, and you make me want to be better just by being you."

Tears pricked at my eyes, and Tia squeezed my hand. "But the press..."

"That will be a challenge. I won't lie about that. But we can face it together, if you want to. And if you don't..." His voice caught slightly. "If it's too much, I'll understand. But please don't let your uncle's words make this decision for you."

I thought about how it felt to be with Floris, the way he made me laugh, how he understood my need for order but gently pushed me to loosen up sometimes, how he looked at me like I was something precious. "I want to. Face it together, I mean. You're worth it."

His exhale was shaky.

I smiled, even though he couldn't see it. "Though I reserve the right to freak out about it later."

His laugh was warm, familiar. "Deal. And Orson?"

"Hmm?"

"I..." He paused, and I could almost see him running a hand through his hair the way he did when nervous. "I love you."

My heart stopped, then started racing. Beside me, Tia squeaked and clasped her hands over her mouth.

"You don't have to say it back," Floris added quickly. "But after everything that happened today, I needed to say it."

My heart pounded against my ribs as Floris's words echoed in my ears. *I love you.* Three simple words that somehow held the weight of everything I'd been afraid to want. "I love you too," I said softly, the words feeling both terrifying and absolutely right. "God, Floris, I love you so much, it scares me sometimes."

His breath caught audibly. "Yeah?"

"Yeah." I smiled, ignoring Tia's flapping hands beside me.

"And not because you're a prince or despite it. I love you because you're you. Because you drag me away from my books when I need it, and you make terrible jokes to get me to smile, and you understand parts of me I barely comprehend myself."

"Orson..." His voice was thick with emotion. "You can't say things like that when I'm an ocean away and can't kiss you."

Heat crept up my neck. "Sorry?"

"No, you're not." He laughed softly. "God, I wish I was there right now."

"Me too." I leaned back against the porch step, looking up at the stars. "Though maybe it's better you're not. You might've punched my uncle."

"Don't tempt me." His tone was only half-joking. "No one gets to make you feel less than amazing. Not even family."

Warmth spread through my chest at his protectiveness. "Mom's handling that part. I could hear her yelling at him when I left."

"Good. I knew I liked your mom." There was a pause, then: "My parents want to meet you, by the way. When you're ready."

My stomach did a nervous flip. "Your parents? As in, the sister and brother-in-law of King Friso of the Netherlands?"

I'd done some research, not wanting to be completely ignorant about his background.

"No, my other parents," he teased. "The ones who run the local cheese shop."

"Shut up." But I was smiling despite my anxiety. "That's... that's kind of terrifying, actually."

"They'll love you," he said with such certainty that I almost believed him. "I may have talked about you. A lot."

"Yeah?"

"To the point where my brother threatened to throttle me if I didn't stop talking about your brilliant mind and adorable curls." His voice was warm with affection. "His exact words were: 'We get it, he's perfect, now please shut up about his eyes.'"

Despite my lingering anxiety, I laughed. "You did not talk about my eyes."

"I absolutely did. At length. Multiple times. They're very distracting, you know. Especially when you're explaining something you're passionate about and they get all bright and intense."

As his quiet laugh filled the darkness, I realized something profound: for the first time since that day on the roof, I wasn't trying to calculate every possible outcome. I was letting myself *feel*. And somehow, that felt like the bravest thing I'd ever done.

23

FLORIS

I couldn't sit still. Not after that phone call. Not after hearing those three words from Orson's lips, words I'd been dying to hear but hadn't dared hope for. The need to see him, to hold him, to kiss him senseless, was overwhelming.

"You're being ridiculous," Laurens said, watching me pace around my room. "It's the day after Christmas. Every flight will be packed."

"I don't care." I grabbed my phone, already pulling up airline websites. "I'll sit in the cargo hold if I have to. I mean, I've survived the dorm washing machines. Pretty sure I can handle being shipped as oversized luggage."

"The press will notice."

"I'll try to keep a low profile, but yes, they may, though it will take them a while to figure out why I'm heading to New Orleans specifically. And as long as we're careful once I'm there, they shouldn't be able to spot me with him." I looked up at my brother, knowing my expression was probably a bit wild. "But at some point, they're gonna find out. I love him, Laurens. And he loves me back."

"You'll have to prepare him."

"I will, but he knows. I've never kept this from him... and he still chose to get involved with me, for reasons passing all understanding."

Laurens tried to maintain his serious expression, but I caught the twitch of his lips. "You're impossible."

"Impossibly charming, you mean." I ran a hand through my hair, probably making it stand up in all directions. "His uncle said some awful things to him yesterday. About how he doesn't belong in my world, how he's betraying his father's memory by being with me. And all I could think was how wrong that was, how perfect he is, how much I needed to be there and tell him that in person. I need to do this, need to see him."

My brother studied me for a long moment, then pulled out his own phone. "I'll call our travel planner. She might be able to find you a first-class seat somewhere."

"Really?" I stopped pacing. "You're going to help?"

"Of course I am." He smiled. "Someone has to make sure you don't end up actually trying to sneak into the cargo hold."

Two hours later, I was in a car heading to Schiphol Airport, a hastily packed bag beside me. Laurens had worked miracles and found me a first-class ticket to New Orleans with only one short layover, in New York. I caught up on some reading on the flight to New York, and later on, messaged with Orson as he woke up. I hadn't told him I was coming, wanting to surprise him, though I'd texted his mom to make sure he'd be home. Diana had responded enthusiastically, even offering to pick me up from the airport, but I'd insisted on getting an Uber. She was already doing me a huge favor by keeping my arrival a secret from Orson.

Luckily, one of the privileges I had as a member of the Dutch royal family was a diplomatic passport, which meant I didn't have to go through the usual long line at border patrol everyone else was subjected to. I made my connecting flight with ease, getting a nap in on the last leg, so I would at least arrive somewhat fresh.

I caught some people snapping pictures of me, both at Schiphol Airport and at JFK, but they all looked like Dutch tourists, not press or paparazzi. Hopefully, it would take a while before those pics made their way to the internet.

The New Orleans air hit me with an unexpected chill as I stepped out of Louis Armstrong International Airport. Even in December, the city rarely got truly cold, I had learned from previous research, but today was an exception. The forecasted temperature was barely above freezing. At least the humidity was taking a break, giving my hair a temporary reprieve from its usual rebellion against gravity.

The Uber ride to their house felt simultaneously too long and too short. The driver seemed to sense I wasn't in the mood for conversation and put on some Louis Armstrong, which seemed fitting. My heart raced with anticipation, my palms sweaty. What if this was too much, too soon? What if showing up unannounced was crossing a line?

But then I remembered his voice on the phone yesterday, the way he'd said, "I love you too," like the words were being pulled from somewhere deep inside him, and all doubt vanished. This was exactly where I needed to be.

The Uber pulled up to the familiar yellow house, Christmas lights twinkling along the porch railings. I grabbed my bag, thanked the driver, and took a deep breath before walking up to the door.

Diana opened it before I could knock, pulling me into a warm hug. "You wonderful boy," she whispered. "He's going to be so happy to see you."

"Where is he?" I asked, suddenly nervous.

"In his room, studying of course." She rolled her eyes fondly. "Some things never change. Go on up."

I took the stairs as quietly as possible, my heart pounding against my ribs. The door to Orson's room was partially open, and I could see him sitting at his desk, wild curls falling over his forehead as he bent over what looked like a textbook. The sight made my chest tight with emotion.

God, I loved him. Every careful, brilliant, overthinking inch of him.

I knocked softly on the doorframe. "So this is what civil engineers do on their Christmas break? Study more?"

Orson's head snapped up, his eyes widening behind his glasses. "Floris?" Orson stared at me like he couldn't quite believe what he was seeing. "How... What are you..."

"Surprise?" I managed, drinking in the sight of him. His hair was even wilder than usual, like he'd been running his hands through it while studying. He wore that soft, green sweater I loved, the one that brought out the gold flecks in his eyes, and his glasses were slightly askew in that way that always made me want to reach out and straighten them.

He stood up so quickly, his chair nearly toppled over. "You're here. You're actually here."

"I couldn't stay away." I stepped into the room, letting my bag drop to the floor. "Not after yesterday. Not after what you said."

"What I..." His eyes widened as understanding dawned. "You flew all the way here because I said I love you?"

"Because you said you love me, because your uncle was an ass, because I needed to see you." I moved closer, drawn to him like gravity. "Because I love you too, and saying it over the phone wasn't enough."

Orson made a soft sound, something between a laugh and a

sob, and then he was moving too, meeting me halfway. His hands came up to frame my face as our lips met, and everything else fell away: the journey, the press, the complications. None of it mattered except this, except us.

I pulled him closer, one hand tangling in those wild curls while the other wrapped around his waist. He tasted like coffee and something sweet, probably the remains of Christmas cookies, and his body fit against mine like it was made to be there.

When we finally broke apart, both breathing heavily, I rested my forehead against his.

"Hi," I whispered.

He laughed, the sound warm and real. "Hi yourself. I can't believe you're actually here."

"Where else would I be?" I brushed a curl from his forehead, savoring the ability to touch him again. "The second you told me you loved me, staying away became impossible."

His eyes searched my face, those beautiful, brown depths full of emotion. "But the press... Won't they notice?"

"They might, yes."

"And you're okay with that?" Orson's hands tightened slightly on my shoulders. "With them finding out about us?"

"I'm more than okay with it... if you are too." I traced his cheekbone with my thumb, memorizing the way his skin flushed at my touch. "Let them see. Let them write whatever they want. You're worth any headline they could come up with."

His breath caught. "Floris..."

"I mean it." I pulled back enough to meet his eyes properly. "I'm done hiding how I feel about you. I'm done worrying about what people might say or think. I love you, Orson Ritchey, and I want the whole world to know it."

"Even if I'm not..." He swallowed hard. "Not what they expect for someone like you?"

"You're exactly what I want. Who I want." I kissed him again, soft and quick. "And anyone who can't see how amazing you are isn't worth our time."

He smiled then, that rare, unguarded smile that transformed his whole face. "Thank you."

"So you're in? You're okay with the possibility of this leaking?"

He pulled up his nose. "That makes it sound dirty."

Fair point. "With the possibility of the whole world finding out about us?"

A deep breath, a flash of panic in his eyes, and then, "Yes."

I kissed him softly on his lips. "Thank you."

"I love you," he said quietly, like he was still getting used to the words. "I really do."

"Good." I grinned, pulling him closer. "Because I flew across an ocean to hear you say that in person, and it would've been really awkward if you'd changed your mind."

That startled a laugh out of him. "You're ridiculous."

"You love it."

"God help me, I do." His fingers played with the hair at the nape of my neck, sending shivers down my spine. "But what about your family? Weren't they upset you left so soon after arriving?"

I shrugged. "My dad was a little perturbed." I was quite proud of learning that new word. "But my mom understood and my brother helped me book the ticket."

"She did?"

I brushed another wayward curl from his forehead, unable to stop touching him now that I could. "They can't wait to meet you, by the way. My mom's already planning a welcome meal for you so you can try some classic Dutch food, and my dad wants to talk water management with you. Though he might be disappointed you're not into football. Erm, soccer."

"That's..." He swallowed visibly. "Terrifying."

"They'll love you." I pulled him closer, breathing in his familiar scent. "How could they not?"

He buried his face in my neck, his arms tightening around me. "I missed you so much," he whispered. "Is that crazy? It's only been a few days."

"If it's crazy, then I'm crazy too." I pressed a kiss to his temple. "I couldn't focus on anything at home. Kept thinking about you, wondering what you were doing, if you were okay after everything with your uncle..."

"I'm better now." He lifted his head to meet my eyes. "Much better."

The way he looked at me, like I was something precious and wonderful, made my heart skip. I kissed him then, unable to help myself. He melted into it, and for several long moments, the world narrowed to this, to us: the warmth of his lips, the way his hands slid into my hair, the soft sound he made when I pulled him closer.

But then my exhaustion hit, and I yawned in the middle of the kiss, making Orson giggle.

"Sorry," I mumbled against his lips. "Long day."

"When did you last sleep properly?" His hands moved to frame my face, thumbs brushing my cheekbones. Those engineer's eyes were analyzing me now, probably calculating my exact level of exhaustion based on some complex formula.

"Uh..." I tried to remember. "I got a nap on the plane?"

He shook his head, fond exasperation written across his features. "Come on." He tugged me toward his bed. "You need rest."

"But I just got here," I protested, even as another yawn escaped. "I want to spend time with you."

"I'm not going anywhere." He pushed me gently onto the bed, then bent to untie my shoes. "And you'll be much better company after some sleep."

I watched him, my heart so full, it felt like it might burst. This careful attention to detail, this way he had of taking care of me without making a big deal of it—it was so perfectly, uniquely Orson.

"Will you stay?" I caught his hand as he straightened up. "Lie here with me for a while?"

His expression softened. "Of course."

We arranged ourselves on his narrow bed, me on my back with Orson curled against my side, his head on my chest. One of his hands played absently with the buttons on my shirt while I ran my fingers through his wild curls.

"This is nice," I murmured, already feeling sleep tugging at me. "Missed this."

I felt rather than saw his smile. "Me too."

"Love you," I managed through another yawn. "So much."

His arm tightened around my waist. "I love you too. Now sleep."

So I did, surrounded by his warmth and his scent and the steady sound of his breathing. The last thing I registered before drifting off was his soft kiss against my jaw and his whispered, "Thank you for coming."

24

ORSON

Professor Dunant was droning on about wastewater management and pollution control, but I couldn't possibly be less interested. Classes had started again after Christmas break, and Floris and I were back in Massachusetts after the most amazing week ever. We'd spent literally ever minute together and while Tia had labeled us nauseatingly happy and had begged to hold off on the PDAs, I had loved every second of it.

I still couldn't believe Floris had flown to New Orleans for me. We'd explored more of the city together, him dragging me away from my books to show him my favorite spots. He'd listened with genuine interest as I explained the architectural significance of various buildings, asked intelligent questions about restoration techniques, and somehow made me feel like my passion for historical preservation was something to celebrate rather than hide.

The memory of his face lighting up when I'd shown him the hidden courtyard of the Hermann-Grima House, one of the city's best-preserved examples of Federal style architecture, made me smile. He'd been fascinated by the original slave quarters that had been preserved and turned into an educational exhibit, asking thoughtful questions about how we could honor history while acknowledging its darker aspects.

"Mr. Ritchey?"

I snapped back to attention, heat creeping up my neck as I realized Professor Dunant was waiting for an answer to a question I hadn't heard. "I'm sorry, could you repeat that?"

She raised an eyebrow but repeated her question about filtration systems. I managed to answer correctly, though my mind immediately wandered back to Floris as soon as she moved on. God, I was happy. Happier than I had ever thought possible, even with the looming threat of press discovery hanging over us. The royal family had a whole PR team, which didn't surprise me, and Margriet, their spokesperson, had released a statement to the Dutch press when they enquired about Floris being on a flight to the US the day after Christmas. She'd told them he was visiting a friend on a private visit, which was true, I supposed. It had bought us some time, but it wouldn't last.

I had spent a couple of hours with her via Zoom for a basic press training. When she had asked me if I had a preferred side I wanted to be photographed on, I'd burst out laughing until I realized she'd been deadly serious. God help me. Both my sides were equally disastrous, though Floris had argued they were equally cute. He *so* needed glasses.

We'd gone over possible questions the press or the paparazzi could ask and how to respond. "No comment" was perfectly fine, Margriet had assured me, which was a relief. I had a suspicion I'd be using that one a lot. She'd told me never to respond to rude comments or questions, online or in person, to put all my social media—which consisted of a Facebook account I hadn't looked at in ages and my LinkedIn—on private, and when responding, never to automatically accept the premise of the question. That last one was still hard for me to wrap my head around, but I'd find out soon enough, I feared.

Much more pleasant, though terrifying initially, had been meeting Floris's parents and brother via Zoom. I'd stumbled and stuttered, but they'd been so kind and nice, truly making me feel welcome. Laurens had shared some embarrassing childhood stories of Floris.

I smiled, remembering how Floris had tried to tackle his brother through the screen when Laurens started telling the story about Floris, influenced by Prince Tore, trying to convince the palace guards he could speak to ducks.

His parents had been nothing like I'd expected royalty to be: warm, funny, and genuinely interested in my studies. His father had gotten particularly excited when I mentioned my interest in historical preservation, launching into a passionate discussion about maintaining centuries-old palace architecture while meeting modern safety standards.

As if he'd known I was thinking about him, Floris texted me.

FLORIS

Save me from this endless lecture about soil composition. I'm dying of boredom.

ME

Pay attention. You'll need this for the exam.

FLORIS

But thinking about you is so much more interesting. Did you know you scrunch your nose when you're concentrating? It's adorable.

Heat crept up my neck, and I glanced around automatically, though of course no one was paying any attention to me.

ME

I do not scrunch my nose.

FLORIS

You absolutely do. I have photographic
evidence.

ME

When did you take pictures of me studying??

FLORIS

I plead the fifth. That's the right amendment,
yes? I've been practicing my American rights.

I muffled a snort.

"Mr. Ritchey, perhaps you'd like to share what's so amusing
about bacterial load in treatment facilities?"

Professor Dunant's voice cut through my amusement. This
time, several students turned to look at me, and I sank lower in
my seat.

"Sorry, Professor," I mumbled, forcing myself to focus on my
notes.

The rest of class passed in a blur of technical terms and
diagrams, though I managed to keep my mind from wandering
too obviously. When we were finally dismissed, I packed up
quickly, eager to get back to our room. Floris had a later class
today, and I wanted to finish some reading before he returned
and inevitably distracted me with his presence.

As soon as I stepped outside, someone yelled, "There he is!"

I blinked, then froze to the spot as photographers came
running, their cameras and cell phones clicking away. A micro-
phone was shoved into my face. "Is it true you're dating Prince
Floris from The Netherlands?"

Panic seized my chest as more reporters converged, their
questions overlapping in a cacophony of demands.

"How long have you been together?"

"Did you know he was a prince when you met?"

"What does your family think about the relationship?"

The training with Margriet kicked in through my rising anxiety. *Don't engage with rude questions. You can always say "No comment". Never accept the premise of a hostile question.*

"No comment," I managed. My hands were shaking as I clutched my backpack straps.

"Is it true you're only dating him for his money?"

That one stung, but I kept my face neutral, remembering Margriet's warnings about showing reaction. *Just keep walking. Don't engage.*

Suddenly, a tall, blond guy popped up next to me. "Members of the press, keep your distance, please," he called out to the press, putting his arm at an angle to physically shield me. They backed off a little, giving me enough space to keep walking. He continued to shield me, guiding my steps when I stumbled.

I'd never been more grateful in my life for someone stepping in to help me, but who was he? He was clearly American, judging by his accent, but too old to be a student. Once we were inside Smelter Hall, I came to a stop, shaking from the experience.

"Are you alright?" the stranger asked, his professional demeanor softening with genuine concern.

I nodded, though my hands were still trembling. "Thank you for..." I gestured vaguely at the door, beyond which I could still hear voices and camera shutters. "Who are you?"

"Nathan DeVos. I'm part of your security detail." He showed me an ID card that looked official. "Prince Floris hired us to keep an eye on things, especially you."

"He what?" I blinked, trying to process this information. "When did he...?"

"After Christmas. He was concerned the press might find you before you were ready." Nathan's expression was sympathetic. "Looks like he was right to worry."

Warmth bloomed in my chest as I realized what this meant. Floris had anticipated this, had taken steps to protect me without making me feel smothered or controlled. He'd known I'd need help but had arranged it quietly, letting me maintain my independence until it was necessary.

"Does he know?" I asked, pulling out my phone. "About the press being here?"

"He's been notified. He's on his way back now." Nathan glanced at his watch. "Campus police has also been alerted. They'll help keep the press off college grounds."

Wow, Nathan was towering over me even more than Floris did. And the dude was ripped. Strong arms, big chest, and a tight stomach that had to be a six-pack under his black shirt. He was wearing cargo pants and what looked to be combat boots. This was definitely a guy you wanted to be on your side.

My phone buzzed with an incoming call from Floris.

"Hey," I answered, my voice shakier than I'd like.

"*Lieverd.*" The familiar endearment made my chest tight. "Are you okay? Nathan said they ambushed you outside class."

"I'm fine." I swallowed hard. "A little overwhelmed."

"I'm five minutes away. Stay inside with Nathan, okay? I'm so sorry, Orson. I thought we'd have more time before they found us."

"It's not your fault." I leaned against the wall, suddenly exhausted. "Though I wish I'd worn a better shirt for my first paparazzi photos."

His laugh was relieved. "Trust you to worry about your outfit at a time like this."

"Well, someone in this relationship has to care about fashion, and we both know it's not you."

"Hey!" Floris's mock-offended tone made me smile despite everything. "I'll have you know my fashion choices are perfectly fine. Hold on, I see the crowd. Be there in two minutes."

True to his word, Floris appeared moments later, slightly out of breath like he'd run across campus. His eyes found mine immediately, and the concern in them made my heart flip.

"Are you really okay?" he asked, crossing to me in three long strides.

"I am now." I let him pull me into a hug, breathing in his familiar scent. "Though I think I understand why you were so worried about the press finding us."

His arms tightened around me. "They can be overwhelming. But Nathan's team will help keep them at a distance, and I had a meeting with the Dean and the head of the campus police a few days ago, and they agreed to ban them from campus grounds."

I pulled back enough to look at him. "You really thought of everything, didn't you?"

"I tried." His hand came up to cup my cheek. "I wanted you to be protected, but I also didn't want to make you feel suffocated or controlled. It's a delicate balance."

"Thank you." I leaned into his touch. "For thinking of me, for arranging protection without making me feel like I needed a babysitter."

His smile was soft. "Always."

"So what's next? Will we have to wait until they disappear?"

"Margriet thinks the best approach is to give a brief statement and then make it clear we're not available for any other interviews."

"Statement? You mean t-talk to them?"

He squeezed my hand. "I will do it, but it would mean a lot to have you by my side."

Standing next to him, that I could do. "Okay."

Floris checked his watch. "It's 2 p.m. Why don't we call it for five? That should give them enough time to set up and give us the opportunity to prepare."

I nodded bravely. "Sounds good."

It sounded absolutely awful, but what choice did I have? Being with Floris meant dealing with this, so I would learn to suck it up.

We used the break to shower, change into something respectable—Floris's words—and go over the statement. Floris had written something, and we called his dad first to get his thoughts, then Margriet to secure her approval. Meanwhile, the Dean's office had allowed us to use the chapel for the press conference, which I thought was somewhat fitting for the announcement of a relationship.

That was probably why I was humming as we made our way over there, flanked by Nathan and another guy named Tim, who was Floris's security detail. Tim wasn't as tall as Nathan, but he made that up by being even more intimidating.

"What are you humming?" Floris asked as we walked across the commons, my hand clamped in his. "It sounds familiar but I can't place it."

"It's stupid."

"Now I'm even more curious."

"The word chapel triggered it. The song is called 'Chapel of Love' and it talks about going to the chapel to get married."

Floris snorted. "Don't you think that's a little soon?"

Heat flooded my face. "I wasn't suggesting... I just..."

"Relax, *lieverd*. I'm teasing." He squeezed my hand. "Though you're adorable when you blush."

"Shut up," I muttered, but I couldn't help smiling. Even with my anxiety about facing the press, Floris had this way of making everything feel manageable.

The chapel came into view, a beautiful Gothic Revival building with tall spires reaching toward the winter sky. A crowd had already gathered outside, cameras and microphones at the ready. My steps faltered slightly.

"Hey." Floris stopped, turning to face me. "We don't have to do this if you're not ready."

I took a deep breath, drawing strength from his steady presence. "No, I want to. They're going to be part of our lives no matter what. Better to face them on our terms."

His smile was proud and tender. "Have I told you lately how much I love you?"

"You might have mentioned it once or twice." I straightened my shoulders, adjusting my glasses. "Let's do this."

Nathan and Tim moved ahead of us, creating a path through the press. Cameras clicked rapidly as we approached, but the security team kept the reporters at a respectful distance. Floris's hand was warm and steady in mine as we reached the chapel steps.

This was it. Time to face our new reality together.

Oh god, the number of reporters and photographers had tripled, and they were now joined by several people with cameras. Like, TV cameras. Thank god I didn't have to do anything. My hand was sweaty in Floris's as we walked to the front of the room, where Floris let go of my hand and took place behind a lectern.

"Good evening, everyone," he said, sounding as calm as if he was talking to a friend. "We have a brief statement to make." He raised his chin. "My name is Prince Floris Willem Maurits van Oranje Nassau, and I'm a nephew of King Friso of the Netherlands. I have been attending Vernon Technical College since August of last year as part of my degree in civil engineering, and so far, it has been an enjoyable and enriching experience. I'm deeply grateful to Dean Carlotta, the staff of VTC, and the campus police for allowing me to fly under the radar and get to experience real life as a college student. That's a gift I will always cherish."

He then looked at me, and I stepped forward and took his hand.

"I'm even more grateful that I have met Orson Ritchey, a civil engineering student from New Orleans, who has helped me settle in and find my way. He has made my life better in countless ways, and I'm proud to have him by my side... as my boyfriend."

That last word triggered a furious round of photos, the incessant shutters sounding like gun shots. I winced, holding on to him a little tighter.

"While I have always been in the public eye as part of the Dutch royal family, Orson and his family are not used to this media attention. I ask for your understanding and your compassion and kindness as he adjusts to life in the spotlight." He blew out a breath. "I will now answer a few questions."

My heart nearly stopped. Questions? We hadn't discussed taking questions. I squeezed Floris's hand, probably harder than I should have, but he squeezed back reassuringly.

"Your Highness!" Several reporters called out at once, hands shooting up like eager students in class. Floris pointed to a woman in the front row.

"How long have you been together?"

"We became friends shortly after the semester started, and our relationship developed naturally from there." Floris's voice was steady, professional.

"Mr. Ritchey!" Another reporter called out. "How did you feel when you discovered Prince Floris's true identity?"

I froze, but Floris spoke before I could panic. "Orson isn't answering questions today, but I will say that he's known who I am from the start."

The reporters seemed to multiply before my eyes, their voices overlapping as they called out questions. Floris handled them with practiced ease, deflecting the more personal ones and answering others with diplomatic skill that would've impressed his etiquette instructors.

"What does your family think of the relationship?"

"My family is very supportive," Floris said, and I heard the genuine warmth in his voice. "They're looking forward to meeting Orson in person."

"And what about the British tabloids' claims about your past—"

"We're not here to discuss past media fabrications," Floris cut in smoothly, his tone cooling several degrees. "I think we've taken enough questions for today. Thank you all for coming."

Nathan and Tim moved forward immediately, creating a barrier between us and the press as we made our way back through the chapel. The reporters called out more questions, but they seemed distant now, like background noise.

Once we were safely back in our room, I collapsed onto my bed, my legs feeling like jelly. "That was..."

"Intense?" Floris sat beside me, pulling me close. "You did great, though. Very stoic and dignified."

"I didn't do anything except stand there trying not to throw up."

"Which was exactly what you needed to do." He pressed a kiss to my temple. "I'm proud of you."

I turned to look at him properly. "Is it always going to be like this?"

He hesitated. "Always? No, but for the first few months, yes. After that, it'll be old news and things will calm down significantly."

I leaned my head against his shoulder, processing this new reality. "Months of this?"

"It'll get easier," Floris promised, his fingers tracing soothing patterns on my arm. "And we have security now, plus the campus police will keep them off college grounds. They'll have to lurk at a distance like the creepy stalkers they are."

Despite my anxiety, I snorted. "Very diplomatic of you."

"I save my diplomacy for press conferences." He pulled me closer. "With you, I can just be me. The me who thinks paparazzi are basically legally sanctioned stalkers with expensive cameras."

"And who apparently arranges security without telling me." I poked his side gently. "When were you going to mention Nathan and Tim?"

He had the grace to look sheepish. "I was waiting for the right moment? I didn't want you to feel handled. Or like I was making decisions for you."

"Hey." I shifted to face him properly. "I know why you did it. And I'm grateful. I can't imagine facing that crowd without Nathan there to help."

Relief flickered across his features. "Yeah?"

"Yeah." I kissed him softly. "Thank you for looking out for me while still letting me handle things my way."

We sat in comfortable silence for a while, the events of the day settling around us like dust after a storm.

"You were amazing today," Floris murmured into my hair, his fingers tracing lazy patterns on my back. "I know it wasn't easy, but you handled it perfectly. Though I still think we should've gone with my suggestion of announcing our relationship via interpretive dance."

I snorted against his chest, grateful for his ability to make me laugh even after the most stressful moments. "Maybe next time," I said, snuggling closer. "For now, can we stay here like this?"

"As long as you want, *lieverd*," he replied softly. "As long as you want."

25

ORSON

Snow whirled past the windows like it was running from something. It kept coming and coming, piling up so high that Floris figured it would reach the second story by morning.

At least it gave us a good excuse to hole up into our room. True to their promise, campus police had kept the press off campus. Well, for the most part anyway. Apparently, some paparazzi had still managed to get some shots of us, walking back after dinner. We'd both been bundled up against the cold, holding hands with gloves on, so it hadn't exactly been the most flattering shot, but whatever.

Nathan and Tim were still next door to us in a dorm room, following us wherever we went. I'd grown used to having Nathan shadow me. He had a dry sense of humor and knew when to cheer me up with a good joke. Also, he was gay, which had been a big shock. And even more shocking: he and Tim were together. Floris had joked they probably hoped this detail would last a long time because it gave them a chance to be together. But we probably wouldn't need them for much longer, since everything had quieted down.

Because of the storm, classes were canceled today, so we were staying inside. I was on my back, my neck propped on the edge of my bed and my fluid mechanics book open on my stomach.

"We're trapped," Floris declared with his usual flair for drama after getting up once more to check on the snow levels outside. "Snowed in... with only one bed."

I snorted. "Do we need to go over kindergarten math again? Because I'm pretty sure we have two beds in here."

He gave me a dismissive wave. "Work with me here. Only one bed sounds much more romantic. Especially when you're stuck with the actual Prince Charming."

"Prince Charming? I had no idea. I didn't sign up for that..."

"It's in the small print. You should always read the small print."

"Does this Prince Charming come with a money-back guarantee if I'm not fully satisfied?"

He put his hands on his hips. "Are you saying you're not fully satisfied?"

I pretended to think about it, so he mimicked an arrow to the heart.

"Maybe you should try again," I suggested. "So I can do a thorough evaluation of your skills and my satisfaction with said skills."

He was still laughing when he all but jumped on top of me. My book slid to the floor as he kissed me slow and long, grinning when he finally pulled back. My insides knotted up. How was this real? How did I have this amazing man, an actual prince, in my room, in my bed?

His hair fell over his forehead, and I brushed it away so I could see his face, the impossible green of his eyes, that princely gleam in them. "How was that?" he asked, as if he didn't already know the answer.

"Not bad. Though maybe I need a longer sample to judge more adequately."

"I aim to please." He moved back in again, his lips on my neck, my cheek, my mouth again, soft and hard and everything between. "And the good news is that this Prince Charming comes with a lifetime warranty."

I snickered as he kissed me again, but then his tongue slipped into my mouth and my laugh became a moan. It wasn't long before I forgot about finals and the storm, before all I could focus on was the warmth of him pressed into me and how perfectly we fit, like a hand finding a glove it never wanted to take off.

I slid my hands up his back and pulled him into me, his kiss deepening, our bodies locked tight. His lips tasted like forever, and I was greedy for more, for everything. We'd been in a sex haze for weeks, going as far as hands and mouths would take us, but he wanted all of me and I was finally ready. The whole thing was building up in my chest, wanting to spill out between kisses. When I couldn't hold it back anymore, I pulled my face away just enough to breathe, just enough to tell him, "I want you to fuck me."

His eyes went wide with delight. "You're sure?"

"Yes. I'm ready for it. I want all of you."

He took my hand, squeezed it in his, then pressed it to his chest like he was making a vow. "I'm gonna make you feel so good."

I laughed, nervous and not. "It might be overwhelming for me."

"You say that like it's a problem."

"It means I won't be able to do much for you," I warned.

"I'll probably come as soon as I'm inside you." He laughed back and sealed it with a kiss that took all the worry and the nerves away.

He sat up, his thighs on either side of me. "We should get the mood right. Nothing says romance like fluorescent lights and the hammering sounds of the ancient heating system."

Before I could even respond, he rolled off me and reached for his phone. He connected it to the Bluetooth speaker he had, then put on some mellow jazz. The overhead light came off and instead, he turned on the little bedside lamp. "There." He nodded, satisfied. "Much better."

Him going through that trouble made me all soft and gooey inside.

He got on top of me and kissed me again. His tongue was gentle and deep, and his breath made the blood rush to my skin, to my head, everywhere. We both knew what was coming and neither of us wanted to rush it, so we took our time. Every kiss lasted a hundred years. Every time he pulled away, we smiled like idiots until the pull got too strong and we had to find each other again. We were pressed together so close, my heart beating fast enough to know it was love and nothing less.

I let myself go soft in his arms. The tension, the anticipation, it all dissolved with every slow kiss. He put his hand on my chest, moving it under the edge of my hoodie and then slowly up to my throat, pulling the fabric with him. I shivered at the thrill of it and sat up enough to let him tug it off.

He moved lower, kissing down my neck and across my shoulder. I wrapped my arms around him, dug my fingers in his shirt and felt the warmth of his skin through it. We were a mess of limbs and hands and mouths, all of it perfect and easy. We broke apart just enough for him to pull my T-shirt off, my skin flushed against the cool air. He didn't let the cold get far. His lips and his hands found all of me, kept me warm and burning for him.

He kissed a trail across my chest, my stomach, everything between, each kiss getting my blood moving hotter, my pulse racing faster. He dragged his mouth back up to mine, took it sweet and deep before moving down my arms. Every kiss made me crazy. My brain was melting into bliss and he hadn't even gotten to the hard part yet. I wanted him. I wanted everything.

"Floris…" His name was on my lips, in my heart all the time now, like an incantation, almost.

He pulled his own shirt off, the flex and pull of his muscles making my head spin. His tattoo wrapped around his arm, the colors stark against his skin, and I loved that I was one of the few people who got to see them. I loved that I got to see all of him. He tossed the shirt aside, then went for his pants, shucking them off before taking me back in his arms.

It was the kind of touch you dream about. The kind you can't believe is happening, like waking up to fireworks and Christmas morning. He moved over me, his skin sliding against mine, his hands gripping my sides, his weight pushing me into the mattress. He kissed me like he needed me, like I was air and water and the only thing in the world.

I couldn't be shy anymore. I reached down and tugged at my waistband, pulled my sweats off while he watched, those green eyes glued to me like I was a present he never expected, never wanted to stop unwrapping.

His hands traced my hip bones and moved lower, taking a hold of my cock and pumping it slow and steady. I groaned and gripped his back, explored his arms, his shoulders, loving the way his biceps felt under my fingers, loving the way all of him felt. I appreciated the curves of him, the lines of his ribs, the smooth heat of his stomach. The round of his ass. He groaned into my mouth when I cupped it, kissing me with a hunger that sent my brain reeling.

I was rock hard, so turned on, I could hardly see straight. He ran his thumb across my tip and wiped the wetness up my cock, stroking harder, making me want to burst. "Are you sure you're ready?" His voice was all smoke and honey, music still playing low in the background.

"Yes," I panted. "Please, Floris."

His touch slowed down. "It might hurt at first," he said, moving his hand lower, teasing me until my head spun. "I don't want you to—"

"I want it."

He took a bottle of lube from the shelf above the bed. I knew what was coming and I wanted it, all of it, more than anything.

"You tell me if it's too much, okay?" He drizzled some on his fingers, then slicked his cock. No condom was needed. We'd both gotten tested again and everything had come back negative, as expected, so we were good to go.

"I will." My voice came out a little shaky, but there was nothing to be scared of. Not with him.

"I love you," he said, and I could hear how much he meant it, how deep the words came from.

Then his fingers were there, working my hole, gently pressing in until one slipped inside. I gasped, feeling tight and open all at once, loving the feel of him. He stayed like that until I adjusted, then worked it in and out until I was wordlessly begging for more. Another finger joined, my muscles stretching and clenching, relaxing around him, wanting him deeper.

How grateful I was for the anal play we'd done that had prepared me for this. I couldn't imagine taking this step without that. The sensation of his fingers inside me, as good as it felt, was still a little odd, but nowhere near as much as it had been that first time. I could thoroughly enjoy it now, getting out of my own head and instead, focusing on how amazing he made me feel.

He stretched me wide, making sure I was loose and ready. His patience was my undoing. "I love you," I said, breathing it out in shuddery bursts. "Love you. Love you."

He pushed a third finger in, and my body took it, shaking and desperate, aching for more. He hit that spot inside me that made me wild, made me crazy for all of him. I clutched his back, pulled him into me. "I want you. Please, I want you so bad."

He stroked my face, his other hand leaving my hole to line himself up. I was wound up, waiting, every nerve sparking, my skin on fire.

"You sure you're ready?"

"Please, Floris." I could hear the want in my voice, so I was pretty sure he could too.

Then he was pushing inside. It was a sweet, glorious pain, burning bright and making me gasp. He didn't move, didn't push, just held still and waited until the hurt faded, his eyes on me, gentle and steady. When it didn't hurt anymore, when the stretch of him was perfect, he moved. It felt so right and real and good that I couldn't believe we hadn't done it sooner. He filled me up like he was meant for me, built for me, his cock sliding deeper with each thrust, stretching me more and making me dizzy.

I clung to him, my hands on his shoulders, my legs wrapped around him. Our eyes held as he set a slow, sensual rhythm that sent sparks through my entire body. Delicious tendrils of pleasure spread out, burning me until everything was on fire.

This wasn't a fuck. It was more, so much more. This was making love.

His thrusts were tender and measured, never pulling too far out, never more than I could take. But I wanted all of it, and I wanted it fast. I wanted to lose myself so completely that I didn't know where I ended and he began. He gave and gave, and I still wanted more, needed him to fill me until I couldn't see straight, until it was too much for anyone else to take.

He groaned and my whole body seemed to rumble with it. Floris worked his hips, each thrust sending me higher, tighter, more breathless. He picked up the pace, driving into me with powerful, relentless strokes, and I couldn't get enough.

I clawed his back, my fingers like live wires, all of me like live wires. The wet slide of him built and built until I couldn't stand it anymore, until it was a wildness in me.

"I love you," I cried, and I did, with everything I had, with everything he gave me. It was overwhelming, and I wanted it that way.

"Gonna come, Orson." His breath was ragged, his voice shaking. "You feel too fucking good."

I reached the stars. Saw them burst behind my eyelids as I tumbled over, came harder than I ever had, gasping his name, everything exploding white-hot and dizzy.

His thrusts were messy and offbeat as he chased after me, panting my name, groaning with his last thrust. "I love you."

He buried himself as deep as I could take him and came hard, grinding into me, his whole body spasming. He collapsed on top of me and I locked my legs around him, every part of us tangled up and breathless.

We stayed like that for a long time, letting the world slowly come back into focus, everything new and different. I didn't want to let go, didn't want to untangle myself from him. I wanted to stay like this forever, wrapped up in his warmth, his smell, his everything. He was still inside me, softening slowly, and I clenched around him to feel that perfect fullness a little longer.

Floris lifted his head from where it rested on my shoulder and looked at me, his green eyes hazy and sated. "You okay?"

I nodded, not trusting my voice yet. More than okay. I felt like I'd been remade, every part of me buzzing and alive in a way I'd never known before.

He brushed his lips over mine, feather-light. "I didn't hurt you?"

"No," I managed. "It was intense. But good intense."

He propped himself up on his elbows to look at me, his eyes bright, his hair tousled and damp at the edges. "You were amazing. It felt so good being inside you like that."

I flushed at his words, at the intimacy and honesty of them. Being vulnerable had never been easy for me, but with him, it came naturally. "It felt right. Like we were always meant to fit together this way." I brushed my fingers through his hair. "I love you so much."

"I love you too." He shifted, pulling out of me gently and rolling onto his side. The loss of him made me ache in a strange, hollow way. But then he gathered me close, tangling our legs together under the blankets. "That was perfect. You're perfect."

I snorted. "I don't know about that."

"Hmm, let's talk about my performance, then. Did I wholly satisfy you? Ten out of ten, would do it again?"

I laughed breathlessly. "Twelve out of ten, gold star, highly recommend. Though I might need you to keep proving yourself, just to be sure."

"Mmm, I think I can manage that." He leaned in and kissed me, soft and lingering. "Anything for my loyal subject."

"Oh, is that what I am now?" I teased. "And here I thought I was the chosen consort."

"Why not both?" He pulled me into his arms, nuzzling into my neck. "My subject, my consort, my everything."

I really liked the sound of that.

26

FLORIS

The library was so quiet, I could hear every breath from the tiny girl sitting next to me. And by tiny, I meant she made my one-meter-ninety-two frame feel like an actual giant. She couldn't have been more than a meter and a half if she stood on her tiptoes while wearing platform shoes. But what she lacked in height, she made up for in breathing volume.

Each inhale sounded like she was trying to vacuum up all the oxygen in Massachusetts. Maybe she was secretly training to be a pearl diver? Or auditioning for the role of Darth Vader in a student production?

I should focus on my textbook instead of creating elaborate theories about my neighbor's respiratory habits, but material science was significantly less entertaining than imagining her as a future deep-sea explorer. Besides, how was anyone supposed to concentrate with what sounded like a miniature steam engine running at full power right next to them?

I tried to refocus on my textbook, but the words blurred together as Tiny Vader took another dramatic breath. Maybe she was practicing for an underwater opera? That could be a thing, right? Though the logistics of singing while submerged seemed questionable at best.

God, focusing was impossible with her next to me. Orson would have no issues with it, of course. He was able to keep studying while I was naked in the room, which I did consider a bit of an insult, to be honest. But it was one of the quirks that made him so adorkable, and it was hard to be upset with him. Make that impossible.

Everything about him was adorable and sweet and perfect. How he never failed to remind me of appointments and tests I had, of due dates for papers. That he set a second alarm because he knew I often slept through the first or fell right back asleep. How he'd leave coffee on my desk during late-night study sessions without saying a word, just a quiet acknowledgment that I needed it. The way he scrunched his nose when concentrating, though he denied doing it. His wild curls that defied gravity almost as much as mine did, and how he'd absently push his glasses up when deep in thought.

Even his obsessive organization and triple-checking of calculations had become endearing to me. Because that was Orson: thorough, careful, always making sure everything was perfect. Not because anyone demanded it of him, but because that's who he was. He approached everything with that same intense focus, whether it was studying for exams or loving me. And god, did he love me well, with a depth and steadiness that made my heart ache in the best possible way.

I was happy. Happier than I had ever thought possible, and it was all because of him. Even the stress of the press coverage hadn't diminished that, though, in all fairness, the articles about us had mostly been positive.

The American media had loved it, of course, a middle-class guy attracting the attention of an actual prince. The compar-

isons with Grace Kelly had been easy to make, and Orson had
been mortified, lamenting that he didn't even possess an ounce
of her grace and anyone who expected that from him would be
highly disappointed.

The British tabloids, however, had been all too happy to use
that damn video to cast doubts about the nature of our relationship. God, would that video ever go away? It had been over a
year, and it was still haunting me.

My phone buzzed quietly, and I smiled, thinking it was
Orson. But then I saw who was calling, and my heart skipped a
beat. Margriet wouldn't call unless it was urgent, which meant
that something was wrong. I declined the call, then quickly
texted her.

> Will call you right back. Can't talk here.

I gathered my things in a rush, then rushed past Tiny Vader,
who sent me an annoyed look. Like she had any right to be
disturbed by my exit.

As soon as I was outside, I hit the call button. "What's
wrong?"

"Nothing," Margriet said quickly. "It's good news, actually,
but I did want you to see it before the press asked you about it."

"Oh?"

"Jason Heald came forward."

My heart stopped. "Jason... What?"

"He released a statement about the video. He's coming clean,
Floris. About everything."

I sank onto a nearby bench, my legs suddenly unable to hold
me. "Why now?"

"He says he couldn't stay silent anymore, not when the press
is dragging up the video again in their coverage of you and

Orson. He didn't want your new relationship tainted by those old lies."

My hands were shaking. After all this time, after the months of speculation and accusations, after I'd kept his secret even when it cost me my reputation...

"I'm sending you the link to his video statement now. Do you want me to stay on the line while you watch it?"

I swallowed hard. "No, I... I need to process this alone. But thank you."

"Call me after, okay? We'll need to prepare a response."

I nodded, then remembered she couldn't see me. "Yeah. Okay."

The link appeared in my messages as soon as we hung up. I stared at it for a long moment, my thumb hovering over the screen. Part of me wanted to ignore it, to pretend this wasn't happening. Things were so good with Orson, with my life here. Did I really want to revisit that night?

But I had to know.

The video opened on Jason's face, looking more serious than I'd ever seen him. Gone was the carefully crafted celebrity persona, replaced by something raw and vulnerable.

"I need to set the record straight," he began, his voice steady despite the obvious tension in his shoulders. "A little over a year ago, a video surfaced of Prince Floris van Oranje Nassau and me outside a London club. The media painted it as an assault, suggesting he had forced himself on me. Those accusations were completely false."

My breath caught. After all this time...

"The truth is, I wanted that kiss. I initiated it. But I was terrified of being outed, of what it would do to my career. So when the edited video appeared, I stayed silent. I let Floris take the blame rather than face my own truth."

Jason's face on my phone screen blurred as tears filled my eyes.

"Floris showed incredible integrity by refusing to out me, even when it meant enduring public criticism and judgment. He protected my secret at great personal cost, and I can never fully repay that kindness." He took a deep breath, squaring his shoulders. "But I can't stay silent anymore. Not when I see the press trying to use that incident to cast doubt on his current relationship. Prince Floris and Orson Ritchey deserve to build their life together without the shadow of my cowardice hanging over them."

My hands were shaking so badly, I could barely hold the phone. After all this time, after the headlines and whispers and sideways looks, after learning to live with people thinking the worst of me...

"I am gay," Jason continued, his voice growing stronger. "I've known it for years but was too afraid to acknowledge it publicly. That night with Floris wasn't an assault. It was a moment of courage that I immediately regretted, not because of him, but because of my own fears. He has carried the weight of my silence for far too long, and I am deeply sorry for that."

The video ended with Jason looking directly into the camera, his expression sincere. "Floris, if you're watching this, thank you. For protecting me when I couldn't protect myself, for bearing the burden of my secret with grace. You deserved better, and I hope this truth brings you some peace."

I sat there for a long moment after the video ended, tears rolling down my cheeks. All the anger and hurt I'd carried, all the times I'd wanted to scream the truth but couldn't—it was finally over. The truth was out there.

My phone buzzed again, this time with a text from Orson.

ORSON

Are you okay? I saw the video.

Of course he had. Everyone probably had by now.

ME

I don't know. Can you come find me? I'm on the bench by the library.

ORSON

On my way.

Less than two minutes later, I heard familiar footsteps approaching. I looked up to see Orson hurrying toward me, his wild curls even messier than usual, like he'd been running his hands through them in agitation. The concern in his eyes made fresh tears well up in mine.

"Hey," he said softly, sitting beside me and immediately pulling me close. "I'm here."

I buried my face in his neck, letting out a shaky breath. "It's over. After all this time, it's finally over."

His arms tightened around me. "How do you feel?"

"I don't know." I laughed wetly. "Relieved? Angry? Grateful? All of the above?" I pulled back enough to look at him. "Part of me wants to be mad at him for waiting so long, but I understand why he couldn't come out before. And the fact that he did it now, to protect us..."

"To protect you," Orson corrected gently. "He saw how much that video hurt you, how it's still affecting you even now."

I wiped at my eyes. "God, I must look a mess."

"You look perfect." He brushed away a stray tear with his thumb. "And brave. And strong. And like someone who kept another person's secret even when it cost him everything."

"Not everything." I caught his hand, pressing a kiss to his palm. "I still got you, didn't I?"

His smile was soft, understanding. "Yes, you did. Though I have to admit, seeing that video was difficult. Knowing what they said about you, how they twisted things..."

"Hey." I squeezed his hand. "That's over now. The truth is out there."

"What happens next?"

"Margriet wants to prepare a response." I sighed, leaning against him. "Something gracious and forgiving, probably. Show that there are no hard feelings."

"Are there?" Orson's voice was careful, analytical. "Hard feelings, I mean?"

I thought about it. "No," I said finally. "Not really. I wish he'd come forward sooner, but I understand why he couldn't. Coming out is personal. It has to happen on your own terms, in your own time. And as a celebrity, it's a thousand times harder. As much as people like to pretend it's okay to be gay nowadays, that's not always the case. Careers have been sunk over coming out."

"You're too forgiving," Orson said softly, but his tone was admiring rather than critical. "He let you suffer through all those accusations, all those headlines..."

"And now he's facing his own headlines." I turned to look at him properly. "Coming out is never easy, even when you're ready. Doing it like this, in such a public way, to protect someone else? That takes courage."

Orson's fingers traced patterns on my palm, a habit he'd developed when thinking deeply. "You really mean that, don't you? You're not only saying it because it's the diplomatic thing."

"I mean it." I leaned against him, drawing strength from his steady presence. "Besides, in a weird way, that video led me here. To you."

His brow furrowed adorably. "How do you figure that?"

"After everything that happened, I needed to escape. To find somewhere I could be myself, without the weight of those accusations following me around." I smiled, remembering our first meeting. "So I came here, became your roommate, and proceeded to drive you crazy with my terrible laundry habits."

That startled a laugh out of him. "You still drive me crazy with your laundry habits."

"Yeah, but now you love me anyway."

"I do." He kissed my temple softly. "So what do you want to do now?"

I pulled out my phone, looking at the missed calls from Margriet. "I should call her back, work on that statement. But first..." I opened my camera and held it up. "Smile!"

"What? No!" Orson tried to duck away, but I caught him around the waist. "I look terrible in photos!"

"You look perfect," I corrected, snapping a quick picture of us together. His wild curls tousled from the wind, his glasses slightly askew, and his cheeks pink from the cold. He looked absolutely beautiful.

I posted the photo to my official Instagram account—the one I rarely used but which had millions of followers—with a simple caption:

Truth and love win. Jason, thank you for your courage. Wishing you nothing but joy and peace as you embrace who you are. Moving forward with gratitude and joy, surrounded by love that makes everything else fade away.

Orson peered at my phone, his eyes widening. "Are you sure about this? Posting us together?"

"Absolutely." I pressed another kiss to his temple. "Let them see what real love looks like. No editing, no accusations, just us."

His smile was soft, a little shy but genuine. "You're going to make me blush in front of millions of followers."

"Good." I grinned, watching the likes and comments already pouring in. "Though I should warn you, my mom's probably going to frame this photo and hang it in the palace. She's been not-so-subtly hinting that she needs more pictures of us."

"Oh god." He buried his face in my shoulder. "Your mother, the princess, wants to frame a photo where my hair looks like I've been electrocuted?"

"Your hair always looks like that," I teased. "It's part of your charm."

"You're impossible."

"You love it."

"Yeah." He lifted his head to meet my eyes, his expression serious despite his smile. "I really do."

My phone buzzed again. It was Margriet, probably wondering why I hadn't called back yet. But for once, the press and protocols and proper statements could wait. Right now, all I wanted was this moment, with this beautiful, brilliant man who loved me not despite my complications but with all of them.

The truth was finally out there. And so were we.

EPILOGUE
ORSON—FIVE YEARS LATER

Amsterdam on King's Day was... orange. Literally everything was orange. From what people were wearing to their wigs, glasses, ties, and other crazy accessories, it was all bright orange. Even trees, bikes, cars, and the famous canal boats were decked out in orange.

"Is this normal?" I asked Floris, staring at the sea of orange surrounding us. We were about to start on a walking tour through the city center, following King Friso and Queen Annette, Floris's parents, and his cousins and brother. Apparently, there would be various activities along the way. Floris had warned me about the possibility of being asked to participate in things like dancing—lord help me—old-fashioned games, or even rope climbing. As he was far more athletic than me, I would happily leave that to him.

"For King's Day? Absolutely." Floris grinned, looking ridiculously handsome in his navy suit with an orange tie. "Orange is our national color. It represents the House of Oranje-Nassau, our royal family."

"I know that part," I said, adjusting my own orange tie for the hundredth time. Floris had insisted I wear it, claiming it was practically treason not to wear orange today. "And I thought I was prepared after seeing pictures and listening to your stories, but this seems excessive."

"Welcome to the Netherlands." He wrapped an arm around my waist, pulling me closer. "Where we're usually very sensible and down-to-earth, except for days like today, where we go completely crazy. Oh, and when the Dutch national football team plays. Or the Dutch skaters are doing well in the Olympics."

I'd visited plenty of times, of course, but never on King's Day. Our schedule had just never worked out to be present for that. And since he was only a nephew of the king and queen, his presence wasn't required. God, I couldn't imagine what it was like for his cousins.

Around us, the crowd was growing, filling the Dam Square with a sea of orange-clad revelers. Music drifted up from various street performers, mixing with the general buzz of excitement. Children ran around with orange-painted faces, while adults sported increasingly ridiculous orange outfits.

"Your people really love the monarchy, don't they?" I observed, watching the crowd's enthusiasm.

"It's complicated," Floris said thoughtfully. "The Dutch are famously direct and egalitarian. We don't do hierarchy or formality well. But the House of Oranje-Nassau has been part of our history for centuries, fighting alongside our people for independence, leading through wars and disasters. Plus," he added with a grin, "King's Day is basically a national party, and the Dutch never say no to a good party."

As if to prove his point, a group below close to us started singing what sounded like a drinking song. I couldn't understand the lyrics. My Dutch was progressing well, though it took a lot of discipline and persistence because that language was damn near impossible, but that was beyond my skill level.

"*We zijn klaar om te gaan,*" Laurens said.

We're ready to go. That was easy to understand. Floris had promised me he'd translate if needed, though the Dutch I had met so far had seemed appreciative and even charmed by my attempts to speak their language, even though I mangled the pronunciation in the most horrific way.

"Remember," Floris murmured as we fell into step behind his family, "be yourself. The Dutch appreciate authenticity more than perfection."

Easy for him to say. He wasn't the one who'd spent the last three years practicing Dutch phrases and proper royal protocol. Though I had to admit, the Dutch approach to royalty was refreshingly different from what I'd expected. King Friso had greeted me with a warm handshake and immediately insisted I call him Friso, while Queen Annette had pulled me into a hug and complimented my Dutch pronunciation, which was either very kind or very diplomatic of her, considering I still couldn't properly pronounce their harsh g without sounding like I was choking.

The procession moved through the streets, where people had set up impromptu flea markets—apparently another King's Day tradition. It was called a *vrijmarkt* or free market, the only day a year where everyone could set up a flea market anywhere in the country and not have to apply for a permit or pay taxes. Blankets and tables displayed everything from used books to vintage clothes to homemade crafts, all with that distinctly Dutch mix of practicality and whimsy.

Floris suddenly groaned beside me. "Traditional games ahead. Please tell me they didn't set up *koekhappen.*"

"What's *koekhappen*?" I asked, then immediately regretted it when his eyes lit up with mischief.

"It's where they hang pieces of *ontbijtkoek*—spiced breakfast cake—on strings, and you have to try to eat it without using your hands." He grinned. "Usually while blindfolded."

I stared at him. "You're joking."

"Nope. And as visiting royalty, we're usually expected to participate." His grin widened. "For the photographers, you know."

"No." I shook my head firmly. "Absolutely not. I draw the line at making a fool of myself in front of international media while trying to eat flying cake."

"But *lieverd*," he pouted, using that endearment that always made my heart flip, "it's tradition!"

"So is jumping off bridges in some places. Doesn't mean it's a good idea."

He laughed, the sound carrying over the crowd's noise. "Fine, I'll do it. You can watch and admire my superior cake-eating skills."

And watch I did, trying not to laugh as Floris, blindfolded and grinning, attempted to catch a swinging piece of cake with his mouth. Even King Friso joined in, to the crowd's delight, while Queen Annette watched the whole thing with an expression of fond exasperation I recognized from my own mother.

"Not as easy as it looks, is it?" Laurens said beside me, watching his brother miss the cake for the third time.

"I'm perfectly happy observing," I replied, wincing as Floris nearly got smacked in the face by the swinging treat. "Though I have to admit, it's pretty entertaining to watch."

"Just wait until they bring out the *zaklopen*."

"The what now?"

"Sack racing." Laurens grinned. "Nothing quite like watching the future of Dutch monarchy hopping around in burlap sacks."

"Please tell me you're joking."

"Nope. Though if you're lucky, they might skip it this year."

Floris finally managed to catch the cake in his mouth, raising his arms in triumph as the crowd cheered. He pulled off the blindfold, his hair adorably mussed, and immediately sought me out in the crowd. His smile when he found me was brighter than all the orange surrounding us.

"Your turn!" he called out, but I shook my head firmly.

"Not happening."

"Spoilsport." He bounded over to me, still chewing his prize. "Come on, it's fun!"

"I'll take your word for it." I reached up to brush some crumbs from his chin, the gesture automatic and intimate. A camera clicked nearby, and I froze, suddenly remembering where we were.

But Floris caught my hand and pressed a kiss to my palm, completely unbothered by the photographers. "Let them see," he said softly. "I want the world to know how happy you make me."

My heart fluttered at his words, at the open affection in his eyes. Five years into our relationship being public, and I was still getting used to moments like these, where our private happiness collided with our public life. But Floris made it easier, showing me how to navigate this strange new world with grace and humor.

"Your Highness!" a voice called out. "Would you and your fiancé participate in the traditional ring toss?"

Floris looked at me questioningly, and I nodded. Ring tossing I could handle. Probably.

"Remember," he murmured as we walked toward the game

set-up, "these photographers are Dutch. They're not looking for scandal or drama. They want to see their royals enjoying the day with everyone else."

He was right. The Dutch press had been surprisingly respectful, maintaining a polite distance and focusing more on capturing genuine moments than manufacturing controversy. It was refreshing after the chaos that had followed our initial announcement.

The ring toss turned out to be more challenging than expected, especially with Floris deliberately trying to distract me by whispering increasingly ridiculous Dutch phrases in my ear. His latest attempt—something about cheese-eating cats riding bicycles—made me laugh so hard, I completely missed the target.

"You're terrible," I told him, but I couldn't stop smiling.

"You love it."

"How do you like Amsterdam today?" a woman called out to me in Dutch.

I swallowed. "I love it. Seeing all the orange is wonderful, and everyone is so nice. I'm having fun. *Het is gezellig*," I added, and that got me a round of approval from the crowd. I'd really come to understand the meaning of that word, and I loved it, even if it was impossible to pronounce with two harsh g-sounds.

"Your accent is cute!" a teenage girl said.

Warmth spread through my chest. That was another thing I'd noticed about the Dutch; they genuinely seemed to appreciate effort, even when it came with mistakes.

"Thank you."

The day flew by, much faster than I had expected, and with much more fun and laughter than I had counted on. The Dutch had a great sense of humor. Direct to the point of insulting at times, but if you didn't take yourself too seriously, it was all good.

My favorite moment, though, was a beautiful rendition of the *Wilhelmus*, the Dutch national anthem, by a teenage girl. Her voice rang out steady and proud as she poured her heart into the solemn song. Out of habit, I put my hand on my heart, something the Dutch didn't do, though they did seem to appreciate my gesture.

By the time we were done and back home in Den Haag, where Floris had bought a house for us, I was exhausted.

"You did great today," he said as we settled on the couch with a glass of wine.

"Thanks." I leaned against him, enjoying the quiet after the chaos of the day. "Though I still can't believe you made me try that herring thing."

Floris laughed, the sound rumbling through his chest where my head rested. "Hey, you can't come to the Netherlands and not try *haring*."

"It's raw fish, Floris. Raw fish that you're supposed to dangle over your mouth like some demented seal."

"But you tried it." He pressed a kiss to my temple. "That earned you major points with the Dutch public, by the way. They love seeing foreigners embrace our traditions, even the weird ones."

I snorted. "Especially the weird ones, you mean."

We sat in comfortable silence for a while, watching the last rays of sunlight paint patterns on our living-room wall. Our living room. Sometimes it still amazed me how naturally that phrase came now, how easily we'd built this life together.

"What are you thinking about?" Floris asked softly, his fingers playing with my curls.

"How different this is from what I imagined my life would be." I turned to look at him. "Five years ago, I was so focused on being perfect, on living up to my father's sacrifice. I never thought I'd be here, in the Netherlands, engaged to a prince and eating raw fish at national celebrations."

His eyes softened. "Regrets?"

"None." I reached up to trace his jaw, still amazed that I got to do this, that this beautiful, ridiculous man was mine. "Though I could do with less orange in my wardrobe."

"Impossible. Orange is clearly your color."

"I'm not getting married in an orange suit. I draw the line there."

Floris gasped in mock horror. "But think of the patriotic statement we could make! The headlines: 'Royal Wedding Goes Full Dutch.' We could have orange flowers, orange cake—"

"Stop." I covered his mouth with my hand, laughing despite myself. "You're terrible."

"Actually..." Floris shifted slightly, and I recognized his "we need to talk about something" pose. "About that. We need to finalize the details. The team needs time to prepare everything."

My stomach did a nervous flip. "Oh."

Our wedding date was set for September fifteenth a year from now, and while I couldn't wait to marry him, I was less enthusiastic about the spectacle it would be.

"Hey." He caught my hand, squeezing gently. "We can do it however you want. Small ceremony, big ceremony, elope to Vegas—though my father might actually have a heart attack if we did that last one."

I struggled to find the right words. "It's not that I don't want to marry you. I do. So much. But the idea of doing it in front of the whole world..."

"Who says it has to be the whole world?" His thumb traced circles on my palm, grounding me. "We could do something small for family and close friends. The palace has private chapels that would be perfect for an intimate ceremony."

I blinked. "We could do that?"

"Of course." He smiled softly. "Contrary to popular belief, royal weddings don't have to be massive state occasions. Not when you're not first or second in line. And while there would need to be some official elements, we get to decide how we want to celebrate our love."

Something tight inside me loosened at his words. "Your family would be okay with that?"

"They want us to be happy." He shifted to face me properly. "Besides, they all love you."

I snuggled closer to him, feeling the tension drain from my shoulders. "A small ceremony sounds perfect. Though your fan club might be disappointed."

"My fan club?" He raised an eyebrow. "You mean those teenage girls who keep sending me marriage proposals on Instagram?"

"And the middle-aged women who comment heart emojis on every photo of you." I poked his side. "Don't pretend you haven't noticed."

"I only notice the comments from one person." He caught my hand, bringing it to his lips. "Usually complaining about my laundry habits or pointing out that I've left coffee cups everywhere again."

"Someone has to keep you in line." But I was smiling, warmth spreading through my chest at his casual affection. "Though I have to admit, you've gotten better about the laundry."

"See? I can be taught." He pressed another kiss to my palm. "So, small ceremony?"

I nodded. "Small ceremony. Though we should probably include some traditional elements, right? For protocol?"

"Some, yes. But we can make them our own." His expression

turned thoughtful. "Like, instead of a massive reception, we could do something more intimate. Maybe in the garden pavilion at Het Oude Loo? It's beautiful in September, and it has special meaning for us."

Het Oude Loo was where I had met his parents for the first time, his friends, and where we'd spent countless weekends getting to know each other away from the press. It was also where he'd proposed, on a crisp, autumn morning surrounded by falling leaves.

"I would love that."

"Have I told you how grateful I am that you agreed to move to the Netherlands for me?" he said softly.

"You have. Multiple times. It's not a sacrifice."

"But it is. You won't get to see your mom and Tia as often. And for your job—"

"I love my job."

I had finished my master's in civil engineering, but encouraged by Floris, I had found the courage to follow my true passion and had chosen to get another master's in historic building preservation engineering with a minor in architectural history. I had loved every second of it, and now I worked as a part-time consultant for UNESCO and advised them on restoration projects of historic buildings. It was a dream come true, and the best part was that I knew deep down, my father would be so proud of me. I was thriving, not merely surviving. All because of Floris.

Floris himself had continued with water management, becoming a specialized engineer who traveled around the world to talk about the importance of flood prevention. I accompanied him whenever I could and had seen places I could've only dreamed of before. I felt incredibly privileged and lucky to have this life with the man I loved.

And somewhere in the south of the Netherlands, in a tiny little town on the river Maas, we had officially opened a new *kering*, a barrier system that would prevent more flooding from happening there... and it was called the Henry Ritchey kering.

Dad would be so proud of me.

* * *

MORE FROM NORA PHOENIX

The next instalment in the Prince Pact series from Nora Phoenix is available to order now here: https://mybook.to/Prince3Backad

ABOUT THE AUTHOR

Nora Phoenix is a *USA Today* Bestselling author of over 60 MM/gay romances. When she's not writing or reading, she's spending time with her son, travelling, or gardening. Originally from The Netherlands, she currently resides in upstate New York.

Sign up to Nora Phoenix's mailing list here for news, competitions and updates on future books.

Visit Nora's website: www.noraphoenix.com

Follow Nora on social media:

facebook.com/authornoraphoenix

instagram.com/nora.phoenix

bookbub.com/authors/nora-phoenix

ALSO BY NORA PHOENIX

Boldwood
EVER AFTER

x♡x♡

JOIN BOLDWOOD'S
ROMANCE COMMUNITY
FOR SWEET AND SPICY BOOK RECS WITH ALL YOUR FAVOURITE TROPES!

SIGN UP TO OUR
NEWSLETTER

HTTPS://BIT.LY/BOLDWOODEVERAFTER

Boldw**oo**d

Boldwood Books is an award-winning fiction publishing company seeking out the best stories from around the world.

Find out more at www.boldwoodbooks.com

Join our reader community for brilliant books, competitions and offers!

Follow us
@BoldwoodBooks
@TheBoldBookClub

Sign up to our weekly deals newsletter

https://bit.ly/BoldwoodBNewsletter